BLIND TRUST

A JANE CANNON THRILLER

BOOK ONE

L.T. RYAN

K.T. CROWE

THE JANE CANNON SERIES

Blind Trust
Collateral

PROLOGUE

SOMETHING WAS WRONG.

Simmons felt it in his bones. And if the agent in charge of the task force hadn't been such a pompous bureaucrat, he would have called it in.

Unfortunately, he needed more than a gut feeling when dealing with Supervisory Special Agent Scott.

Simmons' breath misted in the chilly night air. Seattle never failed to disappoint when it came to a cold, wet December. The streets glistened with ice over cracked, black tarmac. But aside from the occasional vagrant, no one walked this particular block.

Not since the Mazzuca family had claimed the lot as theirs fourteen months ago.

His time spent working undercover for the crime organization had unveiled its share of human trafficking, drugs, and the occasional illegal weapons transaction. Hence the new combined operation with the FBI. Though DEA, Simmons appreciated his new team—minus their annoying supervisor.

Shuffling down the street toward him, an older man muttered to himself as he approached.

Simmons tensed, but the older man drew closer and smiled,

exposing stained teeth. His ragged clothes and faded knit ski cap emanated the scent of something sour.

Simmons blew into his hands and gave a short nod back, one homeless man to another, his own ski cap appropriately soiled, his face dirty to mask his features.

He should have waited for backup to look into this, but something about the entire operation bothered him. The puzzle pieces weren't fitting. He could *feel* it. One of his new FBI counterparts could too. They'd discussed it earlier today, both bothered by that feeling of wrongness.

But then, Jane was uncanny when it came to investigations. Part blood-hound, part she-wolf, the woman had a reputation for solving cases. Though only a junior agent, her close rate put her on everyone's radar, even his own boss's.

Rumor had it Jane had some odd family connection as well. But no matter how hard Simmons dug, he couldn't find it.

A crime family, someone military, maybe a government contact? Simmons didn't know, but with Jane, he wouldn't be surprised at anything he learned.

The rumble of a truck along the road alerted him to focus on the task at hand, so he continued to ignore the cameras mounted to the large warehouse and mumbled to himself as he slowly ambled down the sidewalk, in the shadows, staying in character while the truck passed.

One more nobody the city pretended didn't exist.

The streetlights in this area had been out for months, but the task force's limited surveillance predicted movement in the warehouse as well as the marina behind it. Boats had been coming and going with regularity for the past week, particularly at night.

Yet no one had seen anything specific since the covered dock masked any sight of passengers or transactions on the water. Despite the crimes Simmons had already uncovered, they needed more. Enough to send the Mazzucas away for a long time.

He moved as if drunk past the edge of the warehouse then darted under a broken chain-link fence into a narrow space between the warehouse and the rundown, two-story office building next to it. He'd previously cut through the chain link fence on his last pass two nights ago, allowing him entry to the one spot where the cameras on the adjacent buildings didn't overlap.

A slender person could fit in the narrow space without too much bruising, but Simmons had to angle himself nearly sideways to make his way without getting stuck.

He remained quiet as he moved, stepping over split concrete as he hurried toward the end of the buildings. He rolled his ski cap down, utilizing the mask to better hide his features, and studied the empty lot between the warehouse and the dock.

He saw no one. Not Leo Mazzuca Senior, Junior, or their men. No security. Not even a guard dog.

Odd.

Mazzuca had to be making a move tonight.

I should call this in.

Yet Simmons had no evidence beyond a poorly guarded and apparently empty dock and his gut. He needed something concrete to share with the team, especially with Supervisor Follow-My-Rules-or-Else.

He wanted to text Jane but didn't want her involved unless he had real confirmation of wrongdoing. Though he knew she trusted his instincts, he didn't want to cause her trouble for joining him without Scott's go-ahead.

Thoughts of their supervisor's smug smile, expensive wardrobe, and constant jockeying for power made him grit his teeth. The guy would love nothing more than to fire Simmons from the team for insubordination. He'd already warned Simmons not to go to the warehouse after hours without his say-so, afraid Simmons would screw up their surveillance and blow his cover, even though Simmons had been doing it for a month.

From what Simmons knew, Scott's advancement was riding on this huge bust, and he didn't like sharing the limelight.

Whatever. Simmons trusted his gut. He'd get the evidence to incriminate the Mazzucas. Better forgiveness for moving early than waiting for permission that would come too late. After checking around the corner, he paused while the warehouse's back cameras panned away from the back door.

Once clear, he raced toward the darkened doorway where he typically entered for a day's work after being buzzed in by security.

With the code he'd stolen from Leo's secretary earlier in the day, he let himself inside.

He remained on his guard. Who knew who might be there despite the tomblike silence all around?

The front lobby and adjoining administrative wing lay empty. No desks or filing cabinets. No papers or computers anywhere. Not even any storage boxes.

Impossible. Surveillance would have seen this and reported it in.

The entire organization had vanished. What the hell?

Screw it.

He texted Jane. *At warehouse. Empty. Something wrong.*

His finger hovered over the send icon. The DEA had been surveilling the Mazzucas for the eight months before they'd expanded the team to include the FBI's task force, while the syndicate had been steadily scaling up. Why would they leave now? There'd been no warning of a withdrawal.

An even worse idea surfaced. Were the rumors true? Had the Mazzucas infiltrated the FBI after all?

Uneasy, he sent off the message to Jane and crept down the hallway toward the main office. Leo's private space, off limits to everyone unless the big man invited you.

Case in point, the secretary and cleaning guy who'd interrupted an important phone call two weeks ago had already disappeared. Rumor had it they'd annoyed the boss with all their "sneaking around." They'd vanished. No one had seen or heard from them since.

Simmons paused and cocked his head, listening hard to the silence.

He doubted Leo would be in the office this late at night. And Junior typically spent his nights down at the strip club with the bruisers on staff. A safe bet Leo's office would be empty too, though it was likely locked.

Simmons found the door cracked open.

Wary, he palmed his pistol, an undercover "spare" he'd taken from the armory.

Easing inside the dimly lit office, he found it, too, empty. No furniture and no bodies. Overheating, he rolled up the ski mask to serve as a hat again and slowly lowered his weapon, not sure what to think.

Until he turned around and saw a dark figure step out of the shadowy corner pointing a gun at his face. He hadn't expected this, but it made so much sense.

"Drop it."

Simmons had no chance of getting off a shot before being killed. He slowly knelt and put the gun down, then shoved it away. His heart raced, and dread filled his throat.

The person watching him smiled. "I'm glad you're here. We have so much to talk about."

It took him a long time to die. He just wished he could have given Jane a little bit more to work with before a bullet eventually shattered his skull and tore through his brain.

CHAPTER ONE

ONE WEEK LATER

"SO IT'S REALLY HIM?" The twisted feeling in Jane's gut settled, satisfied despite such a disheartening validation. She wanted to shove her smug sense of I-told-you-so in her supervisor's face.

She'd told him the text they'd received from Dan Simmons hadn't been real.

Over the past couple of months, as she sat with the others in the downtown Seattle field office, she'd spent her time splitting her focus between the Mazzuca case and the other fifteen cases she currently managed. Considering some of her investigations had been ongoing for months and even years, she couldn't just drop one because the task force took most of her attention.

But this news about Simmons…

The last time she'd seen him, he'd laughed at her workload, calling her a lightweight. Then he'd shared some unsettling information he'd learned at the warehouse, news that Leo Mazzuca might be leaning more heavily into the weapons trade than they'd thought.

Simmons had wanted to look harder at some of Leo Mazzuca's

files. Like her, he knew the pieces of their case didn't fit. Mazzuca had grown too careful lately. Too paranoid. Both she and Simmons wanted to know why, especially with the spate of recent activity on the waterfront.

Yet Simmons had gone from intrigued to leaving on vacation? Really? In the middle of a case heating up, while *undercover,* he'd texted the boss that he needed to ditch for holiday festivities out of town?

Perhaps he really had needed time off, but the guy would have at least told her about it first.

Granted, she and Simmons didn't know each other well. They'd only been working together the past two months, but, excluding her two work-friends, she and Simmons had respected each other more than any of the other yes-men on the task force. More than respect, Jane had liked the affable DEA agent. They'd bonded over a good coffee bean and their dislike of bureaucracy—more specifically, their dislike for SSA Scott.

It took effort to look her SSA in the eye without belting him.

"Yes, it's him." Supervisory Special Agent Matthew Scott sighed and in a somber voice added, "Shot and left for dead in a skiff floating off the waterway. Coast Guard picked him up this morning, but it looks like he's been dead for days." After a pause, Scott added, "Looked like he died hard."

She surreptitiously glanced at the other members of her ten-man squad and noticed faces drawn in grief. In anger and a need for vengeance.

"Jane, I need to speak with you in my office."

She met Scott's gaze and nodded. The others watched her leave, no doubt wondering what couldn't be shared among the team.

Though Jane was fairly new to the Seattle field office, having spent her first two years in the FBI at the Resident Agency in Poulsbo, she'd been well-prepared for this larger organization.

Though her uncle liked to say she had more hoops to jump through and people to try to impress, he'd followed that with a laugh.

Because he knew she didn't care about getting gold stars and accolades. She never had.

Jane lived for the hunt. To catch bad guys, keep up on her beloved paperwork, and remain number one on the job. "Competitive" should have been her middle name.

She'd have to tell—*not tell, request*—that Scott keep his briefs and meetings to less than three a day. Did he have nothing better to do than quiz her on her reports? The Mazzuca case aside, she now had Dan Simmons' murder to solve.

Jane bit the inside of her cheek and swallowed her complaints. Instead, she entered the boss's office and waited.

"Close the door, please." He settled behind his desk, not a pen or folder out of place.

Normally, she'd respect such organization. But not with Simmons gone, his killer no closer to being caught while they chitchatted in plush seats.

Office pogue.

She closed the door and took the seat across from Scott's desk at his nod. Had he ever gotten his hands dirty? From what little she knew, Agent Scott had been a Fed since graduating college. No military service or law enforcement background. Just parents with a lot of money and connections.

"We have a problem, Jane."

That's Agent Cannon to you. "Sir?"

His eyes narrowed. The smug bastard sat there in his pristine, expensive suit and his Rolex, both statements of someone on his way up. His hair had been salon-styled, short on the sides and artfully layered on top and brushed to the side, the dark brown complementing his pale complexion. Instead of appearing sickly, his polished image went well with his sophisticated cologne.

The quintessential poster boy for the FBI.

She hated him a little bit for that. He should have looked and smelled like the weasel she knew him to be.

"I know you and Dan Simmons planned to infiltrate the warehouse, despite my orders to steer clear."

"I don't know what—"

He handed her a printout that showed several email messages. They looked to be from Simmons to her, but she didn't recognize the last few past his saying, *See you tomorrow, Jane,* the day he'd disappeared.

She frowned. "What is this?"

"This is proof you intentionally disobeyed a direct order."

She didn't appreciate his tone. Or the accusation. "First, I'm not a toddler. Don't talk down to me like I'm three."

He scowled.

"And second, these aren't my messages." She studied them, aware Simmons' diction seemed off. Jane was a crack investigator. She saw patterns where others didn't. And past the last message from Simmons signing off for the day, she didn't recognize anything.

She surely hadn't received the one sent from his phone that read, *At warehouse. Empty. Something wrong.* Unfortunately, Simmons had in the past texted to her email address instead of her actual phone, mixing up her contact information. So that one might be legitimate.

She tapped the paper, her fingernail blunt and unpolished. "If I'd gotten that, I'd have hotfooted it down there. But I didn't get a text." She shook her head. "None of this is reading right."

SSA Scott stared at her. For a moment, she thought she'd gotten through to him. Then his expression evened, and she knew she'd lost. "I'll need your badge and your firearm. As of right now, you're on administrative leave pending an investigation by OPR."

OPR—the Office of Professional Responsibility. The FBI's internal affairs division.

"Seriously?"

"As a heart attack." Scott waited for her to hand over her badge.

She wanted to shove it down his throat. Instead, she tossed it onto his desk. "My firearm's in my desk." Tucked away in a drawer when she wasn't out in the field.

"Leave it and everything you've been working on. We'll take care of things while you're pending investigation."

She stood, fuming, but tried to keep a lid on her temper. She was slow to rile, but once unleashed, she'd end up saying something that would get her fired. Or doing something that would get her arrested.

And God forbid she act like her hotheaded cousin.

But Jane being Jane, she couldn't leave without a final word. She put her hands on Scott's desk and leaned over, staring down at him. The man was lucky looks couldn't kill.

"You're making a huge mistake. And I'm going to prove it."

"Leave this alone. You're suspended until further notice." He buzzed on his intercom for an escort to see her out of the building.

She turned on her heel, walked to the door, and yanked it open.

"Jane! Don't impede the investigation. Do you hear me?"

She ignored him and stalked to her desk. Grabbing her jacket, she stormed out of the office, not answering anyone's questions or waiting on security.

Jane now had a new set of objectives, which she would accomplish no matter what.

One: find Dan Simmons' murderer.

Two: solve the problem of the Mazzuca investigation.

Three: do whatever it took to heal the cancer that was SSA Scott before he infected the entire squad.

CHAPTER TWO

FOUR DAYS LATER, JANE HAD TO CONCEDE THAT SHE'D NEED TO RETHINK her investigation into Simmons' murder. No one at the task force would talk to her, thanks to her suspension and Scott's orders. Not even Jenn Sullivan or Rob Williams, and they typically skated the edges of propriety, always *just* obeying the letter of the law.

After only four days, she was already climbing the walls. She'd cleaned her apartment, run errands, paid bills, done laundry, and hit the gym twice a day.

She needed to dig harder into the Mazzucas. Unfortunately, she'd gotten nowhere with her usual confidential informants. Her CIs had no idea why the syndicate had up and left Seattle.

That they'd moved out from under the task force's surveillance, limited as it had been, without anyone seeing them leave struck her as beyond impossible.

Jane's bet—the Mazzucas had a source inside the FBI. Not the DEA, as they'd been after the crime family before the feds had joined the team, and no one had ever reported anything amiss. But how to prove it if she had to steer clear of the investigation until OPR cleared her?

She finished wiping down her kitchen for the third time that day.

The tedium of cleaning up soothed her, as did the familiar comfort of home. The one-bedroom apartment in Capitol Hill served her needs well enough. She had a few plants she managed to keep alive. The floors were so clean she could see her reflection in the shiny hardwood.

The minimalist décor suited her, as did the teak wood and Scandinavian style furniture. Though she rarely watched TV, she had one streaming service. The books on her shelves had been read numerous times. Unfortunately, since being suspended, she couldn't seem to lose herself in fiction.

Her idiot cousin liked to say that only pathologically disturbed people contented themselves with repeating comforts. However, a psychologist Jane had once interviewed relegated the reviewing to relieving anxiety.

Jane saw no problem repeating what brought her pleasure. Books couldn't kill you. Books didn't disappoint you.

And speaking of disappointing… She stared at the missed calls on her phone she had yet to return.

She'd been putting him off on purpose. Her uncle must have learned about her administrative leave. Chris North was good like that. The man had connections all over the place and the leeway to do a lot, both legal and illegal, when he had the urge.

She knew he wouldn't step into her business unless invited because she'd set those boundaries before leaving home to go to college, and again when joining the Marine Corps. Uncle Chris had respected her even when she'd joined the FBI against his wishes.

Staring at her cell phone, which she'd also cleaned a few times, leaving it streak free, she bit the bullet and dialed his number, careful not to leave smudges.

Despite what her cousin thought, Jane wasn't a germophobe. She just prized cleanliness and order above all else.

Uncle Chris answered on the second ring. "About time you checked in." His deep voice had that unsettling effect of making her stand straight and tall, as if at attention awaiting orders from her commanding officer.

Annoyed, she purposefully slouched. "Yeah, yeah. I'm fine. I didn't do anything wrong. But I'm bored out of my skull. Will you be home for Christmas?"

Home meaning Bainbridge Island in rural Washington. Situated in the Sound a short ferry ride from Seattle, Bainbridge had plenty of rich forest and property for those who could afford it. Her uncle maintained a large home there they called "the ranch," as well as a bigger plot of land in Central Oregon.

A proper getaway for him and his team when they needed to unwind.

"I'm not actually home at the moment, but Joe and Hal are headed that way. The rest of the guys are with me."

She liked both men. Heck, she considered all her uncle's misfits family. She'd grown up with the members of Team Ten. Joe and Hal were the most fun of the bunch, easily bribable and not prone to snitching.

Even better, her old Resident Agency, or RA, in Poulsbo wasn't far from the ranch.

"I was thinking of going out there for a little bit. I'm bored here."

"I heard you the first time." He paused. "You need any help with the situation? I was sorry to hear about Dan Simmons. He had a great reputation with the DEA."

"Yeah." She didn't know what else to say about Simmons. Grief at his passing still made her uneasy but not exactly sad. Which was good, because Jane didn't do deep emotions. Even anger should be tempered. Accessed sparingly but not exploited.

Jane had learned her lessons the hard way a long time ago.

"Well, then." Uncle Chris cleared his throat. "Just so you know, your cousin might get out there for the holidays. I think she's had some problems with work lately."

"Seems to be going around." Jane sighed. "What has the hothead done now?"

"Jane, be nice," he growled.

Jane counted to ten then said, "I'm always nice. I'm the rational, clear-headed one, remember?"

He chuckled. "Sure you are. You just hide it better is all. Look, I'm heading out for a stint. I'll be back sometime next month. You need anything, just ask. You know the boys will get you anything you want. And keep your head down while you wait to go back to work." I love you, honey. Be safe.

"Will do. And watch your six. I'll be around when you get back." Love you too. Come home soon.

He grunted then disconnected. The master of saying a lot without saying anything at all.

Jane felt better about no longer having to follow Scott's ridiculous orders. With Simmons' death at the forefront of her mind, she couldn't stop thinking that her team had a mole. She also couldn't ignore her cousin's return—cue the inevitable drama. On the plus side, she'd soon see Hal and Joe.

She missed the guys. Missed her cousin too, though she'd be hard pressed to admit it aloud. Though two years younger, Jane typically found herself talking Raine out of a bad idea. It would take several shouting matches, much name calling, and eventual forgiveness before they'd share a beer and some laughs, right before her cousin would be off again on some secret mission. For the Corps, the CIA, or some other alphabet organization.

Raine would never tell, but their uncle always seemed to know when and where his nieces were, and he never tired of telling them he had eyes everywhere. The know-it-all.

With a grudging smile, Jane packed a bag then rechecked the ferry schedule. She had time to combat the ever-present downtown traffic. After saying goodbye to her thriving succulents, she locked up after herself, and, with a spring in her step, pondered what to do next.

She'd make sure to visit with Hal and Joe, but she'd only use their expertise if she failed to get any information from her friend in Poulsbo. The RA had been her first assignment with the FBI, a place full of good memories and lessons learned, mentored by the best—not counting her uncle. A place where she had connections to help her dig into her peers at the Seattle field office.

It was time she stopped playing around and got some real answers.

CHAPTER THREE

THOUGH WET AND COLD, POULSBO, WASHINGTON, HAD HEAVY lunchtime traffic. The storefronts glowed with cheer while the spat of rain that wanted to be snow but wasn't quite cold enough came down in a gentle wash. With only seven more shopping days until Christmas, people hustled to find the appropriate gifts for family and friends.

Jane lifted the collar of her jacket to protect her neck, doing her best to suppress a shiver as the wind sought refuge in the hollow of her throat.

She felt naked without her service weapon, now gone for a solid six days since her suspension.

Last night, she'd arrived at her uncle's ranch, a giant house that could comfortably accommodate a dozen psychotic mercenaries. It felt empty without anyone in it, though a trustworthy crew of housecleaners her uncle had used for years kept it spotless.

Hal and Joe hadn't been by yet. The lack of a mess or spent ammo on the weapons range out back said as much.

She'd chosen the bedroom she normally used when home—her *other* home, she mentally corrected. But she hadn't done more than unpack and fall asleep, tired from stressing about the mess of her current investigation.

The one bright spot in her day had been her friend's agreement to meet her for lunch. And gossip.

Jane smiled as she spotted Special Agent Grace Russo, an experienced senior agent out of the Poulsbo RA. The short, dark-haired woman had been working there for the past ten years. A married mother of two, she had to be one of the most grounded people Jane had ever worked with.

Jane had learned a lot from Grace, and she'd always appreciated the senior agent's willingness to show her the ropes. They'd solved a few key criminal cases during Jane's time at Poulsbo, which had led Jane to favor the criminal side of her work more than the cases involving national security.

"Well, look who finally escaped the office." She waited while the older woman dragged her into a bear hug, squeezing until her bones ached. "*Ooof.* Missed you, Grace."

Grace backed off, grinning, her straight, white teeth nearly glowing in a face lined by age and humor. The laugh lines showed her happiness but couldn't hide the sharp intelligence gleaming from hazel eyes. "I missed you too, you troublemaker. From what I hear, some things never change."

With skin a shade darker than Jane's perpetual tan, Grace appeared to have a Hispanic or mediterranean background. She spoke English, Spanish, and French and had worked in the New York and San Antonio field offices before moving to the Pacific Northwest.

She had a lot of experience and a willingness to help, both traits Jane was counting on.

Grace looked her over. "You're looking a little lean, some stress around the mouth and there in the eyes. But all things considered, I get it."

Jane frowned, not pleased about letting her emotions show. "I don't look stressed."

"You do now." Grace chuckled.

Jane rolled her eyes. "How about we grab something to eat and get out of this wet cold?"

"Sold."

They hustled to J J's Fishhouse, a popular eatery downtown. The gloom outside only enhanced the warm, bright atmosphere and comfort inside. Wooden tables and chairs filled the interior of the overlarge room and booths lined the walls.

After being led to a booth, they sat and considered their menus. The server dropped off their waters, took their orders, and left them alone to study each other. Though Jane had been back to visit, her stays had been brief, and she hadn't had the opportunity to catch up with her friend.

Grace looked the same as always, intelligent, determined, and amused, as if smiling at secrets only she knew. She sipped from her water glass. "Not a whole lot on my end. Just hard at work with the same people you remember. James is still lead, though he keeps hinting he wants me to take over so he can retire."

"Well? Will you?"

"I'm still thinking about it. I'm fifty-two, Jane. I don't know that I want all the hassle James constantly deals with. He's twice divorced and no kids, so he's only got to worry about the work. I'm dealing with work plus a temperamental chef and two teenagers who think they know everything."

"I've met your kids. I don't know that they're wrong about knowing everything."

Grace grinned. "No comment on the temperamental chef?"

"Your husband, your mess."

Grace burst into laughter. "Nice one. Okay, Cannon. Lay it on me. What do you need?"

Jane blinked. "Need? Can't I just come to catch up with a friend?"

Grace said nothing, waiting.

Jane sighed. "I need help."

"What's going on?"

Jane glanced around before quietly filling in Grace on Dan Simmons' death and why she thought it might have something to do with some of the people she worked with. She kept her voice low. "It doesn't make any sense. Anyone with half a brain has to know our target alerted *someone* when they left, yet no one reported it until we found Dan. The task force is looking into it now, but it makes no sense." She puzzled over it. "It has to be someone in the know."

Grace understood. She nodded. "So you want a background check on some of your buddies. Especially the big boss, am I right?"

"Exactly. He's fishy. Which is great if you're at J J's Fishhouse, but not so great in the office." She was suddenly reminded of SSA Scott's fancy cologne.

She much preferred the smell of fish.

The server dropped off their food, and Grace dug into her fish and chips while Jane inhaled her clam chowder. They ate in silence, both apparently famished.

Grace glanced up, looking serious. "I'll do some digging. Carefully. I'll let you know if I find anything."

Jane nodded. She grabbed a list of names from her pocket and slid it across the table. "These in particular. I don't want to think it's any of them, but after what happened, and with any one of them being able to access my computer to send those emails, I can't be sure."

Grace tucked the note into her jacket and cleaned her plate of the last fry. "Man. Wait until I tell Ralph I ate here today. He's going to lose his mind."

"Because he's jealous you ate with me and not him?" Grace's husband had always treated her like a little sister.

"Because he knows he can cook anyone under the table when it comes to seafood. And now he'll be dying to prove it again to me." Grace's eyes sparkled. "This is guaranteeing me some fine meals for the next week at least." She paused. "And speaking of losing their minds, how is that finer than fine uncle of yours? And his friends? Any of them in town and planning to visit us at the office? Chris can stop by for any reason. Any at all."

"Aren't you married?" Jane's uncle had a way about him. A hard-case, but a handsome one...according to every woman he'd ever met.

"Married, honey, not dead." Grace wiped her lips with her napkin. "So, any of them back in town?"

"A few are coming back for the holidays. But I don't think I'll be seeing my uncle until the new year."

"Pity. I used to love when he'd come to visit."

"Yeah, because he'd always get me in trouble with my superiors—you especially—for one reason or another."

Grace chuckled. "That man has a gift." Her smile faded. "But Jane, your situation is no joke. You need to clear your name. OPR will do their best, but when it comes to a solid defense, there's no one who knows you better than you."

"Scott told me to stay out of the investigation." At Grace's knowing silence, Jane nodded. "But of course I won't."

Grace's phone buzzed, and she took it out of her pocket to glance at it. "Shoot. I need to head back."

Jane waved her away. "Go on. I've got lunch. I appreciate your help." She stood to hug her friend then watched her walk away. She sat and finished her meal, contemplating her next steps.

She'd contacted her Poulsbo connection for help, so the investigation into the Seattle field office was underway. Now where should she go? Back to Seattle to talk to her CIs again? Or maybe return to the surveillance area? The Mazzucas hadn't just vanished into thin air.

Maybe a discussion with one of her CIs she hadn't yet tapped might help. Her guy always knew what was going on around him. If anyone knew where the Mazzucas had gone, he would know. But his help wasn't cheap.

Her phone buzzed, distracting her.

She chuckled at the text. *Destruction and the Toy have returned. Hide the women and children. But get your sorry self home, brat.*

Team Ten was in the house. And just in time for the holidays.

Time to make merry and bright...and hide the good silver before the terrifying duo destroyed it during shooting practice.

CHAPTER FOUR

ON THE RANCH, THE MAIN HOME, A SIX-THOUSAND SQUARE FOOT HOUSE, had been professionally decorated to soothe men needing a break from a grueling, dangerous job. Riverstone and steel covered the exterior, the curb appeal ideal for anyone wanting a rustic escape from city life.

Inside, appointed with rich, leather furniture, hardwood floors, and stainless-steel appliances, the mansion could easily have belonged to some millionaire bachelor fond of dark wood and cowhide.

The backyard held a gated pool with a hot tub, as well as a large outbuilding, in which a weapons range had been stationed. The range's basement held a mini-armory, ballistic-resistant concrete walls, protected ceilings, and several five-foot wide lanes a good seventy-five feet long or more. The true jewel of the compound, according to their weapons expert.

No one had ever said Chris North didn't know how to manage his money. Ill-gained or respectably earned, depending on one's perspective, it spent the same. And Chris understood the value of mental relaxation after a harrowing life spent protecting his country and his men, those he considered family.

Back when she'd first come to live with him, Uncle Chris hadn't been a homebody at all. He'd had a small apartment in the city he rarely visited. He'd been deploying all the time, entering hot zones and often barely surviving them. But things changed when he'd become the legal guardian of both a four-year-old and a six-year-old.

As much as he'd attempted to provide stability, he'd gone about it in an unorthodox fashion, teaching his girls to protect themselves like any well-trained Marine.

Jane *oomphed* as another bear hug squashed the breath out of her, though this one lifted her off her feet.

Joe, one of her many honorary uncles, swung her around and laughed. "Destruction" indeed. The six-foot-four marksman could hit anything with a firearm. His weapon of choice was the AI AXSR, a multi-caliber, long-range sniper rifle. At fifty-two years old, with cropped hair, dark skin, and darker eyes, he looked hard and experienced, until he smiled. Then he looked like one of her favorite uncles.

Along with Hal, who waited impatiently to hug Jane as well. He shoved Joe aside and embraced Jane with a paternal warmth, giving her a peck on the cheek as he set her back.

The pair studied her, glanced at each other, then sighed.

"We heard about the murder and the suspension." Joe paused. "Who are we killing?"

Jane knew better than to think he might be joking. She glared. "*I'm* looking into things. I've got this covered." She wouldn't have minded some help, but she didn't have the time to keep an eye on the guys while also working her investigation.

She'd rather herd cats than keep Team Ten in line. They had a tendency to scatter like marbles when left unattended and brought chaos wherever they landed. Her uncle had a knack for keeping their anarchy contained, though his definition of "contained" was *not* the same as hers.

If the problem were left to Joe, he'd mow through the Mazzuca crime family one .30 caliber at a time. Hal would simply wipe out their finances by illegally hacking their banking records. Or he'd plant incriminating files in their computers, mess with their security, then implicate them in something shady they couldn't escape.

Though his way had a certain appeal, she needed to catch a killer and end the Mazzucas' reign of crime the legal way.

Although...

No. Nope. Uh-uh. Law and order is my rock.

Sad that she had to remind herself of that when around her family.

"I mean it," she said to them *and* herself. "I've got it handled. Grace is helping me."

They settled at the mention of her friend. She had a feeling Grace had helped the team a time or two in secret.

Hal sighed. "Fine. Be Miss Independent. But we're here if you need us." Like Joe, Hal looked like he could handle himself. But while Joe looked like a mammoth bruiser who could end a person with one punch, Hal had brilliant blue eyes, blond hair, and a golden tan that put one in mind of surfers and the California sun. His features were almost too pretty to belong to a man.

The team called him Boy Toy, Toy for short. Joe's real name was Randall Finnegan, but he'd been telling "Yo Mama" jokes for so long that Yo had morphed into Joe and stuck.

Hal continued. "Oh, Chris said he and the others should be back next month. Probably." He grinned at her. "If you're nice, we'll tell you what we brought you for Christmas."

Christmas. Crap. She hadn't done any shopping yet.

Joe guffawed. "You owe me five bucks. See that face? That's panic. She doesn't have anything for us."

"First, I am not panicked." What was with everyone seeing emotions on her standard poker face? "And two, I have presents."

"Liar." Hal patted her on the head.

She swatted at him. "Don't make me shoot you."

Joe brightened. "You brought your pistol?"

"It's in the armory." His gift a few years ago, a Sig Sauer P322. The rounds didn't cost much, which was a bonus, and the smooth recoil was tons better than her service Glock. Sadly, she hadn't fired the Sig in nearly half a year, too busy with real life.

"Terrific. We should go hit some targets and de-stress."

Jane wasn't surprised to see Joe's excitement. He lived for the challenge of a bullseye. Though he had no problem taking out threats to the country, he would much rather hit paper targets. He had a true appreciation for the thin line between life and death, no savage killer, but a man who understood and accepted his mission in life to make the world a safer place.

Joe looked at Hal. "Come on, slacker. You know you need the practice."

"Fine. But later, we'll play games. *Video* games."

Joe groaned. "I'm no good at that stuff."

"Look, we shoot at paper targets, no one gets hurt," Hal said. "Then we virtually shoot at digital targets, and no one gets hurt. Plus, you can be an alien, an orc king, or an alt-universe dictator if you want."

Joe thought about it. "Hmm. An orc king? I'm in." He and Hal started for the back door. "Meet us out at the range, Jane."

She watched them leave and shook her head. Some things never changed. In their downtime, the guys gravitated toward the things they liked. The same things they did for work.

Jane had no complaints. Heck, she'd modeled her lifestyle after theirs. As she went to exchange her business suit for jeans and a sweatshirt, she thought about the many years she'd spent acclimating to a family who made a living hunting bad guys.

She'd learned hand-to-hand self-defense and offensive tactics from a young age. Knife-fighting, weapons training, and map orientation had been staples in her teen years. The softer side of feelings and talking out trouble, not so much.

She checked her phone before exiting the back door. The news app revealed a breaking story about two people violently shot in Seattle. A young couple had been gunned down in what looked like a gang-style shooting during the holidays.

She sighed and put her phone down, intentionally leaving it behind.

Life was hard enough. She needed to unwind with loved ones. To celebrate the coming holiday and figure out what the heck to buy everyone. Some fun target practice with the guys was exactly what she needed to relax right now.

She really had missed them and couldn't wait until everyone returned.

But as she joined them in the weapons range behind the house, she wondered if the gang-style shooting had any connection to the Mazzucas, and if her old friends at the Seattle field office might be looking into it.

Or telling the Mazzucas all that they knew.

CHAPTER FIVE

CHRISTMAS MORNING BROUGHT SLUSH, SOME PRACTICAL GIFTS—SOCKS from Hal and a new calendar from Joe, both of which she loved—and a report from Grace that didn't shed light on much. Unfortunately, Grace hadn't found any secrets or scandal lingering around Jane's Seattle colleagues, though she promised to continue digging.

But Jane hadn't been bored while waiting for the holiday to pass. Hal put her through her paces with some challenging games of Scrabble and, according to Joe, other nerdy word games. Joe insisted she practice her marksman skills, finding her lacking, which annoyed her into proving him wrong. She'd doubled up on her weight training. And while running—on a treadmill—she'd pored over every article in social media on the Mazzuca crime family that she could find.

Due to the holiday season, the cleaning staff had time off. So Jane also happily scrubbed and vacuumed and dusted the house, secretly pleased the guys continued to make a mess of the kitchen, giving her an excuse to clean up after them.

On Christmas evening, while Hal went out with a lady friend and Joe played Santa with his family out in Tacoma, she had the house to herself. The fireplace crackled and warmed the chilly living room, the atmosphere cheery since the guys had insisted on getting a real tree, decorated with the ornaments they'd retrieved from the attic.

Jane smiled, spotting a few she and her cousin had made for her uncle and the team, including a few childish drawings of a large group of men helping Santa pull his sleigh. Though members of Team Ten had come and gone, the core group remained.

She appreciated the ease of sharing memories and laughter with Hal and Joe. They didn't demand more than she wanted to offer. She had no trouble being kind to those she loved and appreciated their snarky attempts to one-up her in everything from games to shooting to a few "easy" jogs around the property.

Like Jane, both Hal and Joe understood and encouraged competition. That was why when Uncle Sam needed results, they reached out to Team Ten, the mercs who got things done. Period.

She wanted to get back to that, the ability to do her job to the best of her ability. To take down criminals and serve them justice.

Despite enjoying the holiday atmosphere and reconnecting with family, the part of herself she'd been trying to ignore itched to be more productive than just cleaning house and building muscle.

Her phone rang, and she practically dove for it, hoping for anything to alleviate the doldrums of being away from work so long.

"Yo, spaz, nice you finally answered the phone."

Jane swallowed a sigh at the husky female voice on the other end. "Merry Christmas to you too, Raine."

Her cousin chuckled. "Ho ho ho. So what's going on that I'm missing out on?"

Jane settled into the large chair near the fireplace and placed her phone down, speaker on. "Well, Hal and Joe still can't beat me in a foot race. But Joe's gotten even better with a pistol than he was the last time he was here. I swear he was born with a gun in hand."

Raine snorted. "No kidding. His mom told me he got hooked on a water pistol at age three. The rest is history."

Jane smiled. "I can see that. And Hal has been gorging himself on video games and sweets. Oh, and the ladies. He visited one of his friends the day after he got home, but I think he's out with someone else tonight."

"Boy Toy in the *houssse*." Raine tapered off into a lingering silence, which wasn't like her.

Jane liked silence, introspection, and patience.

Raine could talk the ear off a mule, made it a practice to comment aloud on whatever she thought when she thought it, and had trouble sitting still.

"What's wrong?" Jane asked.

"Nothing."

"Yeah, right." She huffed. "Just tell me. Uncle Chris already mentioned you're having some kind of issue."

"What a blabbermouth," Raine muttered.

"Where are you?"

"I didn't say."

"I know. That's why I'm asking." Jane swore she could hear her cousin shrug through the phone and knew a satisfactory answer would not be forthcoming.

"Nowhere special."

More atypical silence. "But...?" Jane prodded.

A slight pause, then Raine blurted, "I'm thinking about leaving."

"Your unit? You can do that?" Had the Marine Corps changed so much that Raine could leave her current assignment before her tour ended?

"No, dummy. My job."

Jane blinked. "The USMC? But you live for the scarlet and gold."

"I know." Raine sounded miserable. "The last few ops, I, well..." She sighed. "Things have changed. I don't like the direction things are taking."

"Things, huh?" Jane knew what that was like. "If your command is giving you problems, you know you should wait it out. COs come and go. The next spot will be better." Or worse, but Raine would know that. "But then, you're Miss Popular with the higher-ups, aren't you? Use that chatty Raine charm and find a new home."

"It's not that, exactly."

31

"You can't tell me?"

"No." Raine's frustration came through in a growl. "I'm so pissed at what's been going on. And I can't tell anyone."

"Tell Uncle Chris."

"Oh heck, no. He'll bluster and take over, and then I'll have to shoot him."

Jane nodded. "Yeah, probably."

"I just... I wish people would listen when I tell them things."

"More things?"

Raine talked over her. "I'm not like you. I can't just sit back and take it on the chin when my boss puts me on mandatory leave."

Jane straightened in her seat. "Excuse me?"

"I mean, my partner gets shot, I'm all in someone's face, finding out the truth. Making them pay."

"What are you saying?" Jane started to get mad.

"I'm just saying I'd be taking steps to rectify the situation, not hiding out at home."

"I'm doing what needs to be done."

"Yeah, see. That's what I should do. Rectify a few things." Raine muttered something else then added, "I've gotta go. Tell the guys I miss them. Now pull on your big girl panties and make things right. Later, slacker."

Raine disconnected before Jane could yell back at her.

What did her cousin know? Nothing about the situation. Even if Uncle Chris had shared—which he obviously had—he knew less than she did. And Grace hadn't come up with any viable suspects from the home office, which to be honest, relieved Jane.

She didn't want to believe anyone she worked with might be dirty. But unlike her cousin, she knew making a big production out of pointing fingers without proof would get her nowhere. It would only help alert the Mazzucas that she continued to investigate, which would clue in her SSA, and then the jerk would likely write her up for insubordination and finally figure a way to stick Simmons' death on her for good.

Jane thought several steps ahead, playing the long game if not the most satisfying game. She glared at her phone. *Some of us prefer to play it safe.*

Still fuming, she found her uncle's traditional Christmas movie and hit play then as quickly hit pause, unable to watch John McClane duke it out with Hans Gruber all by herself. Some traditions deserved to be followed, and a viewing of *Die Hard* without Team Ten didn't bear consideration.

Grumbling, she tuned in to *It's a Wonderful Life* instead, wondering what life might be like without her cousin to screw up the holidays.

CHAPTER SIX

ANOTHER DAY PASSED, AND JANE WONDERED HOW MUCH TROUBLE SHE'D get into if she happened to hang around the Seattle office and *accidentally* bump into her friends to pump them for information.

Joe and Hal were out doing a favor for somebody. The fewer questions she asked the better, because the conversation before they'd left had been hushed, the legality of the matter no doubt up for debate.

Flipping through channels on the TV, she noted that the police had caught the shooter who'd taken out that poor couple before the holiday. Not a Mazzuca killing, apparently, but some random tweaker on a rant. A second later, in the same tone, the newscaster informed her that shopping had been better than expected over the holiday season, pleasing economists hoping for a better fourth quarter. To top it all off, the Seahawks had won by twelve points, and the stormfront everyone had been expecting moved north instead, giving those poor Canadians more snow to deal with.

And none of that made Jane's life any less boring.

Annoyed with life, Jane turned off the television and grabbed her car keys.

Two hours later, she left one of her favorite downtown Seattle lunch stops with a full belly, stuffed on an English cheese, tomato, and pesto crumpet.

Her phone rang, and she jumped on it, despite seeing the caller ID. "Hey, Uncle Chris. A day late, but Merry Christmas."

"Yeah, to you too. Look, I need a favor."

Trust her uncle to get straight to the point. "Hit me. Unfortunately, I'm swimming in circles. I've got nothing on anyone in the office who might have set me up. I'm twiddling my thumbs while life goes on." *And I'm no closer to finding out who killed Dan Simmons.*

"Exactly. You need to get your butt back in the field. I know you're benched until OPR clears you, but that doesn't mean you can't do some investigative services for a friend of mine."

"Say again?"

"A friend of mine needs help with something that's looking like it's a lot more involved than it should be. I'll let him read you in. Throw on something super casual. Don't look like a federal agent and meet him at the address I just texted you." He disconnected the call, then an address popped up via text.

She glanced down at her jeans and hoodie sweatshirt under a dark jacket. Super casual, check. Though most agents she worked with wore "outdoor casual" on the daily. Comfort, practicality, and maybe a nice sweater to go with the cargo pants and boots.

After plugging the address into her phone, she entered her car and blasted the heat, pleased she'd taken the initiative to head into the city in the first place. If she'd been in Bainbridge and had to wait on a ferry, she might not have been able to get to the place for another few hours.

As it was, she had to maneuver around Seattle traffic before finding the street cordoned off by police cars, barricades, and yellow barricade tape. She'd happened upon a fresh scene, apparently. After parking several blocks away, she returned to survey the area.

Lights flashed, and an ambulance sat sideways in the middle of the street with parked cars lining the roadway in front of several small businesses and residential buildings. Shattered glass covered the area around one of the ambulances. Two bloodied and unmoving bodies lay close by as well.

The tires on one ambulance appeared to be flat, likely from a gunshot, which would also explain the shattered windshield. She didn't notice bullet holes anywhere else, not in the cars parked along the sides of the street or the doors and walls of the nearby businesses.

Not a drive-by then.

She read her text again. Under the directions, her uncle had provided a description of the person to contact. Glancing up, she looked for a man in a long, navy trench coat and gold scarf. Not exactly nondescript. Interesting fashion choice. But he pulled it off, appearing elegant in a standoffish way.

He stood away from the central action near a police car, in deep discussion with two officers. An older guy with short silver hair, a pale complexion, and dark eyes that didn't look surprised at the sight of death so near.

He glanced up as she rounded the barricade to get to him. He said something to the officer next to him, and the woman turned and headed for Jane with brisk strides.

"Come with me," she ordered, and Jane followed her, ducking under the barricade tape until they rejoined the man she'd been sent to assist.

The officers standing nearby melted away, leaving Jane alone with her contact.

"Jane Cannon?" the man asked, his voice deep and raspy.

This close, she saw the fine lines around his eyes. He had to be years older than her uncle, but he looked as if he knew how to laugh. She sensed his authority up close, his military bearing evident in the way he held himself. She'd have pegged him as the man in charge without knowing anything about anyone present, despite him standing apart.

"Yes. I'm Jane. Pleased to meet you." She held out a hand. His firm and dry shake, just long enough to convey trust and authority, said as much about him as his appearance.

"I'm Lionel Gambol. Not affiliated with the police department or FBI."

Jane raised a brow but said nothing. Nearby, she noted the lead CSI, his dark jacket lettered POLICE on the back, giving orders that everyone else seemed to follow as they rushed around.

"You came highly recommended," he added.

"For...?"

"Investigative services." Exactly what her uncle had said. "The murders of these two EMTs make six dead in the past two months. EMTs, doctors, and two nurses. Someone is targeting medical personnel in the city, and I want to know who and why."

"But you're not the police or the FBI."

"Consider me FBI adjacent."

That sounded like something her uncle would say.

"You should know I'm on administrative leave from the Seattle office pending an investigation." Just in case her uncle had failed to mention that. Uncle Chris often left out the parts he didn't feel necessary when it came to doing the job. Pesky little details like legality.

"I understand that. Working this case won't be a problem with your boss or the Agency. You don't need a weapon. This is strictly investigatory. I know you often have insights others miss. And we need that right now."

She watched with him as forensics did their job photographing the scene and cataloguing everything.

She frowned. "Were the bodies found like that?" Both EMTs lay supine, one with an arm over his chest, the other with his arm flung aside, reaching along the street.

"Yes." Gambol studied her. "So you're in?"

She saw no point in making him wait, since she practically frothed at the mouth for something to do while she waited on any information pertaining to who killed Simmons. "Yes."

"Follow me." He walked to the lead CSI, had a few words, then everyone backed away. "What do you think?" Gambol asked Jane.

She crouched by the bodies, aware each had been shot and killed by a bullet to the chest as well as a bullet to the head. Two rounds, placed to kill. No lingering death by internal bleeding. The headshots would have ended them right away.

"Not a random drive-by." She rose and looked around. "There's no damage to the surrounding businesses or cars parked along the street. Looks like the shooter took out the windshield first to stop the bus. The EMTs left the vehicle. But instead of hiding behind it, they rounded the ambulance and headed for the middle of the street." Jane shook her head. "That makes no sense. Any witnesses?"

"In broad daylight, yet shockingly, no." Gambol looked as if he'd bitten into a lemon. "But we've got the surveillance camera from two businesses to check into. Hopefully, we'll find something we can use there."

Jane had a thought. She checked the front of the ambulance, noticed the empty space in front of it, and looked closer at the smudge of blue paint on the front bumper.

She turned to Gambol, the heat of the hunt building in her, fanning the need to find the guilty. "This took planning. I need to see pictures of the other shootings."

"The others weren't shot, but we have crime scene photos of two of them, at least." Gambol nodded. "Let's get you set up. Time to meet the man in charge."

"Not you?" she asked as he led her to his vehicle. She got in, planning to pick up her car afterward.

"Not me. I'm just the connections man. It's time for you to meet Rapp."

"I have to tell you I'm not looking forward to working for anyone like the boss I just left."

"No, no. You'll be working *with* him. Not for him. Think of yourself as contracting your services to the government through me." Gambol shot her a quick grin as they drove away. "Give Rapp a chance. He's not as bad as he might seem."

CHAPTER SEVEN

HAD GAMBOL SAID NOT AS BAD? GUNTHER RAPP WAS *WORSE*.

Jane had met his type so many times before. A typical ex-special forces alpha male with control issues, except he looked to be in his mid-thirties. A little young to be so intimidating.

He came across as hostile, condescending, and maybe misogynistic, and Jane had shared just a handful of words with him at most.

The small coffee shop where they met wasn't crowded. And while they had the corner all to themselves, Rapp seemed to suck up all the air.

She glared at Gambol, who shrugged and gave her an innocent smile before checking his watch.

"Well, I'm off. Jane, you'll report to Gunther." He turned to the tall man next to him. "Jane's working this case with you as a contracted investigator, not as an official government agent. Though she's technically FBI."

"That shouldn't be a problem since this isn't an official FBI investigation, though, is it?" Gunther said in a deep voice filled with sarcasm.

"Gunther, play nice." Gambol gave them both a two-finger salute then left without another word.

Jane studied Gunther Rapp and wondered what she'd gotten

herself into. Though she did need something to occupy her time while she waited for a break in her investigation into her unit, she didn't know if she wanted the headache of placating another idiot boss.

"Let's be clear here," she said.

"Oh, let's."

"First, I'm working *with* you. Not *for* you," she said before he could and deliberately took a seat at a nearby table.

Rapp raised his brows but didn't argue. He left her there and returned shortly with two black coffees. He tossed her some sugar packets and placed a mini pitcher of creamer on the table.

"Why, thank you." Jane shot him a smile with a lot of teeth and took one cup, fixing it to her liking, not bothering to fill the silence with small talk.

Rapp sat down, the suit he wore not disguising the breadth of his shoulders or the muscles hidden by his sleeves. He had short, sandy-brown hair cut for practicality if not style and looked like a warrior with that stubborn square jaw and intense blue eyes. Eyes that looked at her like a wolf considering his prey.

But Jane was nobody's victim. She'd spent years, first in the USMC, then again in the FBI, proving it. She could hold her own, even with a guy who looked like he could bend her into a pretzel.

"Okay, here's what we know." He glanced over as three patrons departed, leaving them alone except for the staff. He continued, his voice low, "You're on leave from your unit due to a suspicious involvement in the death of a fellow agent."

Jane sipped slowly, meeting his gaze.

His eyes narrowed. "You have a record of closing cases. Your name comes recommended by several sources, and since this investigation isn't exactly front and center with the agency, more a fringe case stringing possibly linked crimes together, your involvement carries no risk. Yet."

For a guy who looked like a gym bro, he sounded halfway intelligent.

"Gee, thanks."

His expression lightened, and she had the feeling he wanted to smile but didn't. "I'm leading a small team that's looking into some related violent crimes. I have one agent who's new to the area but used to working violent crime. And I've got a hacker with authority issues currently working off a court mandate by helping us."

Jane blinked. "A ringing endorsement to joining your team."

He grunted and sipped his coffee without cream or sugar. Dark and bitter, like him. She bit back her amusement at the thought.

"What do you bring to the table, Agent Rapp?"

"I'm on loan from another organization for a few months while my superiors fight it out over who FUBARed our last op, because it wasn't me. Gambol needed help with a few cases, and he tapped me for this one." Before she could ask another question, he said, "You can call me Rapp."

"Great. You can call me Agent Cannon." She held out a hand, waiting.

When he took hers, she ignored a spark of disquiet and warned, "I'm happy to help. I'm not happy to take any crap. I work hard, and I get results. All the macho posturing or 'little lady' BS just gets in the way." She tugged her hand free easily. "Any questions?"

He gave her a shark's grin, and had she not been aware of her ability to hold her own, she might have been intimidated. "Sounds great, *Jane*. But so there's no confusion, we have one person in charge. *Me*. Do what you're told when you're told. No hot-dogging. No using this as a steppingstone to unlock a big ball of girl power so you can reign as queen bee. I'm here to solve a case. Period."

"Great to know we're on the same page, Rapp," she said with a lot more sweetness than their dialogue warranted.

He studied her and sighed. "You're going to be a huge pain in the ass. I can just tell."

She swallowed her coffee, her agreement silent but no less adamant. *Screw with me and I'll end you, big guy.*

He glared back at her, and they stared in silence for a few moments, sipping their coffee.

Until Jane said, "So am I going to get notes on the other victims or what?"

Rapp rolled his eyes and pulled out a briefcase she hadn't noticed, one that had been sitting against the wall next to him. He handed her a manila folder.

As she looked through it, she saw four more victims, but all with different causes of death. "So these two doctors died from natural causes. One nurse poisoned, another overdosed. How do they link up?"

"That's what we're still trying to figure out."

"Who lumped them together? They seem unrelated."

"Exactly. Which is why no one is taking them seriously as a serial threat. But Gambol called me in on this for a reason. The only resources I have are the hacker and the agent. I haven't known them much longer than I've known you."

"What a treat that must be for you." She knew it had to be bugging him, a bossy type not in total control of his people yet.

He grinned, a genuine expression of mirth that turned him from annoying to slightly less so. And handsome, not that she had time for that. He set his coffee back down and said, "Gee, it's like we're best friends already."

She snorted. "Right. So obviously you have detailed records on the cases. What do you need from me, exactly?"

"Come to this address tomorrow." He pointed to a sticky note inside the manilla folder she'd been studying. "You can get to work poring over evidence, looking for anything we might have missed. I'll hook you up with Holtz and Rivera. We'll go from there."

"Sounds good."

He drank the rest of his coffee, took the folder back from her after giving her the sticky note, then tucked the folder into his briefcase and stood with it in hand.

She stood with him, irked to see he had several inches on her.

As if he read her annoyance, he smiled. "Need a ride to your car?"

"Nah. I'll walk back." The weather was brisk, but the mile walk would do her good. Plus, it would take her twice as long if she had to drive back. And more time spent with Agent Rapp wasn't on her to-do list, at least not today.

"Sounds like a plan. I'll see you tomorrow, Jane. 0800, bright and early."

"I can't wait."

He laughed and followed her out.

She turned right and walked back in the direction of her car. After some distance, not meaning to, she glanced over her shoulder and saw him watching her.

He caught her glance, nodded, then walked away.

And damn it all, she felt as if she'd lost a game she wasn't aware she'd been playing.

CHAPTER EIGHT

THE NEXT DAY AT 7:45 IN THE MORNING, JANE STOOD OUTSIDE THE locked door of Suite A in a building right around the corner from the downtown FBI office where she normally worked.

Hal and Joe had been disappointed that she'd be spending the next few days in the city, but they understood the appeal of getting back to real work. Having completed whatever they'd been up to, the two of them would likely remain on vacation until Uncle Chris returned.

Her uncle used to have to force them to take time off, but the past few years, the guys had realized they needed to decompress. Working at maximum output twenty-four-seven burned out even the best operatives.

She'd promised to return when she could. They had a few rematches to get to. Poor Joe still thought he could beat her in a distance race. Sucker.

Smirking, she leaned against the wall outside the locked door, content to "hurry up and wait," a circumstance with which she was all too familiar. In the Marine Corps, she'd spent more time being early and waiting around than she could count. Though the FBI was better, she still got caught in the bureaucracy of waiting on superiors and meetings.

Thinking of meetings, she wondered what SSA Scott might be up to. Who he might be talking to. She needed to get with Grace again. Her friend's report hadn't amounted to much more than what Jane had already known about her peers.

Several of the agents in her squad were divorced and paying child support. A few had gambling problems, one of which she hadn't been aware. But Grace showed he made payments on time and was currently in a Gamblers Anonymous program. Her closer companions, Jenn Sullivan and Rob Williams, remained single and nosy about everyone else's business while remaining clean of scandal. A big deal, considering how often they played fast and loose with the rules.

Like Jane, they got the job done, and she respected their work ethic. They never had a problem canceling plans in favor of a case or working through the weekend when needed. Forty hours per week only applied to regular people with regular jobs, not Feds trying to combat violent crimes and protect national security.

They felt like her people, and she couldn't help calling them by last name the way she had her true friends in the Marine Corps. "Sullivan" and "Williams" sounded friendlier to Jane than "Jenn" and "Rob." Weird, but it made sense in her head.

A door slamming and heavy footsteps on the cement floor caught her attention. She glanced up from her phone to see a guy a few years her junior moseying through the hall.

He had shaggy black hair needing a cut, skin a shade darker than hers, and wore a heavy winter coat, faded jeans, and clean sneakers. As he approached, he gave her a leisurely onceover and grinned, showing a crooked front tooth that gave him a charming, nonthreatening appearance.

Slender and standing maybe six feet tall, he didn't move with the grace of someone used to close combat. This had to be the hacker Rapp had mentioned.

"Yo, a new face around the place. I like it." He grinned. "Are you the girl Rapp told us to expect?"

"I am."

"Diego Rivera."

"Nice to meet you, Diego. I'm Jane."

They shook hands.

He demonstrated the code for the keylock at the door then preceded her inside. A narrow hallway opened up into one large room with a bunch of cubicles in the center, surrounded by a few long tables covered in stacks of files.

Along one wall, photos of the victims covered white boards marked with names, dates, and notes. Two doors at the back, on either side of another hallway, led to glass-fronted offices.

A conference room with a long table and a dozen chairs was on the left. The right office likely belonged to Rapp. With the blinds up, she could see file cabinets and bookshelves filled with books and manilla folders, and in the center, a large desk with a computer.

The entire suite had recently been painted a neutral white. She could smell paint along with coffee and a light but floral perfume.

A small, open kitchenette occupied space on the left, complete with two tables and a high-speed coffee maker. A tall black woman stood there, openly assessing Jane and Diego.

She wore a plum-colored pantsuit, her braided hair swept into an appealing bun. Her flawless makeup and attire showcased a strong and confident woman. Jane put her age close to Jane's, early- to mid-thirties, though the woman's sharp gaze said she had experience in the agency. So she might be older.

Maybe this assignment wouldn't be too bad. Something about the woman's intelligent eyes and firm demeanor reminded her of Grace. Then the woman gave her a dismissive onceover and ruined any hope of a pleasant office experience.

Jane mentally swallowed a growl. She wasn't her cousin, needing to prove herself to anyone. She'd been hired—had she, though?—to investigate a series of murders.

Diego introduced them. "Agent Gina Holtz, meet Jane. Jane, this is Gina." Diego fetched an energy drink from the refrigerator, leaving them alone.

"Agent Holtz. Nice to meet you."

"Jane." Gina Holtz nodded but didn't extend a hand, content to sip her coffee and look down her nose. "I'm not sure why you're here, but Rapp said to show you to a desk. Follow me."

Jane followed her to a desk covered in folders.

"This is what we know so far. Each of the stacks is what we've gathered on the victims. There are six of them as of yesterday." She turned to Diego, who'd gone to a desk that looked like something from a movie. Covered in monitors and keyboards, with desktops jockeying for space under the desk, his station resembled the console of a spaceship. "I need you to gather what you can on the EMTs. Their phone records will be here in a bit. But I hit a snag on EMT2."

"We didn't have their names yesterday before Gina went home," Diego explained and slurped his drink. "I'll get it for you."

Jane glanced at her crowded desk, eager to get her hands dirty. After seeing what had been left of the EMTs yesterday, she needed to do something to help catch their killer.

Gina nodded. "I'll leave you to it then." She turned on her heel, then stalked to her desk and settled in at her keyboard.

Jane did the same. What she'd seen yesterday made her eager to know more. She'd bet her next paycheck that the blue on the ambulance bumper had been caused by a hit and run. And that the perpetrator had then shot at the windshield, forced the EMTs out at gunpoint, then executed them one at a time.

A professional hit connected to four other murders. Intrigued, she opened the folder on the first victim, Doctor 1, and got to work.

CHAPTER NINE

AGENT RAPP DIDN'T MAKE AN APPEARANCE UNTIL THE AFTERNOON. JANE only knew he'd entered the office because she heard his deep voice, which distracted her from her research.

Neck deep in the backgrounds of the first two victims, Doctors Ryan Daniels and Julie David, she'd read through their family histories and backgrounds, and nothing seemed to connect. They'd worked at different hospitals in the city, had lived in various places before coming to Seattle—at different times—and practiced different specialties. Dr. Daniels worked in family health and Dr. David in pediatrics.

Her eyes crossed as she confused Daniels with David for the sixth time that morning.

"Hell. What time is it?" she muttered to herself as she rubbed her eyes. She needed more coffee.

"Time you got a watch." Diego smirked at her as he passed her desk, sipping another energy drink. "I know, a dad joke. But it's still funny."

"It's really not," she said, though she grinned.

"Ha! I saw that."

"Saw what?" Rapp said as he joined them. Today he'd dressed in a dark blue suit instead of yesterday's black. Same white shirt and blue tie though. For some reason, he looked both perfectly dressed and out of place in a suit and tie. He needed utility trousers and camo paint on his face, she thought.

A glance behind him revealed Gina engaged in a fierce argument on the phone with someone.

"Diego's trying to be funny," Jane deadpanned.

"Trying?" Diego whined.

Rapp shook his head. "Quit screwing off. Where's my intel on the latest victims?"

Diego made a face and nodded to his desk and a printer that continued to spit out pages. "I've been collecting data." He dropped a stack of paper on the desk Jane was using. "Here. I brought you a present. No one appreciates me."

"Not true," Rapp answered. "Our government appreciates you not hacking into its servers anymore. Legal is a nice, non-four-letter word. Keep using it."

Diego muttered something under his breath and sighed all the way back to his desk.

"Kid needs his meds to stay focused, and I'm not making fun," Rapp said under his breath, though the "kid" couldn't be that much younger than he was. Rapp pulled up a nearby chair and sat. "Report."

"Rapp, I left the Marine Corps four years ago. I don't do one-word orders. Try again." She needed to establish boundaries. Best to start as she meant to go.

He just looked at her, and she wondered if he planned on making a big deal right now. "Jane, could you please *report* what you found, if anything?"

"I see what you did there." When an angry flush started to creep over his cheeks, she figured she'd pushed hard enough. "I've been going through the files on the first two victims all morning. Diego did a terrific job of compiling data."

Rapp relaxed. "He did. Gina too. She went over the in-person interviews then reviewed them again and gained some new information for us."

"Ah, yes. Those are pretty detailed, but I can't find any connection between the first two victims. At all. I'm sure Diego cross-referenced them, but I went over them too. There's nothing in their histories that makes sense. I also read over the reports from the MEs. A heart attack and a hyperglycemic reaction that resulted in death. Neither shout 'conspiracy' or 'murder.'"

"Not until you see that both were injected between their toes with a hypodermic."

"Which isn't conclusive according to Dr. David's—no, Dr. Daniels' report." She rifled through the folders to pull up the medical report on Daniels. "They couldn't determine if that spot was due to a splinter he'd received a few days prior, when he'd been camping, or if it was in fact a needle. Because his wife used sharp tweezers to pull one out and couldn't remember which toes she'd messed with. And the tox screens came back negative for anything suspicious."

Jane sat back and rubbed her eyes. "I'm happy to help with this, but I can't see how it's related. Not even these first two, and I've only glanced at the other files."

Rapp nodded. "I know. I felt the same. But it's there. Trust me."

"You mean trust Gambol and/or his source."

Rapp just looked at her.

"Fine." She grunted. "But we're going to need better coffee than what's in that expensive pot."

He lowered his voice and said, "Don't say that too loudly. Gina's got issues when it comes to her beans." After a pause, he added in an approving voice, "But feel free to express yourself. I'm all for my subordinates working things out amongst themselves."

Subordinate? It was like he was trying to annoy her.

"Just be careful," he continued. "I don't want to think about how awkward the office dynamics could get if people started pulling hair."

"Or punching people in their big mouths," she growled, aware he was deliberately aggravating her.

"Exactly." He stood, serious once more. "When you've schooled yourself on our vics, I have some video I'd like you to watch."

Gina overheard. "I prepped the files for the fun box. Have at it."

"Fun box?" Jane asked.

Rapp nodded. "There's a small room over there, behind the black door."

"Oh, I thought that was the bathroom."

"No. That's down the hall by my office. Men's and women's on either side. I don't care which you use, just *don't leave a mess*," he ended on a raised voice, his focus on Diego.

"The fun box?" she reminded him.

"Follow me."

She trailed him to the black door and after he pushed it open, glanced inside.

A large monitor, surrounded by several smaller ones, occupied a wide desk. A few computer towers sat on the floor by it. She noticed a pedal on the floor and hand controls on the desk.

"It's where we like to view feeds. According to Diego, this setup has better power for speed and sound and whatever else you need to smoothly process video. The monitors are top of the line, and we have access to VHS and DVD players as well. Most of it's streaming, but not all. We've been grabbing all the surveillance video from surrounding areas to the crimes, which hasn't been easy, especially considering the doctors' deaths weren't suspicious at first." He paused. "It's a lot of footage to wade through. Gina and Diego can attest to that. They went over it all so far, though we've found a little more as time has gone on."

"Ah. So this is really why you needed me. For the grunt work no one else wants to do."

"Partly. And partly because, according to Gambol, you're not half bad when it comes to spotting things. Even the smallest detail might help at this point."

She sensed his frustration. "How long have you been on this?"

"Just a month. It doesn't seem like much, but that's already four weeks too many." He paused, and his expression flattened. "One of my brothers is a doctor. Killing people whose job is to save lives rubs me the wrong way. We need to find this scumbag before they kill again."

She nodded. She might not exactly like Rapp, but she couldn't argue with his intent.

And while she waited for answers to her own separate investigation, she had nothing better to do than help catch a killer. Believing her uncle wouldn't have given her name to Gambol if he didn't trust the guy, she put her faith in him as well.

Time to get back to work and find the patterns that would give this dirtbag away.

Before they hurt someone else.

CHAPTER TEN

By New Year's Eve, Jane calculated that she'd spent five days in front of the fun box, which had been misappropriately named.

Her eyes strained, dried from watching hours upon hours of video. Between getting up to speed on the victims, including the two EMTs, as well as perusing content from six different alleged crime scenes over and over again, she concluded that though Gambol seemed to think these were related, she saw no evidence to prove a connection.

The EMTs had definitely been murdered. Video footage proved someone had rammed the ambulance head-on, creating a fender bender mild enough the car had been drivable, allowing the perp to disappear afterward.

The shooter darted out after the impact, firing into the ambulance windshield. The EMTs abandoned their vehicle where the masked perpetrator forced them into the street and executed them. All from a good ten feet away.

Perfect shots. One to the head, then one to the heart for each man. Overkill. Part of a ritual, maybe?

Calmly, the shooter returned to his vehicle, a blue four-door Toyota, and drove away, his bumper only slightly damaged.

More surveillance supplied by Diego indicated the Toyota headed south on I-5 before they lost coverage. LEOs eventually found the vehicle on fire in an abandoned factory in Tacoma.

The sites where the doctors and nurses had been found had little footage, showing weird angles and poor lighting. A few people had used their phone to record the dead nurses, so she got a partial view as they stood around, watching.

She had the best footage of Dr. Daniels—not David—who had collapsed of a heart attack outside a bank.

Jane returned to that one and watched everything again. She'd studied each death numerous times, spending late nights at the office. Hal and Joe had checked in, and Hal had offered to run some special software he'd concocted to recognize patterns.

If she didn't find anything today, she might take him up on the offer. But she didn't think Rapp or Gambol would want one of Team Ten hacking into their servers. Not to mention Hal might still be wanted for crimes he'd committed in the course of work for her uncle. Best to keep him out of the federal loop whenever possible.

She was on her fourth cup of coffee that evening, watching a video of the fourth victim, when she thought she spotted the suspect. Something about the way the guy stood, the slant of his hips, the way he leaned back on his feet a little. How he bobbed when he walked...

She hurriedly inserted a DVD of one of the nurses into the player and watched it on a smaller monitor. *Yes.* There. Him again. She couldn't make out his face, half-hidden by a dark, nondescript ballcap, but she'd swear it was the same guy from the EMT footage.

Scrambling for the EMT video, she noted the way the man in the mask moved. A little jerkier, as if he tried to move differently to fool anyone watching. But she could tell it was him.

After going through all the videos she could find and comparing images, she stuck her head out and called for everyone to join her.

Despite it being close to 8 PM on New Year's Eve, everyone remained working.

"Whatcha got?" Diego asked.

He, Gina, and Rapp crowded into the room behind her. She sat in the chair and pulled up different feeds to different monitors, then pointed at the masked man on the large screen with the EMTs in addition to the other two videos.

"There. He's our guy."

Gina spoke first. "How do you figure? I went through all this and still don't see it. He only appeared in the EMT footage."

"I don't get it either," Diego said, though he sounded hesitant. "Although he does resemble the guy from Nurse2—I mean, Nurse Anna Field."

Rapp leaned in, and Jane caught a whiff of subtle cologne. Or maybe aftershave.

It annoyed her to find it pleasing. She drank more hazelnut coffee to drown him out.

"You wanted an expert on it, I'm the expert," Jane insisted. "And that's him."

"So humble," Gina muttered.

"*I'm* the expert." Diego protested, "I'm the one who found all the footage."

"That we both went over a million times," Gina said.

Jane knew her worth, and she saw what others missed often enough that she had no problem taking credit for work well done. "Well, I notice things. That's why you brought me in."

"Oh, and we don't? We've been meticulously going over these videos." Gina's voice rose, her frustration evident.

Jane shrugged. "What do you want me to say? You missed it."

Gina enunciated her icy reply, "I guess our best isn't good enough, is that it?"

Rapp interrupted, ignoring the drama, pointing at the screens. "No. That's him. Look. She's right. See how he moves? It's our guy at every site."

Getting Rapp's approval changed the tone in the room, the energy suddenly vibrating with excitement.

It came as a surprise when Rapp told them all to go home. "We'll continue the day after New Year's. I'm ordering you all to take a day off."

Diego darted from the room. "Don't have to tell me twice." And he was gone.

Gina paused. "You sure, Rapp? I don't mind coming in tomorrow." She frowned.

"You've been working nonstop for weeks, Gina. Take a day. Trust me. I'll get this info to Gambol and see what he comes up with. None of us will get anything done if we burn out. We'll have trouble getting anyone on the phone with the holiday, anyway."

She nodded. "Happy New Year." She ignored Jane.

Determining that they really did have a connection between the victims, other than Gambol's say-so, gave Jane the warm fuzzies. She smiled at Gina. "Thanks."

That Gina scowled back made Jane feel even better.

She stood to follow the others out and banged into Rapp. "Hey, quit looming."

"Sorry." He wasn't looking at her, too busy staring at the monitors. "Good work, Jane."

"Thanks." She paused at the doorway. "Are you leaving?"

"In a few minutes. Look, I know this wasn't easy." He finally turned to look at her. "But I appreciate your hard work. I'll reach out when we need you back here. Enjoy what's left of the holiday." He paused. "Any big plans?"

"Other than not watching TV for another month? No."

He snorted. "Yeah. The fun box hasn't been very fun, has it? Well, see you next year." He turned back to the monitors and scribbled something on the notepad she'd been using.

Dismissed, Jane left, feeling good. She'd made some progress. And with the time off from Rapp's team, maybe she could circle back to the Mazzucas. Because no doubt they'd made some resolutions. And she was determined to stop them achieving those. No matter what.

CHAPTER ELEVEN

JANE THOUGHT ABOUT SPENDING NEW YEAR'S EVE ALONE, BUT A TEXT from Hal convinced her to join the guys near the Space Needle for fireworks followed by drinks at a bar to celebrate.

The weather cooperated for once, and they enjoyed the fireworks before heading to a popular dive in Lake City. Joe, as expected, got into a fight that Jane solved peaceably with a darts contest.

Hal ended up winning, and the idiot who'd thought he could take on Joe and survive ended up buying Joe, Hal, and Jane a round of drinks. She hadn't expected to celebrate, tired after a grueling day staring at videos, so the beers hit her harder than she'd expected.

She woke up with the sun hitting her in the face, hanging half off her bed, her headache painful.

A familiar groan from her living room told her the boys had delivered her back home, though she had no memory of it.

"You are such a lightweight," Joe rumbled with a laugh.

Hal and Joe and Jane in her tiny but spotless apartment. She would have been freaked out about others, even them, invading her space if she hadn't been distracted by a well of nausea.

Half an hour later, she joined the guys in her kitchen, feeling better after a much-needed shower.

"Aw, look who decided to rejoin the living." Hal sounded way too cheery. To her bemusement, he looked fine if a bit frumpy in his wrinkled shirt and jeans, not like a guy who'd been groaning earlier, sounding two breaths away from death.

Joe looked the way he always did. A muscled giant with a winsome smile who made killer pancakes. And, of course, his clothes looked wrinkle-free.

"Gimme." She motioned for the plate of pancakes he'd fixed.

He grinned. "You're so cute when you're hungover."

She glared, and Joe laughed and slid her the plate. She devoured the food and felt worlds better, especially when Joe handed her a cup of her favorite Earl Grey tea.

Hal propped his chin on his palm, elbow resting on the table, and closed his eyes. "How's the investigation going?"

She filled them both in on what she'd been working on.

They didn't like what she'd found, and neither did she.

"What's odd is how Gambol knew," Hal said. "I mean, did he figure it out after watching hours and hours of video? I doubt it. So who told him?"

"Good question." Joe looked thoughtful. "What if someone warned him about the murders? Like, it's an attack on the city? The murderer maybe contacted him? Because Lionel responds to direct threats. He's not a wait-and-see-and-study kind of guy."

"Wait. You know Lionel Gambol?" She blinked.

Hal opened his eyes and shared a look with Joe. "Jane, we could tell you, but we'd have to kill you."

"Shut up, Hal."

He snickered. "Seriously though. Gambol's a good egg. Takes himself a little too seriously, but he's someone you can trust. He's not political, and he tries to protect the little guy. I like him."

"You would." Joe shook his head. "You still owe him for getting you out of that 'situation' in Riyadh."

Hal cleared his throat. "That's not it. I just like him."

Joe rolled his eyes.

Jane studied Hal. She hadn't heard about the Riyadh incident, though she had a feeling she hadn't heard about most of the things the guys got up to. And she'd sleep the better for it.

"Anyway," Jane continued, "we're getting somewhere on this serial medical responder killer." She'd overheard Diego call the guy the Code Blue Killer and hoped it didn't stick. Giving killers monikers only made them that much more attractive to the press and serial killer groupies.

"It's weird though," Hal added. "Killing doctors and nurses? EMTs? They typically help people. Your unsub is going to have an interesting profile."

He had a point. And that led her to another thought. "Speaking of interesting profiles, do either of you know a guy named Gunther Rapp? He's the agent in charge of Gambol's little task force. The guy strikes me as some ex-military type. I haven't had the time to look him up though."

"I'll get you something on him later," Hal promised. "Are you coming back to the house with us?"

"How long are you guys sticking around?" She really had missed them. Oddly, the holiday made her nostalgic for the old days, when she, Raine, and Uncle Chris would celebrate by shooting weird ammo at funny targets he'd set up. They'd go on treks through the woods on "hunting" parties, looking for Santa and evidence of reindeer, which Team Ten would plant. Or they'd strategize how to invade the North Pole and Santa's workshop in case the elves had plans to overthrow the system.

In retrospect, her uncle had been unconventional, to say the least. But so much fun. Because of him and Team Ten, she had so many fond memories.

"We'll be here for another few weeks at least," Joe said. "Chris said to stand by for a new op, a bigger one, after he's back."

Hal nodded. "He's always got something lined up for us." He sighed. "No rest for the wicked." But he winked to show he loved it.

"Yeah, speaking of wicked… How did we get home last night? I think I might have blacked out."

"You were exhausted, and those three beers put you down hard."

Hal snickered, and Joe joined in. "But you were so cute talking about how much better you are at finding clues and hunting bad guys than 'stupid Raine.'"

She groaned. "You can't tell her I said that. It'll hurt her feelings."

"Yeah, right." Joe guffawed. "You just don't want her to know she can still drink you under the table. Three beers? Honey, that's just sad."

Jane flushed. She'd never tolerated alcohol. "I know. Now hush up about it and I might come back to the ranch with you."

Joe mimed zipping his lip then ruined it by asking Hal, "Can we play that video game again? I was close to beating Jane last time before she stole my treasure and kidnapped my jester."

"Fine by me. But even if you do beat her, you'll still end up losing to me. Then you'll lose to her when you convince her to race again. My man, you're just not as fast as you think you are."

"Shut it, Boy Toy."

"So, Joe," Jane interrupted before they could get started. "If I agree to another race, can we shoot again? I might be able to beat you at fifteen yards this time." He'd smoked her at seven yards and twenty-five, but she had a good feeling about the middle distance.

Joe huffed. "Keep dreaming, girlie." At her glare, he held up his hands in surrender. "But if it helps motivate you to up your pistol practice, let's do it."

Hal nodded. "And Jane, if you're super nice to me—by forgetting Joe mentioned the Riyadh incident—I'll do one better than look up your Agent Rapp. I'll tell you all you want to know about Supervisory Special Agent Scott. All the secret squirrel stuff you're not supposed to know about."

Jane knew the guys hadn't forgotten about her suspension. But she was surprised to see the intensity on Hal's face. A feeling that still burned inside her as well.

I haven't forgotten you, Simmons.

"Okay, Hal. Consider Riyadh forgotten. But Matthew Scott? That one's mine." After a pause, she added, "but we can't tell Uncle Chris. Ever."

They both looked at Joe, the weakest member of their three-person team.

He looked injured but said the magic words. "Fine. Fine. I'll never tell. Happy now?"

Yes, she was. She had a plan. Now to beat Joe at shooting. For once in her life.

* * *

SEVERAL HOURS LATER, Jane got off the phone with one of her newer CIs, a young woman who liked to party with gangsters. She was pretty and talented, working her way from pole to pole in Seattle until she'd landed at Junior Mazzuca's favorite hangout.

They'd dated for a while until Junior decided he could do better. Lola hadn't cared for his attitude. After going down in a drug bust, she'd decided to offer Jane information to stay free of jail.

Tonight, Lola had definitely delivered.

The secret location of the new Mazzuca hangout.

CHAPTER TWELVE

Jane lost, but not horribly, at fifteen yards. And seven. And twenty-five. But she did manage to win their race around the property. Joe might be a heck of a sprinter, but he couldn't touch her when it came to distance.

The exercise put her in a great mood, so that even after three days of no contact from Rapp about finding the Code Blue Killer—because Diego's suggestion fit as well as "that medical guy murderer"—she remained in good spirits while staying busy in Bainbridge Island.

With the guys out and doing whatever they did when Stateside, Jane had decided to head back into the city to clean up her apartment. Their visit over New Year's had definitely put things out of place, and she'd just started obsessing over what she needed to clean when she got a ping on her phone.

A glance showed a forwarded message on a number she used with her CIs, something that couldn't be traced to her personal number without help from a hacker like Hal or Diego.

Excited to finally have movement on the case that had sidelined her and put her reputation in limbo, she drove to the ferry, waited half an hour, and spent her time aboard looking for older news articles on the Mazzucas.

By the time she'd arrived in Seattle, she'd also managed to contact Sullivan and set up a meet.

Of the ten agents working in Jane's unit, she resonated with Sullivan and Williams the most. They were closer to her age and viewed moving up in the ranks the same way she did—that climbing the political ladder was like killing yourself slowly, a poison to the soul as you sold out piece by piece.

Sullivan, a petite blond who rolled in sarcasm and irony like a feline in catnip, was often underestimated and used that to her advantage. Intelligent, fast, and an expert marksman, she was a plus to have on one's side.

Williams, a funny guy of average height and features, had an ability to blend in. He was often overlooked while people talked about all sorts of things in front of him. A friend to everyone, enemy to none. Often undervalued, he made the most of it.

They'd come into the Seattle office at roughly the same time, and they didn't like Agent Scott at all. While Jane had come from the Poulsbo RA and had trained under good people, Sullivan and Williams had transferred from Las Vegas.

When asked why they'd left, they'd both told her Vegas ate people alive. All the gambling, drugs, and prostitution, so many vices in one place, had soured them on Sin City. When learning about openings in Seattle, they'd jumped on them.

More acquaintances than friends upon leaving Las Vegas, they'd bonded here, and even more so with Jane as a happy third. She was probably as close with them as she was with anyone not family.

Another message popped up, and she read it with satisfaction— confirmation that the intel she'd received from her CI on the Mazzucas had been verified by another source.

By the time Sullivan met Jane at Pike Place Bar and Grill, Jane was ready to explode.

"Well, don't you look excitable and casual at the same time." Sullivan smirked as she sat down. Like Gina, Sullivan dressed to impress. The color of her dark pantsuit and pristine, pale pink blouse set off the attractive undertones in her skin, and her eyes sparkled. She looked pretty and capable.

Jane had always been called attractive in a *different* kind of way. She didn't have conventional beauty, but rather an interesting face, whatever that meant. And she'd never been petite at five eleven, though she had an athletic frame and good genes, so she didn't normally have to fight more than an aggressive five pounds here or there.

Jane acknowledged the awkward feeling in her gut when comparing herself to Sullivan and did what she normally did when feeling uncomfortable. She ignored it and focused on what she was good at—the hunt. Because she knew she'd found a piece of a much larger puzzle.

She made small talk until the server took their order and left. "I found them."

"Them?" Sullivan blinked. "Would that be your real parents?"

"Huh?"

"You know, the alien clones who *really* gave birth to you, but left you, an alien changeling, in place of the human baby they stole from the people you think are your parents."

Jane didn't know how to respond to that. "Seriously?"

Sullivan grinned. "I'm on a speculative fiction kick with my book club. I'm hooked on the idea of doppelgangers as the ultimate spies. Think what they could do for us in the Agency."

"I think you're due for a drug test."

"Ha."

Jane grinned then lowered her voice and leaned forward. "No. I found *them* as in the Mazzucas."

"Yeah? Where?" Finally, Sullivan looked intrigued.

"In Tacoma." Jane rattled off an address, and as she thought about it, something niggled at the back of her brain.

"You can confirm this?"

"I can. Two different CIs, trustworthy ones, told me. Neither knows the other. It's no setup." Lola had given her the address, and Mack, a CI Jane had been working with for years, corroborated.

"Oh, I can't wait to follow that up with some surveillance."

The server came with their appetizers, and they dug into spicy poppers while speculating about why the crime family had moved. And why no one had mentioned it.

"Do you think Matthew had anything to do with it?" Jane asked. She picked at the popper on her plate, feeling full. She normally had a healthy appetite, but her instincts told her they were getting close, blunting her need for food and increasing her desire to move, to do something about the situation. She hated having to settle for more hurry-up-and-wait.

"I'm not sure, but I'm leaning toward maybe." Which was more than Sullivan had admitted to before. "I can't be sure, but something's going on with him."

"What do you mean?"

Their food arrived, and Sullivan dug into lunch while she explained, "He's like a different person lately. Secretive. Nosing into everyone's cases more than usual and keeping a bunch of us out of the loop on some of our more major ops. Taking on a lot more himself instead of supervising us."

"That's got to be aggravating."

"You're telling me." Sullivan speared a cooked carrot with more force than necessary. "He's driving me nuts." She added in a low murmur, "And he's stalling on Dan's murder."

"No kidding."

"Yeah. I don't like it. Rob and I have been talking. We're sure Matthew's hiding something."

"I'm going to dig."

"I wish I could lend you a shovel, but I'm booked with all the folders on my desk. Too much to do, and too much oversight to handle on top of that."

"I get it. I really do." She stared into Sullivan's eyes. "I'll find who took out Dan. And I'm planning on doing a lot more looking into Matthew as well."

"Well, if you want, you can start at McGrath's. I overheard him in his office telling someone on the phone that he'd be happy to meet up there tonight at seven."

A lot of law enforcement and federal employees met at McGrath's, a popular bar downtown. A good place to stalk—*track* her boss.

And find some answers before she lost her ever-loving mind.

CHAPTER THIRTEEN

Tracking Matthew Scott should have been more difficult. Jane thought he needed a lesson in how not to be predictable. She knew what he drove, and she waited outside the office for him to leave. She'd been home to change into an outfit appropriate for a night out on the town in case he spotted her that evening.

She trailed him, knowing he had more than an hour before he was scheduled to be at McGrath's. He drove to a dry cleaner then to the library. Jane thought about following him inside but didn't want to be too obvious.

He couldn't do anything even if he caught her following him. She'd convince him that she'd been out for a stroll or a drink. No way he'd assume she'd been following him, not when he'd told her to back off of the Simmons' case. Because Matthew Scott couldn't fathom anyone not obeying his direct orders.

As he left the library, she made a face at him, wishing he could see her. Immature, but it soothed that need inside her to put him down, hard.

With little time before he was due at the bar, she let him go, content to find a place to park away from the bar. Unfortunately, everyone else had the same idea, so she circled the large lot behind McGrath's until a spot freed up.

Jane took a moment to check herself over. Jeans, a cute but casual dark sweater, her hair artfully arranged, a light coat of makeup to complete the outfit. She'd used a clasp to hold back her bangs, bringing attention to her eyes and sharp cheekbones. Normally, she was content to be listened to then forgotten.

But it would work for tonight to blend in. Just one more woman meeting friends at a downtown bar.

She left her jacket behind, stowing her credit cards, license, and keys in her pocket. After locking up, she braved the cold weather and crossed the bar's busy parking lot.

And that's when she saw him. Agent Scott and some man she didn't recognize spoke in the shadows at the far side of the lot, in a low but animated conversation. Scott handed the man a business envelope.

Money? Was he paying the guy off, and if so, why? She wanted badly to close the distance between them to see the man clearly. But she'd frozen in the middle of the parking lot as it was, and didn't want to announce her presence with any sudden movement.

Then Scott glanced her way. His gaze moved past her then whipped right back to her, and his eyes narrowed.

Shoot. Jane looked to the right of him and waved, as if at the couple exiting a vehicle nearby. The moment he looked over at them, she turned and hurried into the bar.

The warmth inside the pub relaxed her, and she used the crowd to her advantage. The place, at just past seven, felt nearly full. She made her way to the ladies' room in case Scott chased after her. She could pretend she hadn't seen him in the lot, like she'd only dropped in to get a drink.

After a solid ten minutes, she exited and started toward the bar. Only to be stopped when he stepped in front of her.

Shoot.

"Well, well. Jane Cannon. What a coincidence."

She contained a wince at his vitriol. "Hello, sir. Fancy meeting you here."

"Nice try. But I saw you following me from the library."

"I'm sorry?" She could play dumb with the best of them. Though her cousin did the innocent expression much better.

"Save it. You're on administrative leave." His voice started to rise, attracting attention. "You have no business—"

"I'm not sure why you're so angry." She frowned, going on the offensive. "I'm here to get a drink and meet someone." *Please, someone be here that I know.* "You already suspended me. How about getting off my—" she would have ended with something crude, likely with one of Joe's favorite sayings, when an arm draped over her shoulder.

She froze, especially when she recognized a familiar cologne.

"Jane. I've been waiting." Gunther Rapp squeezed her shoulder with one muscled arm. "I'm sorry. I'm not interrupting, am I?"

Scott blinked at Rapp, then at his arm around her. "Er, I—"

"Matthew Scott, meet my date" —she couldn't believe she said "date" with a straight face— "Gunther Rapp."

"Hi." Rapp didn't offer to shake hands, and Scott didn't seem eager to engage either. "Oh, Scott. Your boss, right?"

"Yeah." Jane sounded less than enthusiastic.

At that point, someone called out for Scott.

"Apologies, but I have someone to meet as well. Jane. Gunther." He nodded to them both then turned and left.

Rapp leaned down and said into her ear, "You have some explaining to do."

"Me? What are you doing here?"

He escorted her to a tall table by the back. "I was meeting someone and just happened to look up and see you and an obviously pissed-off guy in what looked like an uncomfortable conversation."

Well, he wasn't wrong.

Jane took the seat with the wall at her back and watched Rapp squeeze in across from her, nearly touching the guy behind him. From this angle, she saw Scott across the room for an instant, looking right at her, before people jostled and blocked her view.

"I'm waiting," Rapp growled.

"For what?" No way did she want to admit he'd saved her bacon. She could have figured a way out of the altercation. Probably.

"That's your boss. The guy who put you on leave."

"Your point?"

Rapp shook his head. "I overheard him say that you've been following him."

The obstinate glint in Rapp's gaze told Jane he wouldn't let this go. "Do we have to talk about this?"

"I think we do."

She sighed. "Fine." She summarized what she knew and what she suspected, keeping her voice low, forcing her to lean closer to Rapp than she'd liked. A server brought him something to drink, but Jane only had water, not about to touch alcohol again so soon after the New Year's Eve debacle.

Rapp fastened his gaze on Jane. Talk about feeling under the spotlight. But he was listening to her, nodding as he prodded her to continue.

Once finished, Jane soothed her parched throat with the water, needing the break.

"Well now. That's quite a story."

"It's not a—"

Rapp held up a hand. "You need to be careful with that one." He gave a subtle nod in Scott's direction. "He's keeping an eye on you. He spotted your tail. Even if he buys that you only came to meet me here, he's going to be suspicious. And there's already someone planting evidence in your office."

"You believe me?" Huh. She'd have thought he'd want mounds of evidence to believe someone he'd just met.

He nodded. "Your summary fits with what Gambol told me about everything. Sounds like your criminal investigation stalled before your coworker died. And your boss's defensiveness is off." Rapp's expression turned grave. "I've been where you are. Be very careful, Jane. When you don't know who you can trust, everything can go sideways in a blink."

She nodded, seeing a friendlier, nicer side of Rapp that made her almost like him.

"And one more thing."

"Yeah?"

His overly friendly grin should have warned her. "If you need tips on how to manage overbearing personalities, to be a better people person, I'm happy to help."

"Wait. What?"

"Well, it's got to be tough being the new girl. I mean, the new *person* in the Seattle office. And you're a junior agent too. That can't be easy."

"New person? I've been there a year."

"And you're obviously not great with people. You and Gina haven't been getting along."

"Have you met Gina?" She added before he could speak, "And I'm not that junior. Heck, you don't look that much older than me."

"I'm worlds more experienced."

"I'll bet." She wanted to slug the smugness from his expression.

"Still, you're doing a decent enough job on our tiny task force."

"For a newbie, you mean," she snapped.

"Yes. And on a completely separate note, you look very pretty tonight. And I mean that from a professional standpoint. You seem almost relaxed, your proverbial—and literal—hair down."

"I'm so glad you approve." Her words sounded as frosty as the outdoor temperatures. Rapp, however, didn't seem to read the room.

His eyes twinkled. "It's important that we all take a break now and then, so we don't burn out." His teasing expression left no doubt the guy was making fun of her. "It's healthy to relax. But slow down on all the drinking. Wouldn't want you to get loopy."

She stared at her water then looked back at him. "I should have known better than to think you're a nice guy."

"You really should have." Of course, the insult rolled right off him.

"Jackass." She left in a huff, hearing his booming laugh, and felt Agent Scott's gaze on her all the way until she left the bar.

CHAPTER FOURTEEN

THE WEATHER HAD TURNED COLDER. JANE'S TEETH CHATTERED AS SHE hurried around to the parking lot, needing heat in the worst way.

Had she known Rapp better, she might have laughed at his obvious attempt to annoy her. But then, she didn't know him that well, and for all she knew, he might actually consider her inferior and hadn't just been hazing a fellow agent.

He had helped her with Scott, who remained inside with a few men she recognized from the office. Not from her squad, but agents she'd seen around the building a time or two. So who had that man been in the parking lot? What had been in the envelope?

Lost in thought, she almost didn't hear the shout of warning. She dove out of the way of a roaring car that would have mowed her down had she not flung herself aside, landing between two parked cars.

"Are you okay?" A woman asked as she and her friend hurried to help Jane. "That moron almost hit you."

Falling as she had, face down on the ground, could have been worse. Jane hadn't twisted or broken anything. But as she stood, her cheek started throbbing.

"Oh, looks like it's going to bruise." One of the women winced.

"I'm good. But I wish people wouldn't drink and drive." Jane's thoughts raced.

"No kidding. You sure you're okay? Why don't you come inside with us and let us look you over?"

"Nah. I'm good. I'm going home to ice this." Jane smiled. Her cheek would stop hurting soon. Probably.

The women nodded and wished her well. They waited until she'd climbed into her car and started it up before entering the bar. While Jane appreciated their help, she wondered what might have happened if they hadn't called out in warning.

She'd been lax, not paying attention to her surroundings. Could it be a coincidence that just after tailing Agent Scott, and getting called on it, someone had nearly run her down? Or had some sloppy drunk, or distracted driver, just been behaving badly behind the wheel?

Not one to trust in coincidence, she paid careful attention driving home. She didn't even think about calling Hal or Joe for help. She could take care of herself. Normally better than she had in the parking lot, but still. She felt like an idiot for not taking smarter precautions. She'd change that now.

After safely entering her apartment, she doublechecked her locks before settling in for the night. And that's when the throbbing in her cheek turned painful.

She popped two ibuprofen and made herself eat the last of the raisin toast before it went bad. Adding a glass of tea and ice for her cheek, her night ended better than it had started.

Before she went to bed, she sent Sullivan a brief warning to keep on her toes. If someone really had come after Jane, they might have seen her with Sullivan earlier. No sense in them both being stupid.

With a sigh, she crawled under the covers. But as she fell into slumber, she had a bad feeling she'd forgotten something important.

THE NEXT DAY, Jane felt as if she'd been hit by a truck. Though she hadn't felt it last night, she ached all over. Even worse, her cheek was purple. She must have hit harder than she'd thought.

She took a long, hot bath, doctored with Epsom salts, and felt worlds better. Later, after some eggs and bacon and a nice cup of French press made with decent coffee beans, Jane settled in with her computer, looking over older notes. *Gina can kiss my butt about her nasty coffee.*

She kept coming back to the Mazzucas and wanted badly to call Sullivan to see what the team had found about their new hideout in Tacoma. But one, she doubted Sullivan would tell her on a work phone, where others might hear, and two, it was barely past eight in the morning. Sullivan was not a morning person, and they likely hadn't found a whole lot in that short amount of time.

Coffee in hand, she turned on the television and watched the local news, looking for anything that might jog her mind. She didn't realize she'd been bobbing her knee like a jackhammer until someone banged on her door.

"Hold on, I'm coming," she shouted at the aggressive knocker. Had to be Joe.

But when she looked through the peephole and saw her cousin standing there with a frown on her face, Jane didn't know what to do.

"Open the door. I can hear you breathing," Raine said with no small amount of snark.

"I'm not here."

"Ha ha. Open the door, doofus. I'm not going away. And I can get *louder,*" she said, raising her for voice for the benefit of Jane's neighbors.

Swearing under her breath, Jane yanked open the door and snarled, "What are you doing here?"

Raine opened her mouth to answer and closed it with a snap, her gaze glued to Jane's cheek.

Crap.

"What the hell happened to you?"

Jane yanked her inside and shut the door after her. Now how much to confide to her cousin...?

"You'll tell me everything," Raine said, as if reading her mind. A nasty habit her cousin had always had, that of hearing the truth even when nothing had been said.

"Why should I?" Jane tried for bravado.

"Because if you don't, I'll call Uncle Chris." Raine pulled out her phone and hit several buttons. "Don't push me, because I'll do it."

Jane sighed. "Fine. Sit down, shut up, and listen."

CHAPTER FIFTEEN

"After nearly getting run over, why didn't you go into the bar and ask for help?" Raine seemed to be having a hard time understanding Jane's reasoning.

"I told you."

"Tell me again."

"Simple. I didn't want to give anyone a second shot at me." Jane ticked off her fingers. "If Scott knew he'd rattled me, he'd win. If he saw that I was okay, he could try again before I got home. Even if he had nothing to do with it, I'd become a spectacle in that bar, where a ton of law enforcement heroes would want to help the weak woman who nearly got run over."

Raine sighed. "Okay, that makes sense. Best not to let anyone see you vulnerable."

"Thank you." Jane huffed.

"But you never ask for help, you know. And you need to."

"Who would I ask?"

"Oh please. Hal and Joe are bored out of their minds. When they see your face, all bets are off."

Jane blurted, "You can't tell them. If they know I got hurt, they'll try to take over my investigation. They'll blow it."

"Hey, they're pros." Raine looked hurt.

"Professional problem solvers. *Killers,* Raine."

"Technically, Hal's more of a computer nerd."

"Who has drones drop his bombs for him," Jane growled, since her cousin was missing the point. "They typically destroy their targets. I need my target alive to charge them for the murder of a DEA agent in addition to leaking info to a crime organization. I can't do that with dead suspects."

"You have a point, I guess." Raine didn't look pleased about that. Actually, she looked...tired.

A few inches shorter than Jane's own five eleven, Raine was built on the lean side but healthy and strong. She had skin the same shade as Jane's, but when she tanned, she turned more gold than red. Her long, dark hair was usually kept neat in a French braid but now had been tied back in a ponytail, with whisps of hair curling around her face. She'd dressed casually too, in a pair of jeans and a UW sweatshirt.

A natural beauty with brains and heart, Raine took after their uncle more than she'd like to admit. A hardhead who felt emotions keenly and liked to be vocal in her opinions about everything, Raine and Uncle Chris often butted heads. Jane rarely saw her sad.

And that's what she saw in her cousin's dark eyes. A kind of grief.

"What are you doing here, anyway?" Jane asked more gently than she normally would.

Raine, allergic to sympathy, saw that kindness and stomped on it by growling, "Helping out my stupid cousin, apparently."

"No, really."

"We'll get back to me in a minute."

Jane sighed.

Raine continued, "This is a mess. You have a murdered DEA agent, a potential leak in the Seattle office, and likely someone in your squad working on the Mazzuca case." Raine paused. "How sure are you that this apartment is clean?"

"I went over every inch of the place last night. Found nothing."

"Okay. But you should have Hal..." Raine trailed off when she noted Jane's gaze on the gadget Hal had given her years ago to sweep her house for surveillance devices. "Oh, right."

"I wasn't born yesterday."

"Fine. I'm sorry for worrying."

After a moment, Jane deflated. "No, I'm sorry for not accepting your concern."

"That's a mouthful."

They grinned at each other.

"I did miss you," Jane admitted.

"I bet that hurt to say."

"Seriously did."

They laughed.

"Now tell me why you're here," Jane asked again. "We can talk about me all you like when you're done. But I'm more worried about you, to be honest."

Raine shrugged. "I'm having a crisis of conscience, I think."

"Since when do you have a conscience?" Jane teased, hoping for a smile.

She didn't get one.

"It's like all this interrogation work has turned me into a monster. I know we're trying to protect democracy, to save lives. I'm talking big picture, right? But I'm tired of stepping on the small picture to get there."

Talking in broad terms didn't help. Obviously, Raine had been through something she couldn't talk about, not in specifics.

"Help me understand."

"I'm questioning the validity of some of the missions I've been sent on. I don't see who they're helping or what we're really doing there. And I'm tired of being told to shut up and follow orders blindly."

"But that's part of being in the military." Jane knew it, didn't always agree with it, but she had loved, and still did love, being a Marine. Once a Marine, always a Marine.

"I know. Don't get me wrong. I love it, but I'm not in love with it."

Jane blinked. "Are we talking about the Marine Corps or a guy?"

At that, Raine huffed. "Right? I love the Corps. I love my job, mostly. But some of my bosses really suck, you know?"

"Trust me. I know."

They shared a commiserating nod.

"I think I need a break."

"You think? Raine, you never take leave. You call me a workaholic? Well, right back at ya. I know you're dealing with life-or-death situations in scary places around the world. Terrorism, big scale conflicts. That's a lot of pressure."

"Yeah." Raine started pacing, pulling at her ponytail. She looked so normal, so young, like a woman barely out of college, not some thirty-three-year-old who knew the truth when she heard it.

Jane had always been envious of her cousin's odd ability to ferret out the truth. They'd had her tested at an early age, because Raine seemed to possess a nearly psychic way of reading people. Her uncle thought it had more to do with understanding micro expressions, interpreting the physical reactions of people who fabricated so easily.

In any event, it had made Raine's work in the Intelligence branch of the Marine Corps much sought-after.

"I'm on a short leave,.and I'm hoping to talk to Uncle Chris for some advice when he gets back in a few weeks." Raine stopped pacing and stared at Jane, her mouth firming. "But you need to come clean, if not with the family, then with me. When you need help, ask for it."

"Raine, you are the *last* person I'll ever take advice from when it comes to asking for help."

"That hurts."

"Oh please. Suck it up, princess."

"Who are you calling a princess? You tripped over your own feet and bruised your face, weakling."

"At least I'm not crying about the Marine Corps being too hard. Waa."

Raine shot her an evil grin. "Nice."

"I thought so."

Raine said something else cutting. Jane answered, getting into the spirit of their argument. The stupid squabble made them both feel better as they called each other names and brought up embarrassing incidents from their youth.

As they wound down, Raine offered one more nugget of clarity. "Make sure you doctor that bruise with makeup if you don't want everyone all over your case. You make people want to protect you as it is."

"I'm taller and meaner than most of the people I work with, you know."

Raine scoffed. "Whatever. But seriously, Jane, that new guy you're working with? Gunther Rapp, right?" Raine gathered the keys she'd tossed on the counter, readying to leave.

"Yeah?"

"Tall, great body, nice face, attitude to spare?"

"I guess."

Raine smirked. "He was a big deal in the black ops community for a while. CIA type. Background in Delta or Force Recon before the CIA grabbed him. I'm not sure what he's doing with your task force, but he's the real deal. I never heard anything bad about him. He's something of a legend. Supposedly saved a few guys from dying at heavy expense. I'm just saying, if you can't come to family, you can probably go to him."

Jane realized Hal should have known all this by now, yet he'd curiously said nothing about the guy. Then she noticed that Raine had paused. "But ...?"

"But if he ends up not being on your side, you have to call on us—me, Joe, Hal, whoever's here, for help. Because he will end you and not look back. He's a one-man wrecking crew." Then she smiled and waved. "Later, slacker."

Raine skipped out the door.

"Thanks a lot," Jane yelled after her, feeling out of sorts.

Why would a guy like Rapp, with her uncle's qualifications, be chosen to *find* their Code Blue Killer when he could have just as easily been tasked with eliminating him?

One bullet to the head. Another to the heart.

CHAPTER SIXTEEN

It took another two days for Rapp to call her back in.

Finally. Jane did a great job concealing the damage to her cheek, or at least she hoped she had. The purpling and swelling had spread toward her eye overnight. If asked, she'd say she needed more sleep.

She'd heard from Hal and Joe that Raine had decided to stay at the ranch, unlike her snooty cousin—meaning Jane.

Laughing it off had been easy, especially since Raine had been good on her word and didn't mention Jane's injury.

Hal had also come through with a dossier on Agent Matthew Ronald Scott.

"You never got this from me," he'd warned just before an anonymous email popped into her inbox.

Of course she'd received the file just right before Rapp asked her to come back to work.

Annoyed that she'd have to look at it later, she packed up and rolled into the office just before nine. Later than she liked, but then again, she hadn't been given an exact time to arrive.

"Nice to see you made it," Gina groused as she spotted Jane heading to her desk, now layered with even more folders. The agent narrowed her gaze at Jane but didn't comment on Jane's lateness.

Jane couldn't help that, but she looked decent. Her outfit of jeans, trendy but sturdy boots, and a forest-green sweater was dressier than what she normally wore. She'd left her hair down to mask the eye as well, and if she moved just right, no one would see her face at all.

Buried in more notes, looking through more of the same, searching for connections again, she spent the first half of her day reviewing the decedents' backgrounds.

Diego walked over and looked at her folders. "We're still trying to ID the killer, but no luck yet. He's not in the NCIC, and I haven't found a match to any of the prints that turned up in any other database."

The National Crime Information Center was a nationwide database the FBI maintained. Unfortunately, the unsub hadn't left any prints on the ambulance. They had no conclusive evidence on the guy yet, and clarity issues with the videos around the attack were still giving Diego fits.

"We'll get lucky eventually," she mumbled and continued looking through the folders on the nurses.

Nurse2, Tom Polsun, had been just twenty-nine years old. A favorite at the clinic where he worked. No one had a bad thing to say about him. He'd been raised in Tacoma, and...

Wait. *Tacoma.*

As Diego walked away, Jane dragged out her cellphone and made a call to Sullivan's cell. To her surprise, Williams answered.

"Jenn's phone. What's up, Rebel Cannon?"

She smiled. "Funny guy. Hey, Williams, I'd ask how it's hanging, but then I'd be up on harassment charges too."

"Yeah. Plus, we both know I'm hanging just fine."

She rolled her eyes. "Whatever. Look, I'm trying to contact Sullivan."

"Boss has her." She heard his exasperation. "She'll probably be in there for another hour while she explains, in detail, exactly what she did today, which is exactly what he told her to do."

"I feel for you guys." Poor Sullivan. "Look, maybe you can help me. I gave her some info the other day. Can you tell me the locations of that organization I had you find? Just the ones near some abandoned warehouses."

She jotted down the addresses he rattled off.

"Thanks. I owe you."

"Keep that in mind the next time someone has to pay the tab." He disconnected before she could argue that she didn't drink nearly what he did. The guy was a fish in human form.

But those addresses... She looked through several files until she found what she needed on her computer. The exact location where the unsub's abandoned blue Toyota had been found.

Right where the Mazzuca's had allegedly relocated.

So what the hell did that mean?

SHE SHUT the door behind her as she entered Rapp's office without knocking.

He was on the phone and looked annoyed, his brows nearly meeting as he barked back at someone on the other end then slammed down the receiver. "What do you want?"

Great. Delivering news to an annoyed Sasquatch. Her cheek started throbbing out of nowhere.

He scowled. "I'm waiting."

She counted to five to curb her sarcasm but thought it all the same. *Waiting for a thought to pop into that stubborn head? Waiting for a modicum of dignity? Waiting for divine inspiration to pull your head out of your a—*

"Jane. What. Do. You. Want?"

She let her breath out and focused. "I found a connection."

His gaze sharpened. "Tell me."

She showed him a picture of the torched car. "This is the vehicle our unsub used then ditched. It's in an abandoned warehouse in Tacoma."

"Right."

"Which happens to be located in the new Mazzuca crime family's territory. They picked up and left Seattle overnight after killing DEA agent Dan Simmons, my old teammate."

"Right. Your investigation in Seattle." His gaze shot to hers. "You're thinking our unsub may be part of the Mazzuca organization?"

"I don't know. But I don't believe in coincidences." Like trailing Agent Scott and nearly getting rundown after. She forced herself to avoid touching her cheek. "I'm too close to this, I know. Maybe if you look at it, you can corroborate. Tell me I'm not making unwarranted connections."

"Right. Let's share this with the team."

A safe bet, because his team had nothing to do with investigating an organized crime family.

Or did it? Because, as she well knew, the Mazzucas had a very long reach.

CHAPTER SEVENTEEN

EVERYONE AGREED THAT THERE WERE NO COINCIDENCES IN LAW enforcement. Diego announced he'd dig into the Mazzucas without leaving a footprint, probably by accessing Agency files he shouldn't have had access to.

Jane wanted to ask how, but a glance at Rapp made her keep her questions to herself. Don't ask, don't tell would keep them all safer.

And if it didn't, Rapp could handle it. She just wanted answers. Dan Simmons deserved them.

The connection between her old case and the new case might not be that farfetched. The Mazzucas had dipped their hands into a lot of businesses across the country since making a name for themselves in Philadelphia a few years ago.

Like amoebas, the organization branched out, surrounded, then devoured unprotected communities.

Despite that, the Seattle task force had no plans to let them destroy the Pacific Northwest.

At lunch, she headed for the food cart down the block to grab sandwiches for the crew since it was her turn. Remembering the incident in the parking lot, she kept her guard up.

Despite the cold, the sun shone. She might have enjoyed the walk, but she felt eyes on her. Paranoia? Maybe. She stopped a few times at storefront windows, checking for a follower.

No one. Pulling out her phone, she pretended to text someone as she walked. She kept up the ruse by stopping a few times out of the way of passersby, keeping a side-eye on those nearby.

Her plan paid off. A figure in a large, puffy coat stopped when she did. After a pause, they continued toward her.

They could be anyone.

Maybe even the Code Blue Killer.

Even if it was the killer, how could they possibly know about Jane? Did Rapp's team also have someone on the inside?

Or maybe I'm too suspicious that everyone has a vendetta.

As the individual drew closer, Jane gripped her cellphone, prepared to defend herself. She continued to look down at it, as if engrossed in her phone.

"Excuse me," said a man in a deep voice.

She glanced up. "I'm sorry. Are you talking to me?"

People streamed around them, so she didn't think he'd try anything on the public street. But one never knew.

He held out a card to her. "You dropped this a block ago."

She glanced down at a gift card she'd received in the mail from Sullivan from the office gift exchange. Her suspension hadn't meant the team had forgotten about her.

Her pulse rate settled, and she nodded in thanks. "Appreciate it."

The man in the puffy jacket did one better and pulled his hood back. About her height, with average features and a nice smile, dark skin, and jeans and sneakers that looked on the upside of what she'd normally spend. She put his features in her memory bank just in case.

"Sure thing." He smiled, then turned and walked away, and she noted his gait as vastly different from the unsub's.

Feeling like a fool, Jane ordered herself to stop looking for conspiracies in the shadows and headed to the food cart.

Yet on the way back to the office she continued to feel as if she was being followed. She passed it off as the result of her cousin's warnings.

She knew her own importance, and neither the Mazzucas nor the unsub likely cared that she existed.

* * *

SHE SPENT the next two days looking for more ties between all the victims and praying they'd get a hit on their suspect. Nothing popped. The first victims, the doctors, had turned up a big fat nothing. Since no one had been looking into them initially, as their deaths hadn't been suspicious, it took extra effort to recreate the events preceding their demise.

Diego dug out a slew of pictures and social media posts and offered them to Jane for her review.

She rubbed her eyes, thoroughly tired of computers.

"Go home," Gina said as she packed up to leave.

Despite having worked with the team for two weeks, Jane hadn't received more than a nod and a few sarcastic comments from Gina. Apparently, Gina was holding a grudge about Jane taking credit for what *she'd* actually done by finding an image of the same killer at the crime scenes.

Rapp had been in and out of the office a lot lately, always frowning.

Diego, buzzed on energy drinks, kept to himself while drowning in the rough waters of computer code, streaming content, and security software.

Jane glanced at her monitor and, noting the time, agreed she needed to go home. A Wednesday night with nothing more to do than stare at the walls, yet she'd rather stare at home than look at one more still shot or video of their poor victims.

She left and realized she had to get gas on the way home. Annoyed, she still went out of her way to the cheaper station and filled up. She moved her car from the pump to go in to pay, wanting a snack. She hated it when people didn't think about others needing to refuel while they took their time paying.

Inside, she grabbed an iced tea and a pack of chips. She paused, reconsidering the tea, and stepped out of the way of the couple arguing over whether to buy light beer or the good stuff.

As she knelt to retrieve a pack of pretzels that had fallen from one of the racks, she heard the door buzz open. She stared at the pretzels, wondering if she should swap them for the chips.

An odd stillness settled. Conversation died.

Jane froze, her instincts on alert.

And heard the woman who'd been emphatic about low cal beer beg, "Please don't hurt us."

Jane pulled her foot out of sight behind the snack rack. She reached automatically for her ankle holster. And swore. No backup piece and no service weapon.

She typed in a fast 911 text as she heard, "Empty the register or I'll blow your head off. You too, Coors Light. Down on the ground."

Jane whispered her location into the phone when dispatch answered. Leaving the line open, she slid the phone down the aisle toward the front of the store and the robbery in progress, hoping they'd hear better that way.

Shifting on the balls of her feet, she slipped toward the outside wall of the store. She needed a weapon. Found nothing but paper products, soaps, and useless odds and ends.

Just her luck.

Focused, she sucked in a quiet breath and slowly let it out, edging to the end of the aisle. Still hidden, she glanced up at the convex mirror above the register. The perp held a gun on the young clerk behind the counter and two people face down on the floor.

And here she was. FBI Agent Jane Cannon.

Weaponless

CHAPTER EIGHTEEN

"WHERE'S THE OTHER ONE?"

Jane heard the high-pitched male voice full of nerves and guessed him to be in his late teens or early twenties. A glance back up at the mirror confirmed her guess. He had dirty brown hair and unfocused eyes. The gun in his hand trembled. Maybe inexperience, maybe nerves, maybe something else.

The other two patrons lay face down, their hands behind their heads. He didn't look at them, unconcerned while he stared at the clerk as if the poor kid had all the answers.

He waved his gun. "I said, where is she? And get over here."

"Who?" The poor clerk held his hands high in the air, barely past the age of consent, and walked around the counter toward the gunman. "Please don't shoot. I know the drill. Take anything you want. It's yours."

The man swore, trembled a little, then just as suddenly steadied the gun in his hands as he raised it to the clerk's face. When he glanced toward the far aisle where she hid, she hurriedly backed out of sight before he could see her.

Or so she thought.

"Hey, you. Come here," the robber ordered and flicked the safety off. "Or I'll blow his brains out."

Jane had no choice but to stall for time and keep everyone safe. Law enforcement had already been called, but who knew when they'd arrive.

"Coming out." She rose, hands in the air, and stepped out. She had to see the robber's eyes before being able to read him.

Her time in the Corps had taught her a lot about hand-to-hand combat, but not nearly as much as her time spent training with Team Ten. She knew *exactly* how to handle situations like these, though she'd only been in two like this before.

First rule, don't give your opponent more of an upper hand than he already had.

She stepped closer, slowly, her hands up, and slouched to appear smaller.

Sweat beaded at the gunman's temples. Though his gun hand looked steady, he wavered while staring at her. He looked and smelled like a drug addict, but the sudden clarity in his gaze didn't fool her.

He had the look of a man intent on more than robbery. On *murder.*

"I'm the only other person here," Jane said, trying to look and sound scared.

"Toss me your gun."

She blinked. "I don't have a gun."

"Yeah right. Show me." The robber took his aim from the clerk and centered his weapon on her. "Slowly." His finger tightened over the trigger, ready to fire. "Your side piece too."

At least he no longer aimed at the civilians.

She raised each pant leg to show him nothing but socks. "Is it okay if I open my jacket?"

"Slowly." He didn't sound nearly as frazzled, not like before. She was right. He'd been acting.

Jane slowly unzipped her coat and showed him she wasn't carrying.

"Now the sweater." He didn't flinch or shiver, and his arm remained extended, the gun pointed at her. No jitters for the drug addicted mugger. She didn't think she'd have time to wait for the police to save the day.

Not when this guy planned on shooting someone—likely her.

She raised her sweater to show her stomach.

"Now turn around so I can see you're unarmed."

Sounded like he'd done this before. She moved very slowly, her sweater and jacket up to show she had nothing tucked into the waistband of her jeans, all the while taking tiny steps in his direction. Closer. Just a little bit closer…

The clerk stood still. He'd been down this road before. The couple on the ground remained unmoving, flat statues frozen in fear.

"Good. Now empty your pockets." The robber frowned at the card, wallet, and keys she dropped to the ground. "Where's your phone?"

"I dropped it back there." She nodded to the aisle behind her.

When he glanced toward it, she made her move.

She could have punched him in the throat. But she didn't want to kill him. She wanted answers.

With a burst of speed, she jerked his arm down while punching him in the nose. Heard the satisfying crack. He screamed in pain and fired into the floor.

His eyes watered, and he raised his hands to protect his face.

Using a move Min, another of Team Ten, had once taught her, she took advantage of the robber's disorientation. She deadened his left shoulder and ripped the pistol from him. It skittered a few feet away. With a grim smile, she flipped him onto his back and ended the move with a classic Marine Corps foot stomp to the face.

In a calm tone, she spoke to the others. "Everyone, go to the back room and lock yourselves in. We don't know if he's alone. I already dialed 911, but another call can't hurt. You." She pointed at the clerk. "Duct tape, please." She nodded to a roll near the register while shoving the robber onto his belly.

He sobbed and swore at her for breaking his nose, struggling past the snot and blood down his throat.

The clerk took a few shaky moments to rip a few strips for her, which she used to tie the robber's hands behind his back.

The lite beer woman was crying into the phone, talking to an emergency operator while hustling toward the back with her companion.

"Thanks for saving us," the clerk said before running for the back.

Jane had the situation in hand, but jacked up on adrenaline, she needed a few breaths before she settled. "Robbing the place?" she asked the would-be thief. "Or are you after something else?"

He didn't answer. Just struggled against his bonds.

He had the right build for their Code Blue Killer. Been light on his feet, too. She needed to see him move to be sure, though. They'd have to go over the surveillance footage outside the store for more information. But again, why would their killer be stalking her? It didn't make sense.

She gave him a quick pat down but found nothing in his pockets.

"Who hired you?"

Sirens sounded louder, and the flash of red and blue lights lit up the place.

"Not...hired." He wheezed. "Wanted cash...for drugs."

"Yeah?" She pulled up the sleeves of his scummy hoodie but didn't see any track marks. That didn't mean anything, yet... She looked him over and when moving his hoodie and hair from his neck, spotted a hidden tattoo at the base of his skull. Not a prison or gang tattoo. She made note of it. "What's your drug of choice?"

He tried swearing at her, but as nasal as he'd become, he sounded like a cartoon villain.

Then the police burst through the door and robbed her of the opportunity to ask more questions.

CHAPTER NINETEEN

A GOOD WHILE LATER, AFTER JANE HAD GIVEN A STATEMENT AND MADE sure the others had recovered enough from their ordeal to go home, the officer in charge released her. "Nice work, Agent Cannon. We'll need you to come in to sign the report first thing." He rubbed his tired eyes. "This place has been hit four times in the last six months. I mean, come on."

"Yeah. You'd think the criminals would learn."

"At least management has." He pointed his pen at the cameras on either underside of the overhang on the building. "Installed them the last time they got robbed. But it's been three months since. I hoped not to be back here so soon." He frowned at the back of a squad car where the perp sat, his nose bandaged by the EMTs who'd arrived not long after the cops. "Never had a violent robbery before. No guns. Just threats with knives and pipes. Ah, the good old days."

They shared a grin. "I'll be by first thing to sign the report. Appreciate you guys getting here so soon." She left after checking on the clerk and the couple, who'd be just fine.

But as she drove home, she wondered just how active her imagination had become. Because that robber had known she was law enforcement.

That or he watched way too much *Law & Order*. Either way, she'd get her answers tomorrow then have a long talk with Rapp about what the heck might be going on.

Jane arrived early Thursday morning at the police station to give her statement. Afterward, she asked to look in on the robber.

"Nope. Sorry," the day shift officer answered. He looked at his computer. "We don't have anyone of that description in custody."

"Wait. He's not here? That makes no sense. I broke his nose. You guys took him away in cuffs in the back of a squad car." She paused. "He's on a surveillance camera robbing the store."

"I don't know what to tell you. He *was* here, but now he's not. And when I pull up the file, I get nothing but garbage." He swore. "Need to get IT in again. Man, I hate this system."

Jane tried, but the police seemed as frustrated as she felt. With no one in custody to question, she left for work.

Gina had something pressing and would be in later, but Diego and Rapp were already deep into their computers when she requested an all-hands meeting.

"What's up?" Rapp asked, perched against the conference room desk.

Diego munched on one of the donuts Rapp had brought in as a thank you to the group. Despite being a pain to work with, he seemed to take care of his people. Not her, of course, but Gina and Diego. Jane wondered at Raine's intel on the guy. He seemed big enough to be scary but a lot more civilized than she'd credit most black ops members.

Of course, she only had Team Ten to go by.

"While we're young?" Rapp said caustically before eating a *second* apple fritter, which likely didn't make a dent in his appetite.

"Oh man. Those are fantastic," Diego agreed.

Jane started to rub her eyes before her bruised cheek, now a pretty purplish-green under her makeup, reminded her not to.

Rapp's eyes narrowed. "What's with your face?"

"Nunya."

He frowned in confusion, but Diego smirked and clarified, "That's agent speak for 'none of ya' business," he clarified.

"So many comedians in one tiny office," Rapp muttered, but she'd swear he fought not to smile.

"I have a slight bruise, okay?" She hoped she hadn't rubbed all her makeup away. A subtle glance at her thumb and finger showed a smudge of beige. "Look, I need to tell you something important. Last night, I interrupted a robbery."

Both men stared at her.

She gave them the details, ending with, "And when I went this morning to question the guy, I find he's not in custody. Imagine that." She thought about her impression of the criminal. "I don't think he was a drug addict. I think someone hired him." Then added, "To come after me."

"Why?" Rapp didn't act upset, though Diego swore and promised he'd end the guy's financial score and put him on every call list in existence.

"Diego." Rapp shook his head. "Jane, why do you think he wanted you? That comment about the side piece? Everyone who watches *Criminal Minds* or *Chicago PD* thinks they know how the FBI and police operate. And if he's been in the system before, he'd be familiar with it."

"Don't forget *Reno 911*," Diego added.

Rapp and Jane ignored him, and Jane said, "But he asked *me* to show him I was unarmed, not the two civilians on the floor. He knew I was law enforcement."

"You look like a Fed," Rapp said.

Diego shook his head. "Nah. You only think that because she works here and you're a robot." He flushed as soon as he said it.

Rapp stared at him.

Diego quickly added, "I mean, not knowing her, if I saw her in jeans and a jacket, I'd think attractive chick. Not federal agent."

"Thanks," Jane deadpanned.

Diego grinned. "You're welcome."

"The *point*," Rapp enunciated, "is that Jane might be right."

"Wow. Admitting I'm right. Make note of this Diego."

"Noted." Diego checked the air before shoving the rest of the donut in his mouth.

"We need to find your perp," Rapp said at the same time she thought it.

"I saw a tattoo on his neck. Let me run that down."

"I'll help you." Rapp wrapped the rest of his fritter in a napkin. "I'm going to go change."

"Into someone more professional and approachable, one can hope," Jane muttered.

Diego guffawed but quickly quieted at a dark look from Rapp.

He returned quickly, dressed in jeans and a jacket, looking dangerous but less Fed-like. "Diego, see if you can find out what the police know. Maybe offer to help with their IT problems."

"I don't know if I can legally do that." Diego shrugged in apology. "At least not for the next ten years."

"Do it. Call if you need me. Jane and I are going hunting."

* * *

SINCE WAITING on the database wouldn't yield them answers for a few days, they made a detour.

It turned out Rapp had a few contacts in the city, one of them being a tattoo artist who knew everything about everyone. In less than half an hour, they arrived at a tattoo shop then had to wait for the owner to arrive.

"We need to talk about your safety," Rapp said while they were outside, the sun warming the cold wind that continued to whip Jane's hair around.

"Excuse me?"

"Explain the bruise." He pointed to her cheek. "I can see some purple there."

"Shoot." She grabbed her phone and took a picture of herself, then zoomed in to see a shadow of color under her concealer she thought she'd fixed earlier.

"Boyfriend do that?"

She couldn't read his neutral expression. But she didn't have to. "Oh please. If a man tried to hit me, it would be the last move he ever made."

Rapp grunted. "Well?"

She didn't want to tell him on the off chance he got super pushy and tried to take her off the case "for her own good." She'd heard enough of that from Uncle Chris through the years though he wasn't even her boss.

"Jane, I demand transparency from everyone I work with," Rapp said in a firm voice. "It saves a lot of headaches further down the line. I want my people safe."

Technically, she worked *with* him but *for* Gambol. Rapp didn't seem to see the difference.

"Fine," she growled. "When I left McGrath's the other night, after you helped me out with Matthew Scott, some idiot nearly ran me down in the parking lot. I landed on my face."

He studied her but didn't otherwise react. A good sign. "And last night?"

"I had to get gas, and it was just my luck to head into the gas station that Neck Tattoo robbed."

"You put him down hard. I like that." Rapp nodded, still staring at Jane and starting to make her uncomfortable. "But you never mentioned the McGrath's incident."

"Because I couldn't be sure it was connected to our case. Could have been a drunk driver. No one got any plates. No one followed me home or did anything else suspicious. Trust me. I've been checking."

"Good." He kept staring.

"What?"

"You didn't do a bad job, but you need to stop rubbing your face." He put a gentle thumb under the bruise and frowned. "It's bigger than it looks. Does it hurt?"

At first it had throbbed like blazes but not so much anymore. Daily ibuprofen helped. What didn't help was Rapp putting his giant thumb on her face, however gently. He made her uncomfortable in a weird way she didn't want to think about.

"I'm fine. Stop, already." She took out her phone, saw he'd brushed *more* makeup from her injury, and hurriedly fixed it with the beige powder pack tucked into her jacket.

"Do I need to put you on a safety watch?"

"Huh?"

"From now on, you don't go anywhere alone."

There was no way he could enforce a "safety watch." Whatever that entailed. "Right now, we only have my suspicions about Neck Tattoo. The parking lot isn't a sure thing."

"What is a sure thing is that we have a problem with you not sharing. You should have told me about the parking lot right after it happened. Not later."

He didn't look pleased.

Whatever he meant to add had to wait. A large guy covered in tattoos grinned as he neared. "Yo, Gunther, my man, what's up?"

"We're not finished with this," Rapp murmured before embracing the tattoo artist in a manly hug, the kind that involved a lot of hard patting on the back.

She wanted to find his concern annoying, but part of her liked that her boss—*not boss, coworker*—felt responsible for her.

This is what I should feel working for Scott, who is obviously a bad supervisor.

Jane followed Rapp and his friend into the tattoo shop, more determined than ever to solve the issue of SSA Scott.

"Jane, this is Irv. Irv, Agent Jane Cannon."

"Well, hel-lo." Irv smiled, and she had to admit he was handsome in an I'll-crush-you-and-not-feel-an-ounce-of-guilt kind of way.

"Irv, focus," Rapp growled, and she had to wonder how these two had met.

"Sorry. Shoot, Jane. Tell me about the tat."

She described the sophisticated tattoo, her keen attention to detail one she'd been developing for years. Though small, the lion-dragon tattoo had been crafted by someone experienced with intricate work.

Irv shook his head. "Are you in luck! I know *exactly* what you're looking for."

"Seriously?" Rapp didn't seem to have expected such sudden success.

Excited, Jane waited while Irv dug out a binder from below the front desk and found the exact photo of the tattoo.

He placed the binder on the counter. "This it?"

"Yes. That's it."

He tapped the photo, carefully preserved under a sheet of plastic, and pulled it out. "It's the Momo Dragon, from that popular anime."

Rapp frowned. "Which one?"

The way he said that made Jane wonder. "Do you watch anime?"

Rapp turned red. "It's helped in a few cases, believe it or not."

"Yeah, *that's* why he watched it." Irv snorted.

Rapp glared at Irv and sneered. "Zip it, *Irving*."

"The secrets I could tell you about this guy." Irv laughed, not impressed by Rapp's glower. "Anyways, my cousin did your tattoo, though he normally works in the University District. I remember this tat because he was so proud of himself for nailing the details and because he crushed it while filling in for KJ." Irv flipped the photo over. "Looks like Harding Fellows is your guy. And yeah, that's his actual name. He was supposedly a total tool, but he paid on time. Hold on while I grab his address for you. I guarantee he didn't pay cash for that. Not with all those lines and colors. As small as it is, it's outstanding work, right?" Irv stepped away to wake up his computer and muttered, "Kid gets all his talent from my side of the family."

"Harding Fellows. Gotcha, you bastard." Rapp started tapping into his phone, and Jane smiled with satisfaction.

Finally. An answer to one of their many questions. Now they needed to find Fellows in time to get some useful information from him.

Before whoever ordered him to kill her found him first.

CHAPTER TWENTY

FINDING HARDING FELLOWS TURNED OUT TO BE MORE DIFFICULT THAN Jane would have thought. The police had no luck rounding him up, and Diego's search didn't yield any answers.

The day after that interesting meeting with Rapp's tattoo friend, while they all sat around the conference table in the office, Diego tried using some new software he'd been fiddling around with the night before. He typed some other details of Fellows into the computer.

Not five minutes later, an address popped up. The residence belonged to Fellows' sister, who had since moved. Her forwarded mail led them nowhere, so Diego worked some magic with an algorithm he'd developed to find stubborn people.

That led to a home in Kent.

Jane figured the woman would be hesitant to say anything. And she probably would have been on a normal day. Today, though, her brother owed her money, so she gave them a location before they'd had to ask twice. The phone call had lasted maybe two minutes.

"I know where that is," Jane said, familiar with the area one of her CIs frequented.

"So do I," Gina said.

"I thought you were new to the area."

"I'm originally from here. I've just moved around a lot. I'll go with you to grab him." Oddly, Gina had been acting friendlier than she had in the entire time Jane had known her. Perhaps the woman had finally thawed toward Jane's presence.

Rapp shook his head. "We'll have the police pick him up and sit on him. Then you two can have a crack at interrogating him." He looked from Gina to Jane. "Like I've already said, we go around in pairs. Got it?"

"What about you?" Jane asked, annoyed to have a partner. Especially Gina. She much preferred working alone when she could. "Taking Diego with you?"

Rapp nodded and stood, looking down at her. "As a matter of fact, I am."

Diego looked less than thrilled at the news. "Seriously? Why do I have to go? Where are we going? Will there be food?"

"We're going to talk to the officers at the station that lost Fellows. I didn't like their answers yesterday. Maybe today they'll remember something more. And you didn't find anything on our end, but maybe in person you'll see something that makes sense about their jacked-up computers."

"I hate cops. They have the worst coffee." Diego continued to complain as Rapp led him out of the room.

Gina stared at Jane. "The eye looks better."

Jane swallowed a groan. "Does everyone know?"

"I saw it the other day, but I didn't want to pry." As always, Gina looked perfectly buttoned up, this time in a dark blue pantsuit. The woman had a grudge against jeans.

Gina added, as if in afterthought, "I'm not sure I like you."

"Back at you."

They nodded to each other.

"But we're on the same team, so we'll work together," Gina announced, as if giving Jane no alternative.

Jane appreciated blunt honesty. "What exactly is your problem with me?"

"Other than the fact we were doing just fine before you arrived?

You keep annoying Rapp. I like the way he runs things. Don't screw it up for the rest of us."

"Rest of who? You and Diego? He seems just fine as long as you keep him full of energy drinks, *good* coffee, and donuts."

Gina crossed her arms over her chest. "Your need to be admired and catered to is sad, but I'm chalking it up to your youth and inexperience. Still, you got results, so that's something."

Seriously? We're probably the same age. Jane shook her head. "No, no. Be honest. You're upset because I found something you didn't and that bothers you. You're also irritated with me because you were the only woman here and now you're not."

"I'm not intimidated by other women."

"And you have a thing for Rapp, which now feels threatened. Don't be. I don't play where I work. But hey, you do you."

Gina's eyes widened, and she flushed. "That's ridiculous."

Jane called it like she saw it, and though she hated to stereotype the office romance, she'd seen the way Gina eyed Rapp when he wasn't looking. "Hey, you're both good-looking, intelligent people. I'm sure you'd fit well together. I'm only here to help out before I'm back at the main office."

"Your comments are offensive. I respect *Agent* Rapp. I'm not in love with the guy." Gina vibrated with embarrassment, glaring at Jane.

"Tomato, tom-ah-to. I don't really care. It's your business."

"You're making a mistake. I don't like you because you're only out for yourself, taking all the credit while the rest of us do all the work."

"Look, if you want, I can cheer you on when you find leads and make arrests. Makes no difference to me who finds information as long as we stop this guy from killing again."

Gina swore under her breath, but Jane heard her all the same. "You're taking things out of context. I'm a professional."

"I'm not saying you aren't. But fixating on me isn't helping us get the job done. Are we going to find Fellows or not?"

"Oh, *we're* going to. Because apparently, I have to babysit the new girl. Cannon, just admit what your power plays are really about. You think you're better than the rest of us."

I am better than the rest of you.

Jane surprised herself by not responding. But she didn't fight people out of their depth. Jane had been raised and trained by people who tracked criminals and often killed for a living. She doubted Gina had had the same coaching, as accomplished as she might be. Though trying to knock her out might be fun.

After a pause, Jane asked, "Were you in the military prior to the Agency?"

Gina regarded her with caution. "Yes. Air Force."

"Officer or enlisted?"

With Gina's attitude, Jane would bet officer.

"I was a captain in Air Force Intelligence."

"Interesting."

"And you?"

"Marine captain, Intel as well." Which in Jane's mind, despite their similar ranks and specialties, put her several steps above Gina. But she refrained from saying so since the other, more inferior services, had issues with the obviously superior Marine Corps.

"Ah, now I get it." Gina gave a short laugh. "Knuckle dragger."

"Air Farce."

"Jarhead."

"Chair Force."

They paused to study each other, and Jane mentally transposed Gina's business suit with Air Force dress blues and imagined her lounging at work while drinking gourmet coffee and snacking on imported beignets. She had a feeling Gina was doing the same, envisioning Jane in camouflage utilities digging in the dirt and eating decade-old MREs.

"It would seem we have more in common than not." Gina spoke calmly, ice frosting her words.

"Like the fact that we don't want to wait for Harding Fellows to be picked up by someone else. And for the record, I don't need a babysitter."

Gina scoffed. "Oh, I know. I heard all about how you took down our suspect with just your pinkie finger to save the day. Superhuman strength in addition to that giant brain, huh, Cannon?"

"Just smart is all. And highly capable in hand-to-hand." Jane wondered how fast she could take Gina down, maybe choke her out in a neck hold. The idea held more and more appeal the longer Gina talked.

Gina eyed her warily. "Look. Just do your job without being a glory hound and you won't have to worry about me."

Jane hadn't looked forward to working with anyone on this task force, but Gina made it difficult to be enthused about even tracking down Fellows. "Great. Perfect. You're awesome, and I wish I could be you. Happy now?"

Gina's thunderous expression told Jane they weren't mending any fences, so Jane added without caring, "Now how about you call the precinct tracking Fellows while I talk to my CIs about him? They might have new info we can use. Unless you'd prefer I not call useful contacts, in case I *actually* get information that would help us solve the case, and, you know, make your bestie Rapp happy."

"I really don't like you." Gina stormed out of the conference room to her desk.

Planning to spend as little time with Gina as she had to, Jane checked in with her CIs and found out the police were out in force looking for Fellows, who appeared to be on the run.

With any luck, they'd grab him soon. Because spending more time with Gina worried Jane. At this rate, she'd turn into her cousin and punch the woman in the face.

For once, Jane envied her cousin's ability to say to hell with the rules and go with her gut. But she doubted Rapp would be too happy to come back and find Gina passed out on the floor, her fancy suit all messed up.

As Jane left the conference room, she ignored Gina's glare. She went back to her notes on the victims, and prayed they got word on Fellows before Gina ended up jumping on her last nerve.

CHAPTER TWENTY-ONE

FOUR HOURS LATER, WHEN THE CALL CAME IN THAT HARDING FELLOWS had been arrested, Gina and Jane flew out of the office and into Gina's car. Jane wanted to get their mandatory togetherness over with, so she didn't argue about who drove.

They reached the department in record time and went to interrogate him. On charges of first-degree robbery, a class A felony, Fellows would do hard time once convicted since he'd already been on probation for larceny.

Or rather, *if* convicted. How had Fellows gotten free if not for some grand connections in the first place?

"Let me do this," Gina said before they went inside the interrogation room. "Let's see what he'll tell me without the woman who kicked his butt watching."

Jane nodded, all about the job. As she'd stated, she only wanted to get answers and return to finding the Code Blue Killer. Who made Fellows talk didn't matter—so long as he did. She also happened to agree that her presence might not make him chatty.

She stood in the observation room, accompanied by three other people. A moment later, after conferring with the detective accompanying her, Gina entered the interrogation room where Fellows sat, looking sullen and bruised. An additional officer, one made of nothing but grit and muscle, stood inside for security. Intimidation be thy name.

To Jane's surprise, Gina did a decent job grilling Fellows. The detective with her followed her lead. The two women asking questions finally managed a few pieces of information that told Jane two things.

One, Fellows had no idea how upper management in the Mazzuca family worked. His only tie to the crime organization was a huge debt he'd incurred while gambling, a thing the detective with Gina happily pointed out. Fellows insisted he only knew the Mazzucas from their reputation.

He claimed he'd already paid back his debt, but when Gina accused him of paying it back by trying to shoot Jane, his panicked expression betrayed him. Unfortunately, he wouldn't confess. And other than his gambling debt, nothing tied him to the crime family.

Frustratingly, this crime appeared to have nothing to do with Code Blue. Fellows had no idea why anyone would care about some stupid car burned up in an abandoned warehouse. Everyone knew about the place. Cars found there were usually torched for insurance purposes. Tons of criminals had used the warehouse prior to Code Blue's Toyota ending up there.

One of the detectives watching the interrogation next to Jane murmured, "Unfortunately, he's right."

Another nail in the coffin of that lead.

"I need to speak to Jane Cannon." Fellows nodded at the one-way mirror on the wall inside the room. "I bet she's back there." He said something else uncomplimentary about Jane, but she'd heard worse.

Gina nodded to the officer in the corner, who left and brought Jane in. The other detective departed, leaving Jane with Gina to question Fellows, while the massive officer stood back, watching with narrowed eyes.

"You got lucky with my nose." Fellows' eyes had blackened, and his swollen nose, covered in tape, had to hurt.

"I didn't get lucky. I hit you exactly where I'd intended." Jane sat back, her arms folded over her chest. At ease but ready to strike back if he made a move. Though the deterrent with massive biceps said he wouldn't. "Had you hurt any of the people in the store, I'd have broken your trachea, and you likely would have died, unable to breathe."

He stared at her. "That's illegal."

"No, that would be exercising lethal force to prevent innocent deaths by a violent criminal already on probation. No one would have looked twice at my actions." She could feel Gina glancing at her but didn't react. She just watched Fellows, needing him to know that *she* was the real threat in the room, not the officer in the corner. "What did you want to see me about?"

"I, ah, well, I just wanted you to know I got nothing to do with any of it. Not really."

"I was there. I took your gun away. Try again."

"No, I mean, I just wanted to show off for my friends. The gun wasn't even supposed to be real."

Obvious lies, but he was showing off for someone right now, speaking without his lawyer. For her, or for someone else watching?

"What friends?" Gina asked.

"They took off before the cops got there. They were watching from outside." He nodded at Jane. "I just wanted them to see how dangerous it can be if you mess around with other people's lives. Looking into stuff not your business." He stared into Jane's eyes. "You should have left me alone. Sometimes you need to back off before something happens. Like you get shot. Or you drown. Or worse."

Drown—a reference to Simmons.

She didn't react to the threat, watching in silence until he squirmed. Then she said, "So you're telling me you're working for the Mazzucas. Is that what I'm hearing?"

"What? No. A guy like me? I'm nobody. You gotta be something to work for a class outfit like that." He looked nervous. "I'm just saying a person can't be too careful in this city."

"People who talk about the Mazzucas don't live long, Fellows." Jane shook her head. "I really wouldn't share if I were you."

Gina listened quietly to the interplay.

117

"Hey. I didn't say anything."

"You said everything." Jane nodded. "Thanks. And good luck surviving a night here without cutting a deal." Jane leaned toward him and whispered, "They're everywhere. Watching. Listening." She subtly tilted her head toward the officer in the corner of the room, who frowned back at her.

Fellows' eyes widened, and he cursed at her. Then he yelled at the officer about how he'd said nothing. "You heard me. I said nothing. *Nothing.* I'm not a snitch!"

She stood to leave, and he screamed he wanted a lawyer. He wanted out. He stood, saw the giant officer take a few steps in his direction, then had a meltdown.

She left him to Gina and the detective who rushed back into the room.

In the hallway, she called Sullivan and finally got through.

"What do you want, O Suspended One?"

Jane huffed. "I'm coming back soon." She gave Sullivan a brief summary of the convenience store robbery. "I think the robbery was an attempt on me, courtesy of the Mazzucas. Be on your guard, and let the team know, okay?"

"Damn. Will do. Thanks. We'll look into Harding Fellows."

You will, and who else?

But at least Jane knew the Code Blue Killer had no ties to Fellows and, apparently, no ties to the Mazzucas.

No ties that she could see, anyway. Not yet.

CHAPTER TWENTY-TWO

SATURDAY AFTERNOON, ON A WEEKEND BREAK FROM THE TEAM—AND especially Gina—Jane sat with Sullivan and Williams in a downtown chowder shop. The pair had a lunch break, and since Jane wanted to know more about how Scott had been acting and what the mood was like in the office, she'd bribed her friends with famous clam chowder.

"I feel so used," Williams complained as he slugged down a second bowl of the soup.

"No, please, eat up. My wallet can take it," Jane said, not meaning a word of it.

Sullivan grinned. "Good. Because I have some dish for you on Matthew."

Finally. Info on Scott.

"Man, I hate that guy," Williams muttered and continued to eat.

"Tell me."

"Well, apparently, he caught you stalking him." Sullivan's wide smile made Jane groan. "Or so he thought. He felt badly about accusing you at McGrath's because he saw you with your date."

"He told you this?" Jane had a tough time believing Scott would have confided to Sullivan.

Williams grinned. "Nah. She was snooping and overheard him talking on the phone to his buddy upstairs. Not having the full context, she had to listen for a long time to understand it all."

"Ah. Well, good. So he doesn't think I was tailing him."

"Well, not at McGrath's." Sullivan snacked on cheese bread. "But following him from the dry cleaner and library? Oh yeah. You stepped in that one, kiddo. Oh, and I'm getting dessert today too."

"Count me in," Williams added. "By the way, Harding Fellows, your convenience store robber who emphatically says he's *not* connected to the Mazzucas in any way, shape or form? That guy?"

"Yeah?"

"Well, after you and your, I'd say sexy but I don't want to get accused of harassment, so I'll just say classy, FBI lady friend—who hates you by the way—left, I heard he started singing in exchange for protection."

"Wait. You talked to Gina?"

"No. I talked to Officer Mendoza, who was in the room with you when classy FBI lady interrogated Fellows."

"Oh. Mendoza, built like a brick wall?"

Williams nodded. "Apparently, classy FBI lady wasn't singing your praises to the other detective, who happens to be a friend of hers. Mendoza owed me one, so when I called down there, I heard all about it."

"What did you do to her?" Sullivan asked Jane.

"Nothing. She's just jealous because she was Air Force and not a Marine."

"Ah, interagency competition."

"The Marine Corps is not an agency," Jane said, repeating what she'd been telling the two since she'd known them. "Anyway, I couldn't care less if she hates me. I just want to find out who killed Dan and what Matthew's been up to."

"I'm a little confused," Williams said. "I thought you were suspended."

"I am."

"So how are you involved in all this?"

Sullivan poked him in the ribs. "She nearly got shot by Fellows. Hello?"

"I know that." Williams flushed. "But how does she know classy FBI—"

"If you call Gina Holtz 'classy FBI lady' one more time, I will kick you under the table. Hard."

Williams snickered. "Fine. Gina Holtz, star of the cyber team in Houston for a bit. But she wanted something spicier and transferred out of her old field office a year ago. Rumor has it she's been attached to a bunch of special projects." He studied Jane. "You wouldn't happen to be working with her on anything, would you?"

Sullivan huffed. "And if she was, she wouldn't tell us." Sullivan turned to Jane. "Although she should."

Jane gave in to laughter. "You two crack me up. No, I'm not officially working." Not exactly a lie, but she didn't want to involve these two in her "off the books" work. "I'm helping out a friend of a friend with something."

"Ah." Sullivan nodded. "I knew it. You can't not be busy."

She ignored her. "Honestly, I'm going out of my mind trying to solve the thing with Simmons. I need more on Matthew to make anything stick. Tell me about him."

"Oh, please, Williams, this is all you." Sullivan glanced at him.

"The guy's an egomaniac, a dictator, and a narcissist. What did I leave out?" He snapped his fingers. "Oh, right. He needs to be medicated to calm the frick down. He's been in our faces about everything. Tracking movements, getting reports on top of reports and involving himself in all of our cases. I mean, he's the SSA, but he's micromanaging so hard I'm surprised he can breathe with his nose stuck up our collective asses."

"Rob," Sullivan chastised, but the humor in her eyes told Jane she didn't mean it. "Yeah, Jane. What he said. He's gotten worse since your stalking. I think you shook him up."

"Good. Tell me, is he into any cases I might not be aware of?

Anything you can think of that I could look into while I'm waiting for OPR to find me innocent?"

"You could sneak in and look through his computer," Sullivan offered.

"I was being serious."

"So was I," Sullivan said. "Look, it's been close to a month. Don't you want to come in and get an update? Then maybe Matthew gets distracted, and you get a shot at looking through his computer while Williams or I keep an eye out."

Jane didn't know. That seemed like a big step up from just following the guy. And if she got caught, she could kiss her job good-bye. "Wow. You really went there."

Sullivan shrugged. "Just a thought. But either way, I want dessert. And I want it now."

"The cheesecake looks fantastic." Williams smacked his lips. "I'm so hungry."

"You had a gallon of chowder and seventy loaves of bread." Jane frowned. "This is why I hate picking up the tab with you two."

"Hey, you don't drink. We've got to make things even when we can."

Sullivan nodded.

"Fine." Jane ordered dessert. Perhaps something sweet would detract from the bitterness of being no closer to getting her job back.

And she wasn't due back to the Code Blue investigation until Monday.

She really hated time off. Maybe a distraction on Bainbridge Island would help.

OR NOT, she thought when she arrived at the ranch only to find Hal and Joe stewing about the attempt at McGrath's that her cousin had blabbed about, in addition to somehow learning about the incident at the gas station.

All the care made her queasy. Jane hated being the center of attention, no matter what Gina might think.

Hal demanded she start wearing a tracker at all times so he could find her if need be. Joe came close to tears while hugging her, worried for her future, and mentioned calling in Uncle Chris every other sentence.

Oh man, Monday couldn't come soon enough.

CHAPTER TWENTY-THREE

DESPITE ALL THE HANDWRINGING THE GUYS HAD SUBJECTED HER TO over the weekend, Jane did get some benefit out of it. She'd read through Hal's extensive notes on Agent Scott, though none of it proved the man's guilt.

Supervisory Special Agent Matthew Ronald Scott, the thirty-seven-year-old son of Senator Ronald Scott and Mrs. Belinda Scott née Rupert, daughter of a tech giant worth several hundred million dollars, had graduated at the top of his class at Harvard and spent several years getting a law degree, only to join the FBI, not as a lawyer but as a field agent.

Fast forward twelve years while he fast-tracked his way up the organization. Rumor speculated he might move into another position in the federal government, taking steps to eventually slide closer to the oval office.

Scott had the brains and the drive to succeed, not much of a personal life to speak of, and no scandals or secrets to be exploited. Hal's extensive probing convinced her that tying Scott to any form of misdeed wouldn't be easy.

Money had a way of burying family skeletons.

And thinking about money led her once again to that envelope he'd handed a stranger in McGrath's parking lot. She was dying to know what was in it and why the handoff had been so secretive. Had Scott been behind her near rundown at the bar? Or did Jane continue to see conspiracies where none existed?

For all she knew, her dislike of Scott colored her view on his involvement in the Mazzuca case. Perhaps he was just a bad boss.

Yet her friends also distrusted him. That had to mean something.

Frustrated at her lack of progress and wondering if the OPR would ever let her get back to her real job, on Monday morning, she worked quietly for the first few hours, going through more data Diego had turned up on the victims.

A few times, she felt someone's gaze burrowing into the back of her head and peeked up to see Gina glaring at her. Jane thought about the woman's animosity, realized she didn't care, and returned to her work.

By noon, her head ached from reading through so much information—information she'd already read several times. But in her experience, paying attention to everything often led to the small things that broke a case.

The Mazzucas had to take a backseat to Code Blue, and that ate at her too. Dan Simmons needed closure. Everyone knew the Mazzucas had to be tied to it. Had Sullivan or Williams found out more? And if they did, would they tell her? Probably. She hoped.

"Okay, you and you. In my office."

Jane frowned up at Rapp, who stood glaring at her. "Who, me?"

"Yes."

She followed him and Gina into his office, where he shut the door to give them some privacy. As if Diego wouldn't be watching or listening as hard as he could.

"Okay, what's going on with you two?"

"We don't like each other," Jane said, wanting to get back to work. "Can I go now?"

"What? Why?" Rapp seemed genuinely confused.

Gina answered, "She doesn't play well with others. And she's not really on the team."

Jane shrugged.

"That's where you're wrong," Rapp said. "We're all a team, Gina. We need to come together. We don't have nearly the manpower we need for this case."

"I know, Rapp. But she's prickly. And I'm tired of catering to her."

"How is doing your job catering to me?" Jane genuinely wanted to know.

Gina ignored her and offered a sigh instead. "I don't have to like her to do my job. And we need to be a team. You're right. I'll keep my glaring to a minimum if that helps."

"Yeah, thanks." Rapp frowned.

Gina left. Before Jane could follow her, he pointed at the chair across from him. "Sit."

She stared at him, waiting to be asked.

"*Please* sit, Jane."

She sat and waited.

"Look, I know you're here to help. I also know you like to do things your own way. Your insights are valuable but not replaceable. We're a small group, but we can make do with or without you."

Without her might take longer to catch their killer. He knew that, but he wanted her to know that as well. She sighed. "Fine."

"Good. Now I know we're all frustrated at our lack of progress. But I think we're making headway. We know Code Blue isn't tied to the Mazzucas, but he is targeting medical workers. And he's been pretty quiet since the EMTs a little over two weeks ago. If he's consistent in his patterns, he'll attack again soon. We need to stop him before that happens."

"I'm trying, but I'm getting nowhere with victim records or the phone interviews Gina's done. And her in-person interviews, though helpful, only paint our victims as decent, upstanding people with nothing worse than an overdue library book."

"I know." He nodded. "We're swimming in circles. That's why it's time for a field trip."

Jane caught his excitement. "Oh? Where?"

"To the scene of the next crime."

CHAPTER TWENTY-FOUR

Though Jane appreciated Rapp's idea to try something new, shockingly, Gina continued to argue with him about his plan, thinking her time would be better spent reinterviewing witnesses and friends and family of the victims.

"We can't know where he'll strike next."

Huh. Poor Gina's day appeared to be one big waste of time. That made Jane really look forward to this outing. Plus, she agreed with Rapp. She had a good feeling about his idea. She would have done it before, but in an effort to be a team player, she'd done what was asked instead of going off on her own. And they had so much data to look over, she had more than enough work to do behind a desk.

"I know we don't know where he'll strike next," Rapp agreed. "But perhaps if we scout it first, we'll see what's attracting him to the scenes."

The four of them stood outside the building, preparing to head out.

Diego nodded. "The unsub has struck every two to four weeks in the south and the east. I think he'll move north, in a counterclockwise pattern."

Jane didn't think so. "I don't know. That's feels too easy. He's got to be choosing these medical professionals some other way."

"Then tell us, Jane, how's he doing it?" Gina asked in an uber-polite voice.

Jane shot her a disgruntled look. "I don't know. But I don't think he's motivated by cardinal directions."

"Fine," Rapp said. "We do know he's striking those who work for major medical centers, not the smaller clinics or urgent cares. So we split up."

Please, no working in pairs, she thought as hard as she could.

As if he'd heard her unspoken plea, Rapp smirked at her before adding, "Though I know you'd all love to work together, and we're conscious about safety, we need to cover as much ground as we can. Everyone be on your guard but take a good look around. See what he might see."

He assigned everyone an area, giving Jane the Swedish Medical Center in Ballard out west, as she'd wanted. "And stay out of trouble," he warned.

Jane glanced at him and Gina, both looking stern and official, Gina because she dressed that way and Rapp because he continued to have meetings outside the office. She and Diego looked a lot less impressive, but she liked it that way. Jane wanted to blend in, to move among the possible victims, to see and feel what her prey—the unsub—might feel.

This method of hunting down bad guys had always worked for her uncle and a few of their more vicious members of Team Ten—mercenaries who lived for the hunt with boots on the ground. Drones and computers didn't belong when tracking targets in the mountains or jungles.

She felt the same, getting a rush out of using all her senses to find her quarry. "I'll be good."

"Check in on the hour. All of you." He shot Diego a look.

Diego sighed. "I know. I will. I'm hoping the guys at Montlake will be more cooperative than the techs at Virginia Mason."

"Amen to that," Gina muttered.

Motivated to be doing something, Jane drove through traffic that could have been worse. She parked and did a thorough walk-around, searching for a clue to Code Blue's motives. Without knowing why this guy kept killing medical personnel, she couldn't be sure of where he might strike next.

He'd used poisons to fake heart attacks, actual poison to point at murder in addition to drugs for a fatal overdose, and shot his last two victims. What was next? A hanging? Knife attack? Fire?

She hoped he didn't turn to arson. Thus far, he'd killed six people without wounding or disturbing anyone else.

Studying the area around the hospital, she walked up and down Tallman Avenue, taking note of the parking garage across the street for visitors as well as the nearby buildings and the skybridges as well. Close to busy NW Market Street, she could see a bank, a ton of condos, restaurants, and local businesses.

Plenty of places for Code Blue to linger while studying the hospital and those who used it.

She still wondered how Gambol had known these murders were tied.

Despite being good at her job, she'd never have pegged the deaths as related. The first two doctors hadn't even looked like murders.

Rapp hadn't told her everything. How did they know the crimes were linked...unless the unsub had told them? And if he had, then why the big mystery? Why not let the team know?

The thought occurred to her that maybe Gina already knew.

Jane liked having all the information on a case before delving into it. She could see not telling Diego. The guy clearly knew his computers but only worked for Rapp because of a court order. Jane was on loan, another set of eyes and a brain to work the puzzle pieces.

Why hadn't a serial killer stalking first responders become a larger investigation?

She hated having so many questions without answers.

Rounding the block, she circled back on Barnes Avenue, pausing by some vehicles parked near the cancer institute. Had the unsub lost someone to an illness then placed the blame on all doctors, nurses, and paramedics?

Something to consider, though she knew the others had followed similar investigative avenues before she'd been brought onto the task force.

Putting herself in the unsub's shoes, she backtracked and returned to her starting point, at the main entrance to the complex. She glanced up at the skybridge and saw a few people walking to and fro.

A good place to observe and not be noticed.

Making her way up to the main skybridge over Tallman, she remembered she'd seen another one closer to the emergency entrance, connecting the Tallman emergency building to the main building.

Code Blue's last EMT victims and the violence of their deaths made her think the EMTs meant something more. Though he hadn't started with them, the crime had felt more direct. Up close and personal. He'd fired without hesitation and with deadly accuracy.

Again, a detail that had been gone over to death—no pun intended —without results.

She climbed the stairs in the main building and reached the skybridge. People below came and went, unaware of being observed. Nothing too exciting. Inside the skybridge, a family and two couples clustered near the exit by the parking garage.

She decided to head to the bridge closer to the emergency room. Her scalp prickled. After a pause, she turned around.

A man in a hoodie and ballcap stood at the opposite end, staring down the street. A pair of people in scrubs and jackets walked under them, heading toward the emergency building.

He seemed to be watching them. Slowly, he lifted his head and, ignoring the older gentleman who'd just walked past Jane, looked directly at her.

Nothing about the guy in the hoodie would raise any suspicions.

Except she knew. It was *him.*

The Code Blue Killer.

She'd watched the videos of the EMT shooting so many times,

she'd committed to memory the way the unsub moved, held himself, cocked his head.

Her heart raced, but she forced herself to act casual, glancing past him then back and raised a brow when she saw him still staring at her.

She couldn't see the upper part of his face, masked by the shadow of a ballcap under his hoodie. But she swore she saw him smile before he turned and walked into the parking garage.

Jane didn't have to think.

She started after him and called Rapp, hurrying so as not to lose their guy in the parking garage.

"This is Rapp."

"It's him. He's here. Skybridge over Tallman Ave at Swedish in Ballard. Heading into the parking garage."

She disconnected just as their unsub glanced over his shoulder, met her gaze once more, then bolted.

Jane followed, in hot pursuit.

CHAPTER TWENTY-FIVE

JANE HAD MANY TALENTS, BUT RUNNING WAS HER SPECIALTY. SHE RAN for fun, and she ran to keep in shape. Her races with Joe kept her on her toes, and she gained on the fast-moving killer as he weaved in between parked cars and people, heading down to the second level.

Then the first.

"Stop," Jane yelled and nearly knocked down a security guard who shouted after her.

But she had no time to chat.

She chased the unsub out of the garage and down Tallman, through the traffic, turning several corners.

Barely dodging an oncoming car, she gained on him. He darted away again, and she turned back onto Russell, barreling past an officer holding onto a man in cuffs. He yelled at her to stop, but she couldn't, focused on entering the underground garage into which her perp had vanished before the metal gate closed and locked her out.

She slid underneath, rolled back to her feet and continued. She finally slowed, realizing Code Blue had nowhere to go. He couldn't access the closed elevator, which looked like it needed a code to enter. He couldn't exit through the now locked garage door they'd entered either. That also called for a code.

"I know you're here," she said between breaths. "Come on out. Talk to me."

The killer could *move*. Granted, she'd seen him on video looking lean and limber, but his speed indicated fitness, and the shape of his jaw, what little she'd seen of his face, hinted at youth. Her age or close to it.

Shadows filled the dim garage. She peered into the darkness, listening hard.

She wasn't surprised when he stepped into the open several feet in front of her, his back to the steel gate.

Outside, she noted flashing lights and heard police chatter. Good to help her keep this guy pinned but bad if anyone exited through the elevator to get to their car. She didn't want him to be able to take a hostage or feel too pressured.

And she sure as hell hoped he didn't have a weapon. In hindsight, she should have left his capture to the police. But Jane couldn't have just let him go.

"Jane Cannon. I'm flattered."

She blinked, not having expected he'd know her name. "You should be."

He grinned. Square jaw, somewhat thin face, but she needed to see his cheekbones, his nose, the shape of his eyes and face. Caucasian male and what else?

"Who are you?"

"You call me Code Blue, don't you?"

"You are eerily well-informed."

He laughed, his voice moderately pitched, not too high or too deep. A siren blared behind him before turning off. "We don't have much time to talk."

"Why are you killing medical personnel?"

"That's the right question." He paused, tucking his hands in his pockets.

Wary, she watched him, again wishing she had her service weapon but oddly glad she didn't. She had a feeling he wouldn't have talked if she'd been waving around her gun.

"The corruption. It's all around us." He took a step in her direction. "They were supposed to help, but they didn't."

"What did they do?" she asked, her voice calm. Deliberately, she kept her shoulders slack, her body easy yet ready to move if needed.

He seemed the same, and they watched each other, looking for vulnerabilities.

"You'll see. You'll learn. Hopefully, not the hard way like I did. I only ever wanted to help, to heal. And then I saw what they really do. Conspiracies and cover-ups. Everyone thinks we're crazy, but I've seen the guilty go free. And now they have to pay."

"So the people you've killed? They were all guilty?"

He sighed. "Symbols, Jane. They're symbols of a corrupt power. And they're just the beginning."

"Who are you?"

"Someone the world needs to stop the rot from spreading. I'm just a humble messenger."

The words sounded rehearsed.

She cocked her head. "No. That's not you. That's someone else. Tell me the truth. I'm listening."

"Get this thing open," a cop yelled from outside, too loud to be ignored.

"I'm sorry. We're out of time."

To her surprise, Code Blue ran at her.

Most people would have frozen in surprise, acted too late to do anything.

Not Jane. Being thrown by larger, heavier, stronger opponents over the years had taught her to adapt quickly.

She rolled to the ground and hit him in the knees. He tripped over her. Before he could get to his feet and escape, she twisted and wrapped him in a bear hug, her arm against his throat, her ankles locked around his lower body. She trapped her wrist to tighten the arm bar against his neck, holding tight.

"Easy. I don't want to hurt you," she said, meaning it. She wanted answers, because she sensed his involvement in something larger than just killing medical personnel.

"I know," he rasped. Then he shifted, and the fight was *on*.

They rolled around, but she didn't let go. Her cheek took another smack as he headbutted her, but not hard enough to do real damage.

She had to keep hold of him until the police entered to take over. But the guy was like an eel, wriggling, nearly managing to break free.

Jane finally wrangled him until she sat astride his stomach with his arms pinned to either side of his head. A position she wouldn't be able to maintain for long.

She got her first good look at him now his hood and hat had fallen off.

Late twenties, short, dark blond hair, light blue eyes, handsome features that would be remembered.

"Tell me your name."

"My name is Justice, and everyone will pay until my will be done." He grinned. "Catchy, huh?"

"Tell me," she said again. "Who needs to pay? Not everyone. Who?"

The sound of the garage gate rising distracted her. Her weight and strength in this position wouldn't be enough to keep him down. And they both knew it. "I can help," Jane tried.

"You're sincere, but you're weak. The only thing people like them understand is violence. And blood." He threw her off him.

To her surprise, he raced toward the police, howling for assistance.

"Officer, please! Help me. She's been stalking me, and she has a weapon!"

"On the ground," one of them shouted at Jane while the other cop dragged Code Blue out of the garage, the previously locked gate now fully opened. "I saw her chasing him."

"I'm FBI. Don't let him go!" she shouted, keeping her hands in the air while two pistols remained centered on her. "I'm complying, and I'm unarmed."

"Facedown, on the ground," the closest one ordered.

She had seen too much pavement up close lately. "I will. Please. Keep a hold of him. He's killed six people already." Jane had a bad feeling they'd already lost him.

"Hey! Get back here," the farthest cop shouted.

And just like that, he was gone.

She groaned while one of them reached for her hands to cuff them behind her back. "Go after him! Don't let him go!"

But it was too late. Code Blue was in the wind.

CHAPTER TWENTY-SIX

JUST HER LUCK THAT RAPP AND THE OTHERS SHOWED UP TOO LATE TO help. At least the officers had released Jane without a hassle after verifying her identity, and she hadn't suffered any injuries. At least not major ones, other than the loss of pride at losing Code Blue.

After making sure Jane didn't need medical assistance, Rapp said, "With me," and hurried them toward his vehicle.

"I saw him," Jane announced.

His gaze sharpened. "Gina, get me a sketch artist."

"On it." She called someone on her phone.

They climbed into Rapp's SUV, illegally parked a block down, halfway on the sidewalk, and Rapp darted out into traffic.

Jane tenderly massaged her cheek. She needed to stop landing on her face. "Diego, take this down while it's fresh, would you?"

"Tell me." He recorded her on his phone.

She described Code Blue, keeping his image fresh in her mind, still buzzing off the adrenaline rush.

"I've got an artist enroute to the north precinct," Gina said. "ETA thirty minutes."

"Good. We'll beat them there." Rapp turned at the next street and accelerated. "Jane, tell us what happened. All of it."

"I did a walk around, looking at the hospital from a bunch of angles. Something about the skybridge, the one between the parking garage and the main building, made sense, so I went up there."

"On Tallman," Gina reiterated.

Jane nodded. "I noticed a man looking down at the street. I knew he was our guy. I've spent hours watching those videos of the shooting, studying the photos of the crime scenes. I tried not to be too obvious, but he saw me, smiled, and turned away."

"He smiled?" Rapp sounded intense.

"Yeah. I couldn't make his features out then. He wore a ballcap under the hoodie."

"Color?" Gina asked, though Jane had already told Diego.

She repeated what she'd seen. "A dark blue brim, gray hoodie and faded denims. Converse sneakers, well-worn." Jane went over his description again in her head, adding everything she could think of. Every detail counted. "I didn't smell anything on him. No alcohol, cologne, cigarettes. Nothing. But he was an inch or so taller than me, so say six feet. Maybe 180, 190 pounds? He sounded like an alto, young, likely in his mid to late twenties."

Rapp said, "He smiled at you on the skybridge."

"Yes. I started after him and called you. Then he ran, so I pursued. He's in fantastic shape and *fast*. I raced after him until we ended up in a secured parking level under those apartments on Russell Ave." She frowned. "He got lucky since a car was just leaving, so he slipped in as the garage was closing. I rolled under the gate, and we were locked inside together."

"Not smart, Jane." Rapp sounded disapproving. "You weren't armed. Or were you?"

She didn't want to answer that. "Hey, he wanted to talk. He knew my name."

"What?"

"He called me by name—Jane Cannon." She frowned. "How did he know that? He also knows we call him Code Blue." Rapp didn't look pleased by that. "He's intelligent. He's got a plan." She paused. "This is going to sound weird, but it sounded like he was following someone else's orders."

"What did he say, exactly?"

Her head started pounding, but Jane ignored it and focused on her ability to recall.

After a moment, she said, "Well, first he said, 'Jane Cannon. I'm flattered.' Then I said, 'You should be.'" She ignored Gina's snort. "When I asked who he was, he said, 'You call me Code Blue.' He's getting intel about us somehow."

"I don't like it," Rapp growled.

"Join the club." Jane cleared her throat. "Sorry. Anyway, before I get this backward, I have to tell you he wanted to talk. He had plenty to say about corruption and about getting justice." She concentrated. "He said, 'They were supposed to help but didn't.'"

"Who's 'they'?" Gina asked.

"Someone else in the medical profession was my guess. This is a revenge killing spree. But it's not anything our victims did. He told me that. They're symbols of a corrupt power that's spreading. He mentioned conspiracies and cover-ups. And he added that he's just the messenger."

"So who's really calling the shots?" Rapp asked.

Diego said, "It could just be him. He could be hearing God or voices telling him what to do." He asked Jane, "Did he say he had a boss or partner?"

She frowned. "No, but I got the sense he was carrying out orders that aligned with his mission, yet I don't think they were his idea in the first place."

"But you can't be sure," Gina said, turned around in her seat.

Jane met her firm gaze, no derision there, just direct attention. "No, I can't. But make no mistake, Code Blue was there scouting for his next targets. I'm sure of it."

"Good work," Rapp said. "Keep remembering him. Go over all your details again and again in your head. We'll get his picture down, and Diego will find him."

"I sure will." Diego frowned. "You look like you're in pain, Jane. Are you okay?"

"Yeah."

"Liar," Gina said.

Jane gave a weak chuckle. "Okay, you caught me. My cheek hurts. I'm really tired of kissing the pavement."

"Maybe time to get a social life where you're not on a face-to-face relationship with the ground, eh?" Diego offered.

"Good advice," Rapp said. "But Jane, I don't care what you said before. You're seeing medical after the sketch artist." At Jane's weak protest, he cut her off. "It's either see someone or go home after a great day's work and take at least a week to recover."

"Fine." Jane glared at the back of his head, caught Gina's grin, then glared at her too.

Which made Gina chuckle. "You know, Jane, I might just be starting to like you."

Jane stared back at her, then said to Rapp, "You're right. We need to get me to a hospital. I think I'm hallucinating."

The team shared a laugh before Gina questioned Jane some more.

By the time Jane shared her information with the artist at the police station, they had a face to go with their unsub.

And with any luck, they'd soon have a name.

CHAPTER TWENTY-SEVEN

TUESDAY MORNING CAME EARLY, BUT JANE DIDN'T MIND, PLEASED TO BE back after hours of waiting around the hospital yesterday to get cleared to return to work. Worse than Rapp acting like a stickler for protocol had been him saddling her with Gina while she waited.

As if she couldn't have returned to the office herself. She had a feeling he hadn't trusted her to see a doctor without supervision, and of course Gina would narc on her if she didn't.

A mild headache and more bruising to her face, but since most of it had been healing well enough and they didn't see any fractures— more wasted time on an X-ray—she had a clean bill of health to return to work.

The only good thing to come from her doctor visit was that it allowed time for Diego to grab her car and drive her back to her apartment.

Jane did a light workout before heading into the task force, not surprised at the cold rain that fell. The weather had been a bit sunny lately, so she knew they were due their typical wet winter. Fortunately, it promised to stay warm enough not to ice over.

Inside the warm building that served as her temporary office, she found Gina out, but Diego and Rapp working at their respective desks.

Diego perked up when he saw her holding a cup of coffee.

"Hey, Jane. Come look at what we found."

"When did you find it?" Had no one called her last night to let her know something important?

He didn't answer. "It's our guy. Phillip Keiser."

"You have an ID? Wow. That was fast."

Typically, they'd have to send an image—a photograph, not a sketch—to the Biometric Technology Center, part of CJIS, in West Virginia to the facial recognition unit. And though they found results faster than many other areas of the FBI's crime lab due to the technology used, this result had come back a heck of a lot sooner than she'd expected.

"I know. I used some software a friend of mine's been tinkering with to get a better image off the sketch before sending it in. It helped that our guy was already in the system. CODIS had him on file. He served four years in the Army."

CODIS, the Combined DNA Indexing System used by the FBI and other law enforcement agencies, would have had his information through the DOD since he'd been in the military. A lucky break all around.

"Ah, gotcha. So what do we know about Phillip Keiser?" She sat next to Diego at his desk and stared at his monitor, where a clean-shaven, younger version of the man she'd wrestled the day before looked back at her.

Rapp joined them, looking tired despite his crisp, fresh suit. "Great work you two. Diego, fill her in. I'm just going to sit and listen."

"Listen again, you mean." Diego grinned, brimming with excitement as he read off a report he pulled up on his computer. "Right. So Phillip Keiser, age twenty-seven, is the only son of Dr. Adam and Lena Keiser, deceased. Phillip graduated high school then served four years in the Army before going to college. Unfortunately, his parents died, and he dropped out. Fell off the grid two years ago."

Rapp interrupted, "Tell her about the hit-and-run accident. Who hit them?"

"Who?" Jane asked, picking up on the intrigue.

"Anton Kaminski, August Kaminski's youngest."

"Kaminski? As in the other crime family—if I can really call them that—in Seattle?" The wheels in Jane's head were spinning. The Kaminski name had appeared a few times during her investigations into the Mazzucas but never went anywhere. "So Keiser isn't connected to the Mazzucas but to the Kaminskis?"

"We don't know that he's tied to anyone," Rapp answered. "But the fact is, Anton Kaminski was charged with a hit and run that killed Keiser's parents. But then the charges got dropped."

"And with Phillip not around to protest, no one cared?" Jane ventured.

Diego nodded. "So maybe he's upset the EMTs couldn't save his parents. I don't know. But it's a motive."

"Do we know for sure his parents died in the ambulance? Or did they get to the hospital and the doctors and nurses couldn't help? I mean, he's targeting them all, not just EMTs."

Rapp nodded. "Good questions. We're still looking into it." His phone buzzed, and he frowned at it. "I need to take a few meetings, so I'll be out. Call if you need me." He stood. "Try not to get slapped around today, Jane." Then he headed toward his office.

She scowled at his back then turned to find Diego grinning. "He's not funny. And wipe that smile off your face."

"Yes, ma'am."

Jane sighed. "I need more coffee."

A FEW HOURS LATER, she rubbed her head and, spotting no one watching, popped an ibuprofen for her growing headache. Staring at computers all morning hadn't helped advance anything, so she took a break and followed a hunch she hoped would prove fruitful.

An old professor of Phillip's had been listed in the hit and run case as a point of contact for Phillip. Apparently, the professor had been good friends with Phillip's parents.

She called Professor Lito's number, not expecting him to answer since most people ignored numbers they didn't know. When he picked up, she asked to speak to him face to face on a matter pertaining to a current investigation. He agreed, and before she knew it, she was headed out the door.

She found him in Queen Anne in a lovely Victorian situated on a street that spoke of old money. Despite the season, his yard looked well-tended if dormant. And the charming two-story made her feel at home the moment she stepped inside.

"Thanks so much for agreeing to meet with me, Professor Lito."

"Oh, call me Kyle." The older man had a slender frame, white hair threading dark at his temples, and gold wire frames over intelligent eyes. In khakis and a button-down cardigan, his look screamed academia. He nodded to the attractive white-haired woman smiling next to him. "And this is my wife, Maria."

"Jane Cannon." She shook their hands, careful not to say "Agent" Jane Cannon as she wasn't here under the aegis of the FBI.

"You said this is about a case you're working on?" Kyle looked interested while Maria excused herself from the room.

"Yes. I'm investigating alongside the FBI. This might involve what happened to Phillip's parents."

"Really?" Kyle's eyes narrowed.

Maria returned bearing a tray holding a teapot, cups, and cookies. "I was already making our late afternoon tea. Please have some."

Jane gazed at the plate of cookies. "Are those homemade?"

"Best chocolate chip in the state," Kyle boasted.

Maria blushed. "I just baked them today. I tell Kyle he's spoiled."

"Don't I know it." He smiled at his wife, his heart in his eyes.

Jane didn't know what to make of their affection, as she'd never seen that kind of romantic love up close. But she appreciated the open communication she sensed between them.

"Thank you. I'd love some."

While they settled into comfortable seats in the living area, Jane brought up Phillip.

"Phil? Why, I haven't thought about him in too long." Kyle sighed. "Such a bright boy. And so sad about his parents."

"They were killed in a hit and run, I read."

Maria nodded, but Kyle's pinched expression warned Jane to tread warily.

He nodded. "Yes, a little over two years ago. It was a travesty." He took a sip of tea. "Phil was always such a smart kid. An honor student. He wanted to be a doctor like his father, but he'd also been a fan of the military, like his grandfather, who'd served in the Army. His plan was to do a few years to serve his country then transition out and become a doctor."

"But he didn't. He left college before getting his degree." And without that, he'd never be able to get into medical school.

Maria patted her husband's knee. "His mother was my cousin, who was more like a sister to me. And of course, Phil took some classes from Kyle before he dropped out. Such a lovely and talented boy. It broke his heart when his parents died."

"That boy was so bright and full of life. Losing his parents crushed him."

Maria gave her husband a sad smile. "After he lost his parents, Phillip came to live with us for a while, but then he left. He had to start fresh somewhere without so many memories, he said. He used to call but stopped even that six months ago. I miss him."

"We both do." Kyle clasped his wife's hand, his eyes glassy.

"I saw that Anton Kaminski was behind the hit and run but never prosecuted for it. How did Phil take that?"

Kyle scowled. "That Kaminski brat hid behind his gangster father. Crooked, the lot of them."

Maria sighed. "You've always hated my family."

Jane paused in the act of taking a second bite out of one of the best cookies she'd ever had. "What now?"

Maria shrugged. "Lena, Phil's mother, and I shared the same grandmother. August Kaminski is my uncle."

"Phillip's great uncle?"

She nodded.

Another tie to organized crime. Or was it?

What the hell was going on?

CHAPTER TWENTY-EIGHT

JANE'S REPORT TO RAPP DETAILED EVERYTHING SHE'D LEARNED FROM Kyle and Maria Lito. On the surface, the tie to organized crime spoke of a subversive attempt at criminals to undercut the stability of the city.

But even Rapp thought that might be reaching. Phillip hadn't known about being a Kaminski relative, not according to Kyle and Maria. He'd been a regular guy who'd joined the Army, planned on becoming a doctor, then retreated into his own world after the death of his parents.

She had no proof any of this tied into the Mazzucas *or* the Kaminskis, who were at best minor players.

Yet the adjacent tie to organized crime bothered her.

It bothered Rapp too, so he asked her to do more digging.

With Diego and Gina working their own angles on the case, it was left to her to figure out how Phillip had started down his path toward vengeance. Because maybe if she did, they could stop him from hurting anyone else.

Already, a statewide BOLO had been sent out to pick him up, and law enforcement knew to treat him as dangerous.

But what pushed a young man to turn on innocent people? Why punish medical people who had nothing to do with what had happened to his parents? What was all his talk of cover-ups and conspiracies?

Her nose itched, telling her she'd found something worth digging into.

With Diego's help, she spent the afternoon looking up files on the Kaminski network that might involve Phillip or his family. She found nothing of note. Just a lot of arrests for various Kaminskis dealing with prostitution, drug possession, or petty theft.

The Kaminski family had been around for over a decade but were known mostly for opening restaurants and entertainment facilities where criminals *might* congregate. Some strip clubs, a few underground card games that would ultimately get busted. Small-time crime, staying under the radar.

Studying their activity, she thought they might be smarter than the Mazzucas. They appeared content to work behind the scenes a lot, because the Seattle office was aware of them but had no open investigations. The police kept them in check.

Nor did the Kaminskis tie to other countries. Homegrown American criminals. Not like the Mazzucas, who'd recently made a name for themselves, especially in the drug trade.

She looked through information on August Kaminski. Apparently, he'd been moving around the country for years, shaking things up before settling with family in Seattle. He'd been arrested a few times on misdemeanors in New York and New Jersey before he'd left the northeast to venture west.

From the data Diego had pooled, August had created small businesses in St. Louis, Oakland, and Las Vegas before heading to Seattle to open several restaurants and strip clubs around town. She had a helpful CI within his organization. Although calling it an organization seemed overkill.

August's people didn't seem very structured. Mouthy, loud, and chaotic, more like. He made a decent living but wasn't rolling in money. Or he didn't seem to be. And he didn't show himself to many people, working behind the curtain.

The more Jane compared his family to the Mazzucas, the more she detected a pattern of a puppet master content to pull the strings and never be seen.

How had no one ever looked deeper into them? Or had they, maybe?

Though Code Blue seemed to have no ties to the Mazzucas, he had a definite tie to the Kaminskis. So she followed her nose and set up an interview with the lead detective on Anton Kaminski's DUI arrest in the Keiser accident, along with the ADA on the case. Who just happened to be the retired detective's current wife.

* * *

WEDNESDAY MORNING, she met with Rick Flynn and his wife Amelia. Amelia continued to practice law but now worked in private practice.

The coffee shop in Queen Anne defined the culture of the city with a diverse selection of quirky décor in bright colors and textures, a jazzy, eclectic mix of music playing low in the background, and a casual yet comforting interior, both warm and welcoming.

The small, independent business provided all that as a backdrop to a delicious product Jane didn't mind paying an extra dollar for. The coffee was rich and bold with notes of brown sugar and vanilla, and the pastry had been cooked perfectly, both flaky and delicate with a warm custard inside.

She was definitely adding this to her list of favorite coffee shops.

Jane worked at taking dainty bites instead of falling on her food like a starving woman. "Thank you for suggesting this place to meet," she told Rick and Amelia. "I'm making a note to come back soon."

Amelia grinned, her eyes bright, her white hair making her look sophisticated, rather than older. Her funky blue glasses added to her air of competent chic. "I'm addicted to the scones, which aren't nearly as dry and crumbly as the ones they sell in the grocery store. When

Rick said you wanted to talk about Anton Kaminski, I figured we'd need some sweet to go with the bitter."

Rick grunted. "I'm not at all sorry to be retired from police work, to tell the truth."

"Tell me about the case."

He sighed. "What a nightmare. The kid was sixteen going on forty. Mouthy as hell, and he proudly failed a breathalyzer. He was lit off his ass."

"Rick."

Her husband flushed, and Amelia said, "We're working on not swearing so much."

"Hard habit to break." Rick guzzled his coffee. "Anyway, so the kid doesn't care that he's just killed two people and is bleeding from a gash in his forehead. His buddies in the car thought it was hilarious. They were high on something, not drunk, and worked for Anton's dad."

"The Kaminskis."

Rick nodded. "We'd been looking into the family for years but could never pin anything on them. They own restaurants. They're a little shady but far from criminals. Just ask them." He scoffed.

"No one can't pin anything on them, from what I hear," Amelia said. "Everyone thinks they're small time, but I think they're just really, really smart."

"I'm beginning to see that." Jane took another bite of heaven before pushing her plate to the side. "So Anton kills Dr. Adam and Lena Keiser. Their son, Phillip, was twenty-four at the time. He took it hard."

"I remember him," Amelia said. "The poor kid was lost. So angry. His parents had been wonderful people, and then they were gone."

"So the hit and run killed them?"

Amelia paused and looked at her husband.

Jane frowned. "What am I missing?"

Rick answered after a pause, "You know what? I don't care anymore. I can tell you this, Jane. I was on scene, and those folks were still alive when the EMTs picked them up and transported them to the hospital. Barely, but still, alive. They somehow got rerouted a few times and landed at a hospital a half hour farther away than Harborview."

Harborview, not Swedish Medical Center, Jane thought. So Phillip hadn't been lying about the dead being symbols. If he carried a grudge, why not target Harborview?

"Did the EMTs botch the rescue?"

"I have no idea, but we couldn't find the bodies for *a few days*," Rick said, his disgust evident. "In addition to that, we somehow 'lost' the evidence on the Kaminski kid. The breathalyzer data, his clothes, the car, all either disappeared or caught fire in an unfortunate accident."

"What?" Jane looked at the pair across from her. "Someone ruined the evidence?"

"You say ruined, I say covered it up," Amelia answered. "And not only that. I was ordered to drop the case by the DA. We'd lost the evidence, but it was an obvious attempt to distract us from the guilty party. I wanted further investigation."

"We all did." Rick nodded.

"But we were all ordered to let it go."

"Well, isn't that interesting?" Jane sipped her coffee. "But hold on. Let's backtrack. The bodies of Phillip's parents *disappeared?* Were they ever found?"

Rick scowled. "Oh yeah. But get this. When we found them days later, they were missing some vital organs."

"Say what?" This case kept getting weirder.

"Yep. Missing brains and hearts, if that doesn't beat all. Hearts, I get. But who the heck is looking for brains on the black market? Weird collectors?" He huffed. "Anyhow, it tied into this." Rick plucked a folder from a carryall beside him and tossed it on the table. "Have at it. I never could figure out how this connected to some baby casino in Vegas."

"Vegas?"

"It's all in the file. If we can help you after you read that, feel free to ask. But I think you'll learn as much as we did when you go through it." Rick nodded at the folder, which contained a thick stack of papers and several thumb drives and CDs.

Vegas? Missing organs? Phillip's parents had reappeared, missing their hearts and brains.

And the EMTs had been shot twice—once to the head, once to the heart.

CHAPTER TWENTY-NINE

By the time Jane went through all the paper documentation in the file Rick had given her, lunchtime had come and gone.

Leaning back in her chair, she studied the list she'd made, facts that turned into questions that turned into *more* questions.

Phillip Keiser killed six people who work in medicine. None of them killed his parents.

Phillip is related to August Kaminski, head of a small crime family that's swimming under everyone's notice.

Anton Kaminski killed Phillip's parents.

Anton Kaminski was never charged with their deaths.

Adam and Lena Keiser's bodies were found with organs missing.

No one was ever indicted for the crime of stealing their organs.

Ten people were arrested in the Harvester case—a similar crime of organ theft that tracked back to Las Vegas and ended in Seattle. Three went to prison and are still doing time there. The others either vanished or died soon after being charged.

None of the organ theft suspects were our victims. Two doctors, two nurses, two EMTs, and four hospital administrators.

Which meant Phillip had four more people to kill. Maybe.

She pulled up one of the thumb drives on her computer and

studied the organ theft case. A name on the investigating report looked familiar. Jon Haversham. Hold on. Not the new ASAC at the Seattle office? It had to be a different guy.

"Jane, you got a minute?" Rapp called from his office. For once, his door remained open.

"Hold on a sec." She googled the name Haversham, corrected it to Jon Haversham FBI, and stared in recognition. Then she quickly dialed the main Seattle office.

"Hello. This is Agent Jenn Sullivan."

"Sullivan? It's Jane. Hey, do you happen to know if our new Assistant Special Agent in Charge of the Seattle office is the same Jon Haversham who worked in the Las Vegas office?" Where Sullivan and Williams had worked.

"One and the same." Sullivan's voice warmed. "He was a mentor for a lot of us in Vegas. And now he's the ASAC at our cozy little HQ." She lowered her voice. "And one of Matthew's besties."

Jon Haversham, one of the three Assistant Special Agents in Charge of the Seattle Field Office. Holy crap.

"Thanks. I need to talk to you later."

"I need to talk to you too. We should meet up."

Jane nodded to herself. "Let me know when and where."

"Will do. I'll text you." Sullivan hung up.

Jane just sat there. Haversham had clout and was SSA Scott's best buddy. He'd been around when the organ theft had been hushed up in Seattle. From all official accounts, the Keisers had passed away due to a car accident. Not because their bodies had been desecrated.

Phillip knew. She had only found out because she'd been digging. No one else seemed to care about a buried case. All the criminals in the Harvester ring had gone to prison or died.

Yet Anton Kaminski had gone free after the DUI that injured Phillip's parents.

She could see how the cases were tied but couldn't yet figure out what it meant.

"Cannon, my office," Rapp shouted.

Lost in her thoughts, she jolted and hurried over to him, ignoring the way Diego smirked at her and Gina gave her a disdainful once-over.

"You called, Rapp?"

"Yeah. What's new? I could see the smoke coming out of your ears from here. You found something."

She nodded, filled him in on everything she'd learned, and out of breath, sat back to see what he made of it.

He had been writing notes as she explained, and now he studied his notepad. "This is bizarre."

"Yep."

"So Phillip Keiser is killing people as a message to the organ thieves? That means he's got four more people to kill, likely employed in medical administration."

"Maybe."

Rapp gripped his hair in frustration and leaned back to stare at the ceiling.

"I have a question."

Rapp continued to lean back but nodded at her. "Shoot."

"How did we find out these cases are linked in the first place? No way Gambol just thought they connected. Did he run some kind of diagnostic program to figure that out? Is that something Diego did?"

"No." Rapp stared at her. "This can't leave this room."

"Who am I going to tell?"

He snorted. "Right. And besides, Gina and Diego know."

"Oh, so I'm the only one out of the loop." She huffed. "Figures."

"You're a late addition. Gambol brought you on as a favor to someone."

Uncle Chris. She hoped her cheeks didn't turn as red as they felt. So now she was a charity case? She thought she'd been brought on for her expertise.

"But I'm glad he did," Rapp continued. "You've helped us a ton on this investigation. We have a suspect and multiple leads we didn't have before. But don't let that go to your head."

"Sure, sure. So what can't leave this room?"

"Gambol was contacted by an anonymous source that told him to look at all six deaths as connected. Mind you, at the time, the EMTs hadn't been murdered yet. We'd just found Nurse2."

"Someone planned it."

"Yeah. From what you said, it seems Phillip is on his own mission, but he's doing someone else's work."

"Maybe. He could have been the one who called."

"He could have." Rapp nodded. "But this tie to organ theft, Las Vegas, and the Kaminskis means something."

"I know. I'm just not sure what. I suspected the Mazzucas for a while, but it seems like they're just related to Dan Simmons' death."

"Maybe."

She groaned. "We have a lot of maybes. I don't like it."

"Me neither. Let me mull on this. We should get the others to look at it too."

She agreed. "Something's really been bothering me though."

"Besides Gina?" he teased.

She ignored him, and his grin widened. "How did Phillip know my name? And that we dubbed him Code Blue? Only us four and Gambol know that, right?"

Rapp straightened in his seat but didn't appear alarmed. "Not exactly. We're keeping this low key, but plenty of LEOs have been questioned in regard to this investigation. And I think Diego said something around the police when we picked you up at the parking garage in Ballard."

"Shoot. But wait, that was after Phillip had already mentioned it."

"Then maybe Gina or Diego said it around someone else. I know I didn't." He frowned. "Gambol wants this investigation to be quiet, but it's not classified. And honestly, I want *more* help on this, not less. We're running out of time." He muttered, "Something he and I have been arguing about lately."

So Rapp and Gambol were butting heads. She wanted to know how the pair knew each other, but it wasn't her place to ask.

"Running out of time?"

"I'll look into this. Are you feeling okay?" He glanced at her cheek.

"Right as rain." A stupid thing to say, because that made her think of her cousin, Raine, who she didn't want to talk to anytime soon.

Rapp nodded. "Good. Keep doing what you're doing. We'll have a group meeting tomorrow to catch up. And Jane, be careful. The attempt on your life wasn't related to this case, but it's still a threat."

"Trust me. I haven't forgotten." How could she with Hal and Joe constantly demanding she check in when not at work?

"Good. Let me know if you need anything."

She nodded and left to grab a late lunch. All the while, her mind kept circling back to Phillip and his odd ties to organized crime, conspiracies, and cover-ups...like that hushed-up DUI and the Harvester case in Las Vegas, worked on by ASAC Jon Haversham.

What would Sullivan have to add to that? She couldn't wait to find out.

CHAPTER THIRTY

"You really do take me to all the best places, Jane," Sullivan said by way of greeting.

At eight o'clock at night in January, darkness blanketed the city. A pale moon gave little light, adding to the mystery of a gentle rolling fog creeping over the ground below.

The main ferry terminal, located at Colman Dock, Pier 52 on the Seattle Waterfront, was anything but empty. Upstairs and outside the building, she and Sullivan leaned over the railing, looking down at the line of cars waiting to board.

"Hey, you picked the place." The terminal had decent foot traffic as the ferry continued to bustle people back and forth to Bainbridge Island and Bremerton from the city until well after midnight.

"Well, I might have a date on the island."

"On a school night?" Jane teased.

Sullivan laughed. "Yeah. I've been seeing this guy for a few weeks. It's nice. But I'll be staying over at my aunt's. I'll be sleeping at *her* place, not his, since you're too shy to ask."

"And because I don't care."

"I'm hurt."

"Yeah, yeah." Jane liked Sullivan. Finding a female friend, of which she didn't have many, who both understood and appreciated what she did wasn't easy. Sullivan lived the life and had a sense of humor about it. Jane liked that.

"So why are we here gossiping like old ladies? And why shouldn't I have brought Rob?"

Jane frowned. "I didn't say you couldn't bring him."

"Oh. I kind of thought this was hush-hush."

"It is. But Williams is okay. Isn't he?"

Sullivan nodded. "Right. Well, maybe I held back because I didn't want to him to know about my date. He's a little..."

"Into you?" Jane said wryly. Everyone knew about Williams' crush on his fellow agent.

"Yeah." Sullivan sighed. "I don't want to make him feel bad." She shivered in her coat. "But whatever. Tell me why we're here talking about Jon Haversham and some serial killer you're looking into."

Jane stilled. "How did you know about the serial killer?"

"Code Blue?" Sullivan snorted. "Creative name there."

"I didn't name him."

"Yeah, well, it's a hot topic at the office."

"But who told you?"

"I forget. But rumor has it they brought in some new hotshot to handle the task force. Then Matthew mentioned your date, and I put two and two together."

"You didn't believe I was dating the hotshot?"

"No. Because if you were, you'd never go someplace where tons of government employees hang out. You'd go somewhere private for snuggles with *Gunther Rapp.*" Sullivan gave her a sly grin. "Are you working that angle? If so, *go, Jane.*"

"Shut up."

Sullivan laughed. "Okay, sorry. You wanted me here. Talk."

"Haversham. He's good friends with Matthew."

Sullivan nodded. "What's the big deal? We all know Matthew's headed on to bigger and better things. All those family connections and money. I do understand why he's been working so hard to close this case with Simmons. A DEA fella dying under his watch isn't good." She paused. "But honestly, I think he actually cares about Dan. He sounded broken up about it."

"Because he's guilty?"

"I don't know. But I do know he spoke to Dan's boss. He told Haversham it was one of the worst conversations he'd ever had. As in, a true tragedy."

Jane had her doubts about Scott's sincerity. "Right. But back to Haversham. When you worked in Las Vegas, do you remember cases involving the Kaminski family? Or maybe a big organ theft ring?"

"The Kaminskis? No. But the organ theft thing was huge. You don't remember the Harvesters case?"

"No, but I've been reading about it."

"Yep. It made big news before they hushed it up. Some creepy doctors arranged to make a ton of money selling organs on the black market. Turned out they had contacts throughout the states and overseas. They'd get orders for organs, kidnap and kill donors, taking whatever they wanted. I think there were close to a dozen people involved."

"Ten, and Haversham was on the case."

She nodded. "He co-headed it. But that was four or five years ago, right?"

"Yes." Jane's mind whirred. "You're sure you never heard the name Kaminski?"

"Before coming to Seattle? I've heard it more than a few times here, but they're nowhere near to taking on the Mazzucas. They have no real firepower. And calling them a crime family or organization is an insult to families and organizations everywhere." She chuckled. "But I do know some interesting intel on Haversham, if you're interested. Though Rob could probably tell you more. He—" The sound of firecrackers distracted them. "What the heck is that?"

More noise, and cement chipped at their feet.

Sullivan and Jane dropped.

Gunfire.

Near them, people scattered and screamed.

Jane swore. "Those aren't firecrackers."

"Where are the shots coming from?"

Something struck the ground to the right of Jane, hitting the edge of the platform close by. She peered over the ledge to see one shooter, holding a rifle aimed *at her*, standing between small cars in line for the ferry.

"Down below—" Sullivan swore as a round struck between her and Jane. "And over there!" She nodded to two people, a man and a woman, firing pistols from the building some twenty or so yards away. Sullivan pulled out her weapon.

"They're aiming at us. We need to move." Jane also wanted to get the gawkers and civilians standing around to safety. "Get to safety!" she yelled at the people staring at them with blank expressions.

She and Sullivan darted away, running for the stairwell for some cover while shots continued to explode around them. Sullivan couldn't return fire because too many people ran between her and the shooters.

Sirens screamed, growing closer.

Below, a loud exchange of gunfire filled the air, likely from the Washington State Troopers who'd been checking on the vehicles boarding the ferry.

"Drop your weapons," she heard someone yell.

Sullivan grabbed a nearby crying woman who stood frozen in fear. She nudged her toward the stairs and fired back.

Jane tackled a young man just before a bullet drilled into the post behind him. "Head down and away," she told him, watching him crawl away in terror down the stairs.

The rest of the civilians had scattered. The shooting ceased, the gunmen nowhere to be found. So she turned to check on Sullivan.

And found her friend bleeding on the ground.

CHAPTER THIRTY-ONE

"Seriously, I'm fine," Sullivan growled at the closest paramedic wrapping her leg.

"You don't look fine," Jane said.

Sullivan glared but ignored her and said to the EMT, "The bullet barely grazed me. Just hurts. Yes. It was a bullet after all."

"Ma'am, please don't move. Let me just—"

"Guy, I appreciate your help, but..." She gave him a polite and appreciative earful, trying to get down to the cops buzzing all over the terminal grounds.

Rapp stood by Jane's side. He'd been nearby and seen the lights of responding vehicles just before Jane had called him. Since she didn't know if the shooting—aimed at her and Sullivan—had to do with Code Blue or the Mazzucas, she decided to err on the side of caution by calling her not-boss.

"Thanks for letting me know," he murmured. "You sure you're okay?"

She gave him a look.

He sighed. "Fine. God save me from stubborn agents. You said it looked like they'd targeted you and Agent Sullivan?"

Jane nodded. "I'd bet on it."

"Then I think it's time to get a police presence by your apartment."

"I've got it." She hated to call her family for help on this, but she didn't want to get stuck with some annoyed cops having to swing by at all hours.

"I don't think you do." Rapp frowned.

Williams' arrival interrupted them. He looked panicked as he stared at Sullivan, the bloody ground, and the exasperated EMTs. "What the hell happened to you?"

"Jane."

"Jane did this?" He turned to Jane with wide eyes.

"Very funny. I didn't shoot her, though now I'm thinking about it. We think it was the case you guys are still working." He'd know which one she meant.

Williams looked her over, then blinked at Rapp. "Who are you?"

"The hotshot," Sullivan said.

"Oh, right." Williams relaxed. "Glad you're here. I'll take care of Jenn. Be safe, Jane. The boss is on his way too." He helped Sullivan to her feet and guided her down the stairs, likely to the ambulance.

Jane followed and watched him get in with Sullivan, arguing that the flesh wound at her thigh could get infected and she needed to suck it up and get ready to have support. Period.

Matthew Scott suddenly appeared, looking as put together as always. He saw Jane and frowned, then frowned even harder when he noticed Rapp with her. But he only nodded before heading to the local law enforcement lead.

Jane glanced in the direction of her car, hoping Rapp might take the hint and go his own way as well.

He didn't.

"You're clear to leave." He told her what she already knew. She'd already talked to the police. No one seemed to know where the shooters had come from or what they'd been after. Since she couldn't say for sure she'd been the target, she hadn't shared that detail with them. Fortunately, no one but Sullivan had been injured. And the wound appeared minor, despite all the blood.

"I'm tired and hungry. I'm going home."

"I'll escort you. And that's not a request."

She would have chewed him out. Jane wasn't a baby and didn't need watching. But as this was the second time she'd been shot at, only a fool would say no to another set of eyes to look out for her.

"Fine. But I've got backup coming. Seriously."

"Uh-huh. Sure." Rapp directed her to his vehicle. "I'll have your car delivered to you later. Address?"

She gave it to him then sat in the passenger seat and let the warmth and rolling sensation of the SUV lull her. Overly tired, Jane wondered if shock might be setting in. Her adrenaline had been pumping like crazy, but now that the danger had passed, she felt drained.

The next thing she knew, Rapp was calling her name and gently shaking her. "Jane."

"Huh? What?"

He gave her a soft smile that didn't belong on his face. He normally gave the impression of a hardened marksman out to annihilate his target. Even a smirk or sarcastic twist to his mouth would fit better than whatever that was.

"Come on, butt-kicker. Let's get you inside." He put his game-face back on, looking like a guy one wouldn't want to meet in a dark—or light—alley.

"I can take care of myself." Yet she felt sluggish.

"I know. But I'd do this if you were Gina, Diego, or Gambol. My team, my responsibility."

"Not yours. I work with you, not—"

"For you," he interrupted. "Yes, yes. Now let's move." He hurried her to her door and stashed her inside while he swept the place, not giving her much time to argue.

The warmth of her apartment felt so good, she decided to ignore his high-handedness.

"I'm going to call a few friends who can handle themselves to back me. You can go now."

"Go ahead. I'll wait." He watched her call Hal.

Hal never picked up on the first ring, except this time he did. Odd. He sounded tense. "What's wrong?"

"What's wrong with you?"

"Jane."

She sighed. "Nothing's wrong, exactly. But I might need some backup before my boss assigns some poor cops to patrol my street. I don't need babysitting."

"I didn't say you did," Rapp answered.

"He's there? Good. Are you hurt?" Hal sounded serious.

"No, not at all. I'm fine but tired. There was a shootout at the ferry tonight."

"That was her?" she heard Joe in the background. Well, that would save her from a second call.

"I was involved, yes. But I didn't start it." She ignored the ghost of a grin on Rapp's face. "A bit of added protection for a little bit wouldn't hurt."

"Put Rapp on," Hal said, which surprised her but shouldn't. Hal had never given her any info on Rapp, but he clearly remembered Rapp's name.

She must have paused too long, because Hal growled, "Jane..."

"Fine." She thrust the phone at Rapp. "Hal wants to talk to you."

Rapp raised a brow but took the phone. He answered in yeses and nos then handed the phone back.

"Hal?" Jane scowled. He'd hung up.

"They're on the way. I'm just going to wait for them to get here."

"You know what? I'm done arguing. I'm going to shower and pack a bag. I have a feeling they'll want me at the ranch tonight."

"The ranch?"

"Family home on Bainbridge Island."

"Ah. Mind if I put the TV on?"

"Knock yourself out." Jane closed herself in her bedroom, neatly placed her clothes in the hamper, then took a hot shower that helped soothe her sudden jitters.

She'd been shot at. Again. Once could be bad luck. Twice? *Really* bad luck.

And as much as she didn't like being reliant on others, if you couldn't turn to family when it counted, who could you turn to?

She made herself leave the hot shower, dry and dress in comfortable sweats. After packing a bag, she decided to put her head down for a few minutes. Rapp could entertain himself for a little bit while she focused on settling down.

But she woke to low voices arguing.

She jumped to her feet, fully alert when she heard Joe outside her door adding, "I'll kill you and won't blink twice."

CHAPTER THIRTY-TWO

"What the heck is going on here?" Jane asked as she hurried into her living room.

Hal stood, leaning back against the front door and conveniently blocking Rapp's exit.

Joe stood nose to nose with Rapp, both of them looking massive since Rapp had removed his jacket and rolled up the sleeves of his shirt, showing off muscled forearms and broad shoulders.

To her surprise, he looked amused and not scared. Even Jane took a moment when Joe got angry. A teddy bear at heart, on the outside, he looked like a mix of angry giant and rabid killer.

"Jane, I had no idea you were a Team Ten fan," Rapp said.

"Huh? You know who Team Ten is?"

"They have quite a reputation."

"Fan? Please." Hal smirked. "It's the other way around. We worship the ground she walks on." He didn't seem at all bothered about the macho posturing in front of him.

Joe seemed one finger squeeze away from a kill. "We really do. Our girl never needs to worry about anything. Or anyone." Joe gave him the smile. The one that said *I can bust your head open like a grape from any distance.*

Jane didn't understand all the hostility. "Joe. You realize he's not the one that shot at me."

"I know who he is."

She was missing the subtext, obviously. "You know Rapp?"

"I'm her boss." Rapp announced.

She cleared her throat.

"Okay, not her boss since she keeps associating Gambol with that title. I'm the guy calling the shots on our assignment. I consider her one of mine. So you don't need to threaten me, Randall. I'm invested in keeping her alive."

Hal actually hooted. Joe's first name was a closely guarded secret.

Joe's brows gathered, his thunderous expression intensifying. "Don't you threaten me, boy."

"Boy? I'm not that much younger than you. Unless you're seventy and don't look it." Rapp didn't appear threatened.

Jane frowned. "How do you know Joe's real name?"

Hal laughed. "That's a big secret, Rapp. You going to explain?"

Jane got the feeling all the men in the room knew one another. Yet she remained in the dark.

"I know because it's my job to know."

"The kid ran into us on a few ops," Joe explained to her. "Now he thinks he's a big deal because he learned a few of our names."

Rapp looked away from Joe and studied her. "Which one do you belong to?"

"All of us," Joe said.

Jane sighed. "Chris North is my uncle. Officially," she added when the guys looked hurt. "But all of Team Ten are my family."

That soothed Joe's ruffled feathers. "Exactly. So watch your step with our girl."

"Step? Randall, I'm here because I'm watching out for her." Rapp's easy smile faded. "But someone is clearly after her. Mazzucas or our killer, I'm not sure which. This is more than someone trying to shut down a case. I'm not sure what yet, but I'll find out."

Jane felt beyond embarrassed that all the big, strong men in the room felt the need to watch over the little woman. "Hey," she barked.

"I can take care of myself. Rapp, I'll be safe enough with these guys. But I'm not off the case."

He looked right at her. "Never said you were."

"Okay then." She nodded. "I'll be in later tomorrow."

Rapp ignored the stern looks from Hal and Joe. "Make it Friday. And before you argue, I want you to do your best to think. What is it you know that you don't know you know?"

"What?"

Hal nodded. "Valid question. She's on it. I'll help."

Rapp considered him and nodded. "Ah, right. The Toy. Heck, yeah. We'd love your help on this."

Hal preened. He'd be tough to live with for the next few days.

Joe opened his mouth, but Rapp cut him off. "My only goal is for my people to remain safe while we catch a killer. Do what you need to, not that you need me telling you that."

Joe nodded, his expression odd as he glanced from Rapp to Jane. "So you're not a couple?"

"What?" Rapp and Jane said at the same time, sounding horrified.

Wait. Why is he upset? I'm a treasure. He should be flattered Joe suggested we're a thing. Not that Rapp's ever going to be that lucky.

Joe seemed pleased at the reaction though. She just wished Hal would stop grinning like an idiot.

"Okay then," Joe growled. "Jane's protected. Shut this down fast, Rapp. Before I have to."

"I'd like to. Trust me. If I had my way, I'd..." Rapp glanced at Jane. "I'll talk to Gambol. See if he wants this done my way—your way—or by the book. See you on Friday." Rapp nodded to her. "Hal. *Randall.*" He snorted with amusement when Hal stepped between him and Joe. "Talk to you soon." He sauntered out the door, not looking back.

Joe kept rumbling beneath his breath, and none of it was complimentary. "I can't believe you're working with *him.*"

"What's wrong with Rapp? Besides the obvious, I mean?"

Hal cocked his head. "What's the obvious?"

Jane ticked off her fingers. "He's arrogant, standoffish, way too mysterious, and obviously some special ops whiz kid now playing at being a Fed."

"Well, that hits all the right marks," Hal agreed. "Joe's upset because he thought, wrongly, that you two were dating." Joe made a noise, but Hal continued, "He doesn't think Rapp will watch out for you, but he's not a bad guy to have at your back." After a pause, he added, "Although he's not someone you want with a knife at your neck."

Jane huffed. "Who is?"

"Good point." Joe wrapped an arm around her shoulders, engulfing her. "You make sure he stays on your good side, sweetie. If he does anything you don't like, you let me know."

"Don't like?" Then his meaning settled. "Oh geez, Joe. Seriously. We are *not* dating! He's my not-boss."

"Not-boss?"

"I work for Gambol. I work *with* Rapp. And with any luck, I'll work for a new supervisor at the field office just as soon as OPR clears me."

"Right." Joe and Hal shared a look.

"What?"

"Never mind," Hal said with emphasis that made no sense to her.

Joe shrugged. "Forget it. I'm just being paranoid and protective. But nobody shoots at our Jane and gets away with it."

"Especially not twice," Hal said. "Now let's head home. That's if the ferry is back on schedule yet. What morons shoot up the ferry and expect it not to be a huge mess?"

Joe agreed. "Messy."

"Very messy." She smiled, no longer adrenaline-fogged from earlier.

Because with family around, Jane was unstoppable.

And it was time the Mazzucas, and whoever else was out to get her, realized that.

CHAPTER THIRTY-THREE

"I would have told you two, but it just happened." Jane didn't know why she had to keep apologizing. The guys had let her sleep it off the night before, but Thursday afternoon, they expected details on everything.

"Okay, Joe's being a little pushy." Hal gave him a look that seemed to calm Joe down. Joe could get super protective, but that was part of what Jane loved about him. He very much put family first. "But we're concerned. We had to hear from Raine about your assassination attempt at the gas station."

"They didn't send an assassin after me. But he worked for the Mazzucas. And I'm not sure those events were connected, but that wasn't too long after my near run-down at the bar. But again," she said hurriedly before Joe interrupted, "I couldn't be certain that was tied to the Mazzucas. I'm still not. Though I am wondering if maybe Scott had something to do with the gas station. Are you sure you can't find anything tying him to the Mazzucas?"

Jane still secretly wondered if her fixation on Matthew Scott's guilt wasn't just because she disliked him.

"You saw what I dug up on him. And I went deep." Hal shrugged. "There's just not much there. He's a Boy Scout."

They all sat at the kitchen island, taking a water break after an earlier jog. Jane had needed the run to clear her mind, and Joe refused to let her go by herself, even at home on the ranch. But when she'd asked Hal for help with her overprotective guard, he'd told her that he would have done the same if he didn't dislike running so much.

"I know you went deep. I just don't like the guy. I think I want him to be guilty." She laid her head down on the table, frustrated.

"Look, you've gone as far as you can go on both cases you're working, right? Let's brainstorm," Hal suggested.

"Or shoot things."

They both regarded Joe with humor.

"Go shoot something, Joe. I'll stay here, under guard, and talk to Hal."

Joe sagged in relief. "Thank God. If I had to listen to you two yammer about more conspiracies without just taking out the problem, I'd lose it." He left in a huff.

Jane stared after him. "I'm a little worried about this sudden desire to shoot first and ask questions later."

"Part of the problem might be that he learned his niece is dating an older guy his cousin—"

"Which cousin?"

"Penny."

"Oh, I like her."

"Well, Penny hates her daughter's boyfriend. Joe doesn't like him much either, but Joe can't say anything because Shantelle will freak out on him as only a sixteen-year-old can."

She understood. "I guess I'm the placeholder for all his protective tendencies, huh?"

"Well, you know he considers you family." Shantelle wasn't actually Joe's niece but his first cousin once removed. Joe didn't care. He kept it simple. If he loved you, labels didn't much matter.

Hal added, "Just cut him some slack. He cares about you. Plus, I don't think you've ever been in this much danger when we were both here to do something about it."

"Okay, I'll admit you have a point there." She knew she'd do whatever it took to help either of them, though her skills didn't quite match theirs. Her talents lay in the ability to trap and track, not kill.

"So what are you going to do next?" he asked.

"I need to find Dan Simmons' killer. I need to figure out why someone wants me out of the way so badly. I wasn't the only one involved in the Mazzuca case. It was the entire unit. So why target me?"

"How do you know the others haven't been targeted?"

"Sullivan and Williams never mentioned it. I'm sure they would have."

"Yeah? Want me to look around?"

She hated to say yes, but she had nowhere else to turn. She swallowed hard. "If you would."

He beamed. "Be right back." Hal returned moments later with his souped-up laptop that might very well be able to read minds. The monster hacker had no problems getting around firewalls and national security to find answers. Diego could take lessons from him.

Normally, Jane wouldn't use him or Joe in a case. But things had gone beyond normal.

She could and had majorly annoyed people in the past but not enough to warrant killing her. Although she should probably ask Gina and Scott about that.

"What's that scary smile for?" Hal asked as his fingers danced over the keyboard.

"Just thinking about people I know who might want to kill me."

"So many."

"Ha ha."

Hal grinned. After a few moments, he turned the laptop around. "Jenn Sullivan's emails look pretty tame. Rob Williams' too. And I've been reading the rest of your team's correspondence. Not much going on, except Sandy seems like she's having an emotional affair with Josh."

The pair on her team had been pretty cozy following Thanksgiving. "That tracks."

"Yeah. Wait. Hold on." He turned the laptop around and continued typing. "Hmm. Read this."

She joined him to read a bunch of emails from Scott to the ASAC, Jon Haversham. Scott had no idea what to make about the gun violence aimed at his people. Interesting that he still considered her "his people."

"Doesn't look like your butthead is guilty."

"He's not my—never mind." She knew better than to get in a stupid argument with Hal. "What are you typing now?"

She watched as he infiltrated Rapp's Agency email account. In it, Rapp kept talking to Gambol about getting more agents on the task force, about updates on the danger they faced, and the fact Phillip Keiser knew more than he should. He also asked about getting Diego a raise and gave kudos to Gina, who might ask to stay on in Seattle once he left.

Jane suppressed an odd pang at the thought of Rapp leaving. Although typically, once a case closed, so would the special task force. Did Gambol plan on making the task force into its own squad? And why did she care if he did? It wasn't as if she planned on staying. She had a job waiting for her at the field office. Hopefully. Still, this assignment had been entertaining as well as challenging.

"Now this is interesting." Hal pointed at her email.

"You're hacking me now?" She blinked as she read aloud, "Wait. When did this come in?"

"Yesterday. You need to keep up."

She read aloud. "From anonymous: *You'll never stop what's coming. There's too much at stake.* What does that mean?"

"Probably the same thing it meant when they sent that message to Gambol." He typed something and showed her Gambol's screen. "I cheated and looked through his emails the other day. I remember seeing that same message."

"Nice, Hal. If he finds you going through his emails, you're in trouble." She didn't know much about Lionel Gambol, but she knew enough not to mess with him.

"Oh, trust me. I know." He started to say something else when Joe rushed back into the house.

"She's home!"

Jane looked at Hal, who looked back at her and shrugged. She pointed to herself. "I know?"

Then Raine walked through the front door carrying a huge seabag over her shoulder. "Well, well, the gang's all here."

"Raine?" Jane hadn't seen her cousin in nearly two weeks, but she'd assumed Raine had been staying somewhere on the property. "I thought you were here already."

"I left a few days ago to grab some stuff. I, ah, might be back for good. I'm on terminal leave now."

Hal blinked. "Terminal? I thought you were taking some time to figure things out, not totally leaving the Marine Corps. Oh boy. Does Chris know?"

Joe swept Raine into a big hug.

As if Hal had summoned him, Jane's uncle called. She saw the caller ID and winced. "He does now." Before she could think twice about it, she picked up the call and held it out to Raine. "Raine? I think this is for you."

Raine managed to crawl out of Joe's embrace to grab the phone. "Yeah?" She winced at the shout that answered.

Hal and Joe shared a commiserating shrug then vanished from the room like ghosts.

Jane would have done the same, because she could hear her uncle screaming at her cousin through the phone despite it not being on speaker.

"Oh no you don't." Raine grabbed Jane's collar. "You threw me to the wolves."

"Technically, wolf."

Raine tucked the phone against her chest to muffle her uncle's roaring. "You put me in this mess. You're in it with me."

"Hey, I was nearly killed the other day. I don't need this kind of stress in my life."

Raine tugged the phone back to her ear and released Jane. "You'll be nearly killed again if you leave me with this psycho." She put the phone on speaker in time for Jane to hear their uncle loud and clear.

"Psycho? *Psycho?*" Uncle Chris shouted. Explosions and screaming sounded in the background. "You want a psycho? I'll give you a psycho!"

Jane settled into what promised to be a royal butt-chewing. But hey, at least it wasn't at her expense.

CHAPTER THIRTY-FOUR

THE CALL WENT AS EXPECTED. UNCLE CHRIS DEMANDED ANSWERS Raine refused to give, citing "It's my life and my decisions. Butt out."

That went over like a shark in a kiddie pool.

Raine seemed dispirited, not willing to fight back the way she normally would. Jane took over while her cousin stood in front of the fridge, staring blankly at its interior.

"She's having some issues right now," Jane told her uncle.

"I know that," he snapped. "Talk some sense into her. She's the best in her field right now. The Corp needs her. Hell, she can ask for whatever she wants if she reenlists. Despite what the military says it can and can't do, they'll move mountains to keep her. Raine's fast-tracking to bigger and better things."

"She needs time." Jane added quietly, "And I think she needs to evaluate if this is the best thing for her."

"Exactly."

"I meant her staying in. She needs a break at least."

"Fine. If she needs it, she—" He paused to yell away from the phone, "Hondo, you can't keep blowing crap up. I wanted a peek into that building, and now we're out of luck."

She heard Hondo over the rumble. "There's one more. I think.

Malcolm is…" Something exploded. "Uh, I'll go talk to him. Malcolm, bro, I think that's an IED. Go left." A pause. "Your other left!"

Uncle Chris growled, "Jane, I have to go before one of these idiots kills himself or the rest of the squad. Help Raine out, okay? Before she does something she can't undo."

He disconnected.

Jane turned to her cousin, who sat at the kitchen island with a dispirited attitude, slurping down a strawberry yogurt.

"I thought you were staying here while on leave, thinking about things. You went back to close down shop? Getting out for good? Have you given yourself a chance to think about it?"

Raine's hair stuck up all over. Her jeans had stains, and rips showed through her tee beneath her camo jacket. What the heck had she been up to the past two weeks?

Jane asked in a softer voice, "So you just decided to rip off the Band-Aid and make it permanent?"

"I guess."

"What happened?"

"Does it matter?" Raine gave her a bitter stare. "You'll just try to talk me out of it because Uncle Chris told you to. Suck up."

Jane knew this pattern. Raine's go-to when cornered or upset was to lash out.

I will not respond in kind. I'm the calm, mature one here. She needs advice, not judgement. Or mocking. No mocking. But what came out of Jane's mouth was, "Stop being a baby and tell me what happened. I know you're having issues blindly following orders. But that was never your problem. You only do what you want to do."

That was obviously the wrong thing to say because Raine straightened and threw her half-empty yogurt container at the refrigerator.

Pink yogurt splatted and glopped down the stainless-steel door.

"I *do not* do what I want to do."

"Raine, what's going on?" Jane tried not to sound tired of her cousin's antics, but Raine's *constant* need to be talked off the ledge grated on Jane's nerves.

Raine glared. "Back off."

"Great work thinking things through, as usual."

"You missed my birthday."

Instant remorse filled her. "Sorry, but I—"

"And you missed Mom's celebration." The annual trip to the ceme-tery where Cleo North lay buried.

Jane winced. "I'm really sorry about that, but in my defense, I was getting shot at."

"You sure do know how to make friends, don't you?"

"I'm sincerely sorry about missing Aunt Cleo and your birthday."

Raine sniffed. Not one for tears, she gave off more of a moody sense of frustration. "You owe me a gift."

"I do. But none of that explains why you would leave an organiza-tion you love. I know you've had a rough time with some classified assignments. Are you feeling guilt? Regret?" She paused before adding, "Shame?"

Raine's cheeks flushed, and her eyes blazed. "We can't all be perfect little go-getters! You got suspended from your stupid job and you're still trucking around like a happy little camper. Need me to shine your boots, Special Agent Moron? Sure. Need me to file some papers? To look through spreadsheets and mine data for you while my career swirls down the toilet? Aye, aye, Sir." Raine snapped off a violent salute.

Jane counted to ten in her head, determined not to engage. "So it's shame. What did you do?"

"You have no idea what it's like to make life and death decisions you can't take back."

"You're right," Jane said, not bothering to hide the sarcasm. "I totally couldn't have shot the guy who shot at me, or punched him in the throat, or asked Joe to snipe my jerk of a boss because he benched me. This entire family is one lucky charm away from being a fruit loop, but we sift through our feelings, seek balance through careful consideration, and make the best choices we can."

"First, you're mixing your cereals." Raine gave a harsh laugh. "I love it. A psychology degree you did nothing with and you're *still* trying to give advice. You're pathetic. Life isn't black and white, genius. Live a little and you'll see it's all about shades of gray."

"Just because I'm not some emotionally unregulated *psycho*" —she tossed in the Uncle Chris reference because it would further annoy Raine— "who flies off the handle at every turn doesn't mean I don't know what life is. Some of us prefer to be calm, centered, and intelligent versus, 'Hey, I have a feeling about this. Let's go bomb something.'"

"I have a feeling I'd like to share with you, you sanctimonious shrew." Raine took an angry step in her direction. But before she could launch herself at Jane, Joe was there, scooping her into his arms and walking away with her while she ranted, "You're dead. So dead, *Pain* Cannon!"

Hal slid into the kitchen and glanced at Joe carrying away a squirming Raine. "She still using that old insult? The one she used when she was fourteen?"

"She's been regressing. I think she forgot it used to be Plain Jane Cannon. Now it's Pain Jane. Or Pain Cannon? I think she's confused." And thirty-three years old acting like a toddler throwing a tantrum, but that was beside the point.

"She's stressed. Ignore her."

"Oh, like you two did? Cowards."

He gave a weak grin. "We were being strategic. She needed to loosen up a little."

"You're welcome for taking the hit." But now Jane felt bad, because she knew her cousin would be embarrassed later for making a fool of herself.

A petty part of Jane enjoyed that, but her wiser self wished she'd been able to help instead of making Raine's mood worse. She sighed.

Hal sighed with her and pulled her into a side hug. "Now how about we look at the data I found on Jon Haversham and see who's really on the up and up and who needs to be shot down?"

"By shot, you mean…?"

"Taken down a peg. Legally. While still alive. *Obviously*, not violently."

She didn't trust Hal's fake smile. Jane narrowed her eyes and poked him in the chest.

"Ow."

"I'm glad to hear you're going the non-killing, law abiding route. Because Uncle Chris is already ticked at Hondo and Malcolm on whatever mission they're on. Things were blowing up and bodies were flying."

"Oy."

"Exactly. I think his head might explode if you or Joe kill anyone else on his watch."

"Noted."

Thank God.

CHAPTER THIRTY-FIVE

FRIDAY MORNING, PLEASED TO BE BACK AT WORK, JANE SETTLED IN AT her desk. She'd ignored Rapp's inspection and satisfied nod. The gesture hadn't been sexual or romantic. More like a gesture from a stronger superior to his weak little subordinate.

After taking orders from the guys and her uncle and being yelled at by her cousin, she didn't have the bandwidth to tolerate more nonsense. Since Rapp's attitude felt like a twin to her Uncle Chris's, she snapped, "Take a picture. It'll last longer."

Gina shook her head. "*Annnd* she's back. Yippee."

Jane mentally flipped her off but fought back a smile as she woke up her computer. Annoying Gina almost made up for Rapp being Rapp.

He grunted at her before moving back into his office.

Jane's odd irritability made her pause in reflection. Her typical, calm, collected professional persona contrasted with Raine's railing at life when a straight line sometimes curved. Lately though, especially with this group, Jane felt her patience being tested.

Her phone buzzed. A text from Sullivan. She immediately returned the call. "Oh wow. I'm so sorry. I meant to call and check on you but got sidelined by my family. How are you?"

"Not great." Sullivan sounded stressed.

"Is it your leg?"

"It's not that."

"What's going on? Are you at work?" Jane could pop over for a few minutes and catch Sullivan up on what she'd learned about Haversham in person.

"I'm being escorted out of the office, and the building, because I've supposedly got mob ties."

"*What?*"

"Apparently, I'm the mole in our unit."

"Scott is an absolute moron. I'm heading over. Stay there." Jane hung up, grabbed her coat, and left before anyone could ask questions.

She found Sullivan sitting in the lobby of the building.

Incensed, Jane would have stormed past her and given Scott a chewing out, but Sullivan stopped her.

"Let it go. He's got bigger problems than me if he thinks my absence will solve anything."

"How are you feeling?" Jane studied her. Sullivan appeared fine, dressed in loose trousers and a sweater. But when she stood with her tote bag and headed for the door, her limp grew more pronounced.

"Here. Let me carry that."

"Good." Sullivan handed off her bag, though Jane saw through the cheery demeanor to defeat. "I was hoping you'd volunteer."

They left in Jane's vehicle and headed to her favorite crumpet shop down the road.

Once seated, Jane insisted Sullivan tell her what had happened.

"Well, Matthew was decent after I'd been shot. He acted supportive and horrified that I'd been wounded. He even met me at the hospital and praised me for helping out." Sullivan scoffed. "Like, that's my job to protect and serve. Duh."

"Right."

"So I went home. Rob helped. I think he was more freaked out than I was." She paused. "I was a little keyed up afterward. Took me a while to wind down, but then I slept like the dead."

"Same."

"Anyway, I'm obviously not going to be a hundred percent for a while. The divisional nurse put me on restricted duty. I was planning to spend most of my time at my desk. It's not like I don't have a dozen other cases needing attention, right?"

Jane winced at the thought of all her cases lingering while OPR took their blasted time getting to the truth. With any luck, Scott and the others were keeping up with her work.

"No biggie, though," Sullivan continued. "I've been deep-diving into some older cases anyway. Then that SOB comes to me this morning and tells me I'm suspended! That there's an OPR investigation on me too. They rush me out of the office before I can blink. And then some pushy chick who's *also* pending an investigation insisted I bask in shame and wait for her in the lobby."

"Dramatic, but who— Oh, the pushy chick would be me."

"I swear, you've infected me." Sullivan tried to sound amused, but Jane heard the unspoken hurt at being sidelined.

"I'm so sorry. We'll get this fixed. I swear."

"It's tied to Dan Simmons."

"Yep." Just when Jane and Sullivan had met to discuss Scott and Haversham. "Hey, you never did tell me what Haversham did. Or what you found on him." Hal had found nothing but stellar reports about the guy.

"Oh, that's right. I was looking through older case files. Did you know Jon Haversham spent time in Vegas when August Kaminski's name started circulating there? Nothing ever came of it. Then he moved to Seattle. Kaminski, I mean. But Haversham was in charge of the case file on Kaminski. I find that interesting."

"So do I."

"I talked to Rob about it. He remembers working some of that case as well."

"I thought you two arrived in Vegas together."

Sullivan snorted. "We're not joined at the hip, you know. I got there a year after he did. And yes, we bonded—*platonically*—as coworkers. Rob's one of the smartest guys I know, but he always gets overlooked. He says it doesn't bother him, but it would bother me."

Could Williams have turned mole to get back at a system that didn't value him?

Sullivan scoffed. "I can read that small mind of yours. No. The mole isn't Rob."

Jane tried to look innocent. "I would never think that."

"Yeah, right." Sullivan took a healthy drink of her tea. "I'm trying to think of who could be feeding the Mazzucas information. Because we know someone is. I just can't think of anyone in our unit. Maybe it's someone outside."

"You know, before I looked into Haversham, I would have said it was him. He's in a position of power to make things happen behind the scenes. And none of us would know."

Sullivan blinked and whispered, "The ASAC?"

"But no. The guy's as clean as a whistle, and yeah, I know that's majorly cliché. But it fits. He's a real do-gooder with an outstanding record. Served eight years in the Navy before joining the Agency. Doesn't have any money or connections behind him, just a lot of recommendations from people who've worked with him. He's not our guy, I don't think."

"You never know."

Jane nodded. "I agree. But I really don't see Haversham helping organized crime. A friend of mine who's good with computers also did a deep dive into Dan Simmons, just in case he had a beef with someone he'd previously put away. But nothing stood out, and everyone in Dan's organization loved him. It's got to be one of us on the Mazzuca case."

Sullivan scowled. "But everyone in our squad is decent. Even Sandy and Josh's weird work-spouse dynamic feels oddly normal. They're not exactly hiding anything from the rest of us unless they're having sex. And I don't want to know about that."

Jane grimaced at the thought.

"Is it Matthew? He stands out as the most viable candidate to me. I mean, who does he think he is, accusing me of being a sell-out?"

"I don't know. But I think it's time I got serious about the Seattle field office."

"Oh right. That place where you still have a job, even if it's temporarily suspended."

"Funny." Jane had a plan, but she didn't want to involve Sullivan. What she had in mind wasn't exactly aboveboard. "On another note, whatever happened with your failed date Wednesday night? Did you let him know why you didn't show up?"

"He totally came over to take care of me yesterday!" Sullivan launched into a story about her new boyfriend that Jane tried to listen to without looking bored.

All the while, she tried to figure out how to bribe Hal so he'd do her a favor without mentioning it to Joe, Uncle Chris, or worse, *Raine*.

CHAPTER THIRTY-SIX

IT TURNED OUT THAT HAL DIDN'T NEED THAT MUCH CONVINCING. JANE just had to play a few rounds of some new video game he was beta-testing for a friend without complaining. Apparently, the friend needed some "newb" who wasn't very good to give valid feedback.

Despite being offended—she considered herself decent at video games—she nevertheless accepted his terms. Though the not-complaining part might be tough.

Saturday evening, Jane sat with Hal in the back of a rental van down the street from Matthew Scott's two-million-dollar residence in North Capitol Hill. The large home had privacy despite its proximity to its neighbors, a rooftop deck with views from the Olympics to Lake Union and Downtown Seattle.

Had she been less content with her life, she might have felt envy at her boss's ability to afford something on such a scale. But it was way too much house for one person or even two, if Scott had a significant other no one knew about. She preferred something small and practical.

"You bugged everything?" She stared at the shifting feeds on the monitors in the van. "How did you get in without being spotted? This neighborhood is like a beehive that never stops buzzing."

"Don't you worry about that. I've been a surveillance expert for more years than you've been alive."

"What? Since you were a teenager?" Although knowing Hal, he'd been hacking into systems from birth.

"If I don't want them to notice me, they don't." They sat in an upscale sprinter van and not some murder van with no windows. In this neighborhood, they wouldn't attract attention. "And before you ask, don't. This vehicle is on loan from a friend who will remain anonymous for certain reasons."

"Reasons like he's wanted by the law? Or reasons like you stole his van and don't want anyone to know?"

"Yes."

She rolled her eyes but couldn't help laugh. Hal was ridiculous and talented in the best of ways. The guy lived under a lucky star. Nothing bad ever seemed to stick to him, certainly not the various charges aimed his way through the years.

"I know, I know," she said in apology. "Don't ask questions. Sorry. I'm just nervous." She couldn't be tied to this. Not that anyone would associate her with Hal. Or she hoped they wouldn't. Just because Hal and the others on Team Ten maintained a shadow profile in the U.S. didn't mean they couldn't be identified.

Though Team Ten didn't officially exist, people knew of them. Rapp had known, but then, that said a lot about him—that he knew of a bunch of off-books mercenaries often employed in secret by the government.

To be fair, Uncle Chris hadn't tried too hard to isolate himself from Jane the last few years. She had a feeling he wanted people in high places to know she had connections.

Funny how her uncle trusted military might a lot more than he trusted law enforcement. Jane knew they all had good and bad points, but that calling to protect the greater good appealed to her in whatever way she served.

"You don't have to sit here for this," Hal said. "Heck, I don't either, technically. But it feels more fun this way. Like we're on a stakeout."

He grabbed a bag of gourmet popcorn and two cans of soda from the minifridge next to him. "Complete with all the chow."

"This is sad. You're as bored as I am at home." She accepted the drink.

"Well, that and I'm giving Raine some space. She's out of sorts, needing something to punch. I'd rather it was Joe than me."

"Good call." That wasn't exactly why Jane had opted to spend her Saturday night in a van with Hal, but she did appreciate the distance from her moody cousin. "You know, I get that she can't tell me what went down to sour her on her job. But she's not great at expressing her feelings."

"Pot, kettle. Hel-lo."

"I'm an open book."

He just looked at her as he shoveled in a few handfuls of popcorn and said with his mouth full, "Do you believe the lies coming out of your mouth?"

"Hey, not being a fan of drama doesn't mean I'm a liar. I choose to detach emotionally from the job so I can focus on what's important. Raine takes everything to heart."

"Because she has to get deep to see the truth."

"Maybe." She popped open the soda and took a swig. "Or maybe she's just a hothead like Uncle Chris who runs around *feeling* everything to death instead of being objective and getting the job done."

"I will give you fifty bucks to say that to your uncle's face."

"What am I, stupid?"

He chuckled. "A hundred? A thousand?"

"Do you have a thousand?"

"Joe does, and he owes me."

"Oh?"

"Yeah. That boyfriend of Shantelle's... I found some dirt on the guy. She's no longer seeing him."

"Hal." Jane shook her head. "You need to let the girl make her own choices."

"Hey, don't blame me. I just passed the word. I'm not involving myself in anyone's business. Well, just yours." His smile blinded her. "You owe me *big*. If your uncle knew you were using my talents, he'd insist on billing Uncle Sam for my services."

Not to mention rubbing it in her face that she'd finally caved. He'd been telling her to use the family's talents for years, but she'd always resisted, trying to keep on the straight and narrow at work.

"Oh stop. You know this isn't official." Her face heated, the embarrassment at what she'd stooped to not beyond her. "I'm desperate. I tried all the legal ways of finding out if my boss is scum. I got nothing."

"That's right. And that's when you come *to me*," he ended in a low, creepy voice.

"I swear, if you rub your hands together and crow like a dastardly villain, I will sock you one."

He grinned but didn't give the evil laugh she knew he wanted to.

"Please note the personal security feeds of our target. He's home, and he's alone."

She watched as Scott pulled into his driveway, waited for the garage to open, then drove inside before the garage door shut behind him. Hal scrolled through his many views of the man's house, and she watched as Scott walked inside and up the stairs into his living room, then up again to one of his four bedrooms.

When he pulled off his tie and started to change clothes, she studiously looked away.

"He's not a bad looking guy, I guess," Hal commented. "If you like the professional hot yoga and gym type. I guarantee none of that muscle is from actually being out in the field and running from insurgents."

"Since when are you a combat snob?"

"I'm not. I prefer no yoga and no gym. Give me a hand-to-hand workout or a fast walk and I'm spent."

"Just let me know when he's dressed."

"Prude." Hal drank loudly, gave a gentlemanly burp, then tapped the screen. "He's back. And joy, he's calling someone."

Haversham, as a matter of fact. As Scott moved into the kitchen to get some food, Jane perked up when she heard Sullivan's name mentioned in the conversation that he'd put on speaker.

"I'm telling you, Jon. It was the right move. She had to go. And now I'm ready for what comes next."

And so was Jane.

CHAPTER THIRTY-SEVEN

"It was a risky move, Matthew. They tried to kill her," Jon Haversham said.

"I'm not so sure about that."

She heard some static. Jane wished Hal had a better angle, but the miniature camera he'd planted in the living room that looked through to the dining room and kitchen didn't have the best definition. She could see Scott frowning until he turned his back on her.

"Relax. We'll hear what we need to." Hal adjusted something, and the conversation grew crystal clear.

"What do you mean?" Haversham asked. "The report on the attack at the ferry listed Jenn Sullivan as the gunshot victim."

"Yes, but she was there meeting with Jane Cannon."

A chuckle, then Haversham said, "Your penance for sinning so much in your youth."

"Is he wrong though, do you think?" Hal murmured.

"Shh."

Scott huffed and warmed his food in the microwave. "Very funny. Jane is a wildcard. I wish she'd come clean with whatever Dan told her."

Jane's heart raced.

"We both know the Mazzucas found him out. They used you to do it," Haversham said quietly.

"I know."

That was it. The confession she'd been waiting for.

"If I'd been a little faster on the uptake, if I'd realized they were reporting everything back to Leo Mazzuca, I'd have taken Dan out of rotation. But I thought we'd compartmentalized what our mole had access to. I thought we had time."

Hold on. What?

"Look, we both knew it was a risk. If I'd thought they knew about Simmons, I'd have ordered you to pull him out. He wasn't supposed to be engaging with the crew at the warehouse, not without eyes on him at all times. Why was he down there that night?"

"I don't know. I'm not sure Jane knows either. That email exchange between her and Dan was obviously fake. But even if she had knowledge, she wouldn't tell me." He frowned and removed his plate from the microwave, then walked to his spotless dining room to eat while he talked to Haversham. "I get the impression she doesn't like me."

"None of them do."

Scott muttered something under his breath as he ate one bite at a time, cutting his food into small pieces. He ate like a robot, controlled, precise.

Jane actually liked him a little bit better for that. But not much.

"Matthew, doing your best to keep on top of everything your squad is doing isn't making you any friends. You're micromanaging."

"But I need them to know I'm watching so they won't see *you* keeping an eye on them."

Clever.

"Although, if you think about it, making yourself a common enemy should make the squad tighter."

"So they can retaliate against me?"

"Exactly. We're closer to finding out who's been keeping the Mazzucas up to date on our progress. But we need a little bit more before we close in. I've narrowed it down to three—maybe four—names."

Scott put down his fork. "I just can't believe it's any of them. Not on this squad."

What four names? I thought he was convinced it was Sullivan. Jane tried to understand Scott's actions. Apparently, he and Haversham had suspected someone in her squad of being the mole a lot longer than she'd suspected anyone.

Dan had come to her with questions about something not right with their investigation. She'd never expected him to go off on his own to investigate the night he died. Or that someone else would imply her involvement.

With ten members of the squad remaining, minus her, that left nine suspects minus the five Haversham didn't think responsible. She wanted to count Sullivan out but couldn't. That would be the obvious move. Despite what she hoped, she could only cross Haversham, herself, and now Scott off her list of possibly guilty.

She let that stew as she reviewed the team. Could Jim Broderick, Ian Tann, or Greg Minton be the mole? She didn't want Williams and Sullivan to be guilty. But she had no proof they weren't. And what if there was *more* than one Mazzuca plant? That would put a whole new spin on this.

"I need answers."

"Jane, look." Hal nodded to the monitor, and she stared at Scott's face as he frowned at the phone.

"I tapped into his phone's camera." Hal nodded. "Because I am amazing."

"You truly are."

She watched Scott's face as he spoke, seeing his frustration while she heard it. The more he spoke, the more she doubted he had anything to do with Dan Simmons' murder. Instead, he'd been doing all he could to clean up the squad before something terrible happened again.

She not only heard but saw him beat himself up for Simmons's death, for Sullivan's injuries, even for Jane being suspended.

"It really is the best thing for Jane though," Scott said. "I think Gambol's got her working for him. I saw her with Gunther Rapp." He gave a self-deprecating smile. "I almost believed they were dating when I saw them at McGrath's. Except I caught her following me earlier."

Shoot. He hadn't bought it.

"Do you think she saw you paying Guillermo?"

Jane jotted down the name.

"Maybe. But he's still going to follow Jim and Ian for me, and his brother has Greg and Sandy under surveillance." *Guillermo was some kind of PI?* "She hasn't given up trying to find out who killed Dan Simmons, I do know that. But I can't have her in the way. Not if they're actively after her now. I don't think that attack at the ferry was anything but a shot at Jane."

"I knew it." Hal stared at her. "They were gunning for you."

She shrugged. "I suspected, but they came at Sullivan too. And how did they know we'd be there?"

"They were probably following you. But I should have a look at your car and phone again to be sure."

"After this."

He nodded.

"We need to wrap this up," Haversham said. "I can't hold Bob off much longer."

"I appreciate it."

"I know. But I wouldn't be backing you up if I didn't think you were our best shot at cleaning out the muck in our HQ. I'm tired of constantly being one step behind."

"Me too." Scott sighed.

"You've got two more weeks. Don't waste it." Haversham hung up.

Scott pushed away from the table and walked into his living room, where he promptly threw himself onto a designer sofa and kicked back, groaning.

"My head hurts." He rubbed his temples and swore under his breath, but she thought she heard her name mentioned.

"How am I hearing him?" she asked. From the angle of the camera, she figured it must have been hidden above the fireplace.

"I bugged the house for sound too. Just in case."

"I really owe you."

"Yep. But Jane, I think you owe someone else just as much." Hal glanced at Matthew Scott now looking a lot less like a bureaucratic bully and more like a tired man just trying to do what was best for everyone.

"Aw, heck. I don't like this at all. Before this is all over, I'm probably going to have to apologize to him."

"Or you could just be really, really nice when you're eventually cleared of all charges."

Jane cringed. "I'd rather say a quick 'sorry' then avoid him for a while."

But this news did serve its purpose.

Jane wouldn't worry about Matthew Scott anymore. Knowing he was on track to find out who killed Dan Simmons made her feel better. She'd still push for answers, but she wouldn't get in Scott's way.

Instead, she'd do her best to help him find their Mazzuca spy. And she'd help Rapp and the team find Phillip Keiser before he struck again.

"Outstanding." Hal brushed his hands together, having demolished the popcorn. "Now let's go home. We can start on the video game tomorrow."

"So soon?"

He frowned. "Yeah. And don't even think of using work as an excuse. You owe me."

"I know. I always pay my debts." Thoughts of apologizing to Raine and Scott hit her hard. "Even if I would rather get a root canal."

CHAPTER THIRTY-EIGHT

Determined to find Phillip Keiser, Monday morning, Jane and the others poured over any and all data centered around the Kaminski *crew*—a good a word as any to describe the crime group.

Led by August, who had three sons. The first two by a wife who'd died and Anton by a woman who remained unnamed. Several cousins and other distantly related soldiers filled out the ranks. Henryk, the oldest son at twenty-five, and Marcel, twenty-four, helped in the strip clubs. Anton, the youngest at eighteen, tended to create chaos, though he was known to swing by the restaurants and help cook, oddly enough.

The distant Kaminski relatives and soldiers led to dead ends regarding Phillip Keiser. Rapp had arranged a police patrol around Professor Lito's house, just in case Phillip might go there for help.

Jane wanted to talk to Phillip again. She had a feeling the guy hadn't said all he'd had to say before the police had interrupted him.

Law enforcement had stepped up security around several of the large hospitals as well, everyone alert in case Phillip made an appearance.

Jane continued to study the victims' files, looking for any incident that stood out, something that would have put them on Phillip's radar.

There had to be a reason other than blind misfortune that they'd been targeted. She *knew* they weren't random.

Frustrated at her lack of answers, she paced the large office, trying to collect her thoughts. Gina and Rapp gathered by her desk, both in casual attire for once.

"We're going out to check on potential sightings of Keiser," Rapp announced.

"I'm still trying to figure out how he chose his victims." Jane stopped by Diego's desk, and paused, curious about a name that popped up on one of his monitors.

"Call if you find something." Gina followed Rapp out the door.

"Bossy, isn't she?" Diego asked as he swiveled on his chair. He stopped and focused once more on the monitor to his right. "See these? Interactions our victims had with different people the week leading up to their deaths. And that's not a for-sure timeline, because Phillip could have met with the vics before. A month, even two." He groaned, sounding dejected. "There's too much info. Just not enough that's pertinent to fill in the gaps."

"Yes, but with your help, we found out who our unsub is. That's huge."

"True. I did do that, didn't I?" Diego grinned. "So, want to thank me by going out on a date this week?"

Jane blinked. "With you?"

"Why not? You're not married. Not engaged." He glanced at her ringless fingers. "No boyfriend?"

She frowned.

"Girlfriend? Hey, I don't care. I'm an admirer either way."

Jane stared at him for a moment. Though only a few years her junior, Diego felt worlds younger.

He sighed. "I get it. That's a no. No sweat. I still like you, Jane."

Easiest to just pretend they'd never had the conversation. "Can you pull up information on Phillip's father, Dr. Adam Keiser?"

"Sure." A new screen popped up with a summary of Dr. Adam Keiser's life.

Sad that the life of a man who'd helped so many could be condensed into a few paragraphs, his death a random traffic statistic.

Jane read down the list of accomplishments, pausing when she saw that he and his wife had co-owned a bakery in Fremont for a time. She let that sit, staring at the name of the bakery. They hadn't investigated Phillip's parents too deeply, more concerned with Phillip's victims. Just a casual background search on Dr. Keiser, trying to see where he'd done his residency and follow-on clinics, hoping for some rhyme or reason to Phillip's choice of vics.

Yet Lena Keiser had been lost to the Harvester crime ring as well. And she'd owned a bakery—Best in the State Cookies.

Her cousin, Maria Lito, made the best chocolate chip cookies in the state.

Something clicked in Jane's mind, the beginning of a pattern that didn't yet make sense.

"Diego, I'm heading out to check on something. I'll be back. I have my phone."

"Everyone leaves me." He sighed.

"While I'm gone, do me a favor and get as much information on Lena Keiser as you can. She's related to the Kaminskis, but I'm not sure of her maiden name. It might be Kaminski. It might not."

"On it."

She left him, excitement stirring at the knowledge she'd taken one step closer to the truth.

When Jane arrived at the address of the old bakery, she found it boarded up.

An older woman sweeping the front step of a flower shop next door glanced at her. "It's been closed three months now. The new owners tried to make the bakery work again, but it could never come close to the magic of Lena Keiser."

"Oh?"

The woman stopped sweeping, happy to chat. "I've been in business for seventeen years. When Best in the State Cookies moved next to me, my income tripled from all the foot traffic. I was doing great for over a decade. I like to say they helped build my business. Then Lena passed away a few years ago, and Maria couldn't keep it going without her."

"What happened to Lena?"

The woman started sweeping again. "Hit and run accident. Some fool teenager. I don't blame him. I blame his parents for not keeping a better eye on him."

"How did Lena's family take it?"

"Her husband died too. He was in the car with her when they got hit. Their son never was the same. Such a sweet boy. Or man, I should say. He was in college at the time. Peter...no, Phillip. He had a mental breakdown and disappeared. I hope wherever he is he's all right."

"Sad story." Jane studied the front of the store. The front banner had faded. It wasn't Best in the State Cookies, but some cartoonish logo with chocolate chips floating around it.

She said goodbye to the woman and walked down the block and around to the alley behind the stores. Jane needed to see it inside. Her intuition screamed at her to give it a look.

Her cousin could often hear the truth when interrogating people. She watched the person talking and read their nonverbal cues, heard different intonations when they answered and had learned to study their breathing as well. Jane saw patterns in behavior and in the details that didn't always mesh. Her instincts often gave her a boost where others would notice nothing.

And right now, she needed to get inside this abandoned bakery.

The back door should be locked, but she tried it anyway.

The doorknob turned. She pushed it open and stepped inside, closing it behind her.

The early afternoon sun lit up the space, and she imagined its former charm. Black-and-white floor, red stools, and expansive white granite countertops. A cookie bar with framed pictures of treats hung on the walls.

And there, at the front counter near the register, sat an 8x10 family portrait of Phillip and his parents smiling at the camera. A plain, black flip phone lay in front of the picture. On a piece of paper next to it, he'd written a phone number in bold block numbers and spelled out: *CALL ME.*

She tucked her hand in her pocket and touched her phone but didn't pull it out, conscious of a small video camera in the corner of the ceiling that might or might not be active.

Donning gloves, she flipped open the phone to dial the number on speaker.

Silence. Then a familiar voice. "Hello, Jane Cannon. Miss me?"

She smiled. "Why yes, Phillip. I do."

CHAPTER THIRTY-NINE

"You know, I was beginning to think you'd never find me."

"I still don't know where you are," Jane said. "But I know we didn't get to finish our discussion. You had more to tell me."

"Have you ever lost anyone, Jane? Can I call you Jane?"

"Sure. And yes, I have." She needed to keep him talking while she let Rapp know she had Phillip on the phone. Yet she was loath to pull out her cell if he could see her, worried he might stop talking. She could try to hide her actions but couldn't chance making him suspicious.

"I lost my parents in that horrible crash."

"But you didn't go after the person who hit them. And that puzzles me." Not that she wanted to give him a new target, but there had to be a reason Phillip had no interest in Anton.

"Oh, I did. At first. But the kid had just turned sixteen and was drunk off his ass. He's my cousin several times removed, if you can believe that."

"Really?" Maria had been wrong. Phillip did know about his relation to the Kaminskis.

Phillip tsked. "Please, Jane. Give me some credit. I was a medic in the Army, did you know that? I served and planned to continue to serve once I left the service. I'd finish at UW and go on to medical school."

"So I heard."

"I'm intelligent. I get that from both of my parents."

Jane could feel his terrible grief in the pregnant pause. "I'm sorry for your loss."

"I think you mean that." Phillip sounded both sad and elated at the same time. "It's refreshing to know that not everyone in law enforcement lies." After a pause, he continued, "I couldn't kill my cousin. No matter how Uncle Kyle and my dad felt about Mom's family, they're blood. Heck, Dad was the one who instilled that loyalty in me."

"He was a healer, Phillip. And so were you. 'Do no harm.' Isn't that the first rule of medicine?"

"Yes, it is. And those doctors, nurses, and medical people broke it when they killed my parents. They could have survived the crash. But not what was done to them in that excuse for a clinic where they were *butchered.*" His breathing grew choppy.

"That was wrong."

"It was. I tried to let it go when my parents were killed. I would have probably. Maybe. I don't know. But when I found out that they were used for body parts, and that the police and FBI covered up the crime, I had to fight back. That's not right. That's not justice."

"You're right. Completely."

He sat with that a moment. "Thank you."

"But Phillip, you're killing innocent people to get revenge. Why do that? You're not punishing the guilty."

"But I'm making sure people know. It took you so long to realize it's all connected. We had to make you see."

"Who is *we?*"

"He tells me what to do. I do it."

"Who is *he?*" Was Phillip delusional or did he have an accomplice? "And how do you know who to punish, Phillip? Why Dr. Ryan Daniels and Dr. Julie David? Anna Field, Tom Polsun, Mike Stevens, Tony Alvarez? Those were people just like your parents who have families left crying over them."

"They're gone for a greater purpose. So that we remember, so that these mistakes won't ever happen again."

"Please, Phillip. Come in. Stop hurting people. It's not too late. We'll get your message out."

"I'm not done yet, Jane. There are four more who must die."

Clearly, Phillip wasn't well. She took her phone out, deciding to chance that he might see her.

"Ah-ah-ah. No calling anyone else while we're talking. That's rude, Jane."

Bingo. The video feed was live, which also answered how he'd known she would be the one on the other end of the line. She tucked her phone back into her pocket and looked around the bakery as if just now spotting the obvious video camera.

She waved at it. "Apologies."

"Accepted. Hey, I'm waving back at you, though you can't see it."

A polite killer. How nice.

Maybe he'd appreciate a helpful, polite FBI agent. "What can I do to help you stop killing, Phillip?"

"Nothing. What's done is done. It's a travesty, but we can make things right. *I* can make them right."

"Is *he* telling you to do this?"

"He doesn't have to. We're all God's children."

Jane didn't know what to believe. At turns, Phillip sounded incredibly intelligent then off his rocker. Was he acting alone? "Phillip, did you call this in to let the FBI know about your work?"

"About Justice, you mean?"

"Yes."

"I cannot know his plan. I am the arm, the tool he uses to make it right. Aunt Maria really misses my mom, you know?"

Jane rolled with the change in conversation. "I know. I met your aunt and uncle. They're very nice people."

"They are. I'm sorry this will hurt them. But it can't be helped. And it's so much bigger than me."

"That's what I'm afraid of."

Phillip laughed. "I like you, Jane. I'm sorry about our fight in the garage. I don't like hurting women."

"Then don't."

His tone changed, lost all warmth when he said, "But I will. I'm coming for the others. If you get in my way, I will end you. For I am Justice."

He disconnected.

She stood there, thinking about all he'd said and didn't say. One thing struck a chord. A small, perhaps coincidental turn of phrase or not?

After calling in to get forensics on the scene, she turned off the recording she'd started the moment she'd dialed the flip phone.

With any luck, they'd get something useful from it.

And she'd figure out if he'd meant to drop that major clue or if he'd done it by accident.

"It's a travesty, but we can make things right. *I* can make them right," Phillip had said.

Echoing the exact same wording his uncle had used.

CHAPTER FORTY

Back at the office, after Jane had replayed the recording for everyone and they'd listened twice, she looked up when Gina interrupted to take a call.

After a moment, she hung up, not happy.

"Well?" Jane asked.

"Professor Lito and his wife are gone. So's their car. They left their phones behind."

Sometimes when her brain fixated on a detail, the way it had when Phillip had called the mess a "travesty," Jane knew to pay attention. She'd heard that same description before, when Kyle had spoken about the Keisers' deaths.

Anyone could use the same word, but "travesty" wasn't that common. Kyle acted like he hadn't talked to Phillip lately. But Jane thought he had.

"Shoot." Jane scowled. "We should have put someone on them."

Rapp shrugged. "We have no proof Lito is part of the murders. He and his nephew obviously spoke. Perhaps the use of the word 'travesty' is just something Phillip picked up from his uncle."

"No. It's not."

"How do you know?" Gina asked.

"I just do."

Gina snorted. "Nothing like a lack of proof to tie murderers together. 'I just do' never works in court."

"Good thing we're not in court then, isn't it?" Jane said, not appreciating Gina's tone.

Gina shook her head. "Look, we still don't know if all this talk of some 'he' is a real person or not. Because I've listened to this a few times now, and I have to tell you that Phillip sounds mentally unstable."

Rapp agreed. "Yes. He's also methodical. And no matter who's telling him to kill, he's planning to do it again. At least four more times."

Jane glanced at Diego. "Hey, can you run all our victim's names against Kyle and Maria Lito?"

"Yep." Diego hustled out of the conference room to his computer.

"Great. So what now?" Gina asked.

"What did you find when you went looking for him?" Jane asked.

"A lot of nothing. We're haunting the hospitals though. Hopefully, our presence will deter him. He's after administrators, right? So we've warned them to stay inside as much as possible and to use hospital security and a police presence to get them in and out of the building."

"That's good."

Rapp sighed. "I'd suggest leaving one hospital open to draw him in, but he's too smart for that. Even if he is getting advice from voices in his head, he's slick. He knows how to avoid leaving a trace."

"If not him, then his partner." Jane still didn't like it though. "Not partner. That's not the right word. This voice is directing him to get justice. He said, 'It's much bigger than me.'"

Gina argued, "God is much bigger than any mere mortal. We can't assume he's working with a partner."

"We can't assume he's working alone," Jane argued right back.

"Good points. Unfortunately, you're both right." Rapp stood. "Let's find out as much as we can about the Litos."

"I'll look into Kyle," Gina said.

Jane nodded. "I'll take Maria, though I have to tell you. I don't think they're in on it. Phillip clearly said he's sorry this will hurt them."

Rapp shrugged. "Yes, but Jane, they took off. That's suspicious. So we'll look into them, and I'll get August Kaminski and his sons." Rapp left and headed to the kitchenette for coffee.

Jane felt caffeined out. And a little depressed. She'd liked Kyle, and he'd lied. He'd acted like he hadn't talked to Phillip lately. But Jane thought he had. And maybe he knew what Phillip was up to and didn't like it, so he'd called in a warning to Gambol. Or he liked what Phillip was doing and wanted the FBI to know.

It would be interesting to learn how Gambol had gotten the first message. To his email address? A private line? By phone?

She chased after Rapp and cornered him in his office.

"You look a little intense there, Jane. What can I help you with?"

"How did Gambol hear about the cases being connected?"

"He was emailed."

"To his private email address or a government address?"

"Hold on." Rapp made a quick call then hung up. "To his fbi.gov address."

"Which wouldn't be too difficult to learn if Gambol were anyone else. But he isn't a regular department head or division chief. So why contact him? How many people know who Lionel Gambol is?"

Rapp grimaced. "Not many. Very few people in the Agency have the clout to get him involved in anything. From what I gather, he usually involves himself. I need to talk to him again."

Jane started to leave, done with that angle, when another question nagged at her. "Hey, Rapp."

He paused in the act of dialing. "Hey, Jane."

His fake excitement made her want to laugh.

Instead, she schooled her expression into one of disinterest. Unfortunately, that only made his smile widen. "Cut it out."

"Sorry." He cleared his throat and looked menacing.

"Better. Question for you. What do you know about Jon Haversham?"

The abrupt change in subject startled him, she could tell. But he put his phone down and waved her to the chair across from his desk. "Why do you want to know?"

"His name's come up a few times, mostly in relation to the Seattle field office, of course, and my friend Jenn Sullivan, who is now suspected of being the squad's mole."

"Sullivan. The blond who got shot?"

"Yep."

"How exactly has Haversham's name come up?"

"Well, it was something Sullivan mentioned. She and another friend came to Seattle from Las Vegas. Haversham was there when the Harvester case happened. Do you remember hearing about the black-market organ theft case?" She still didn't. The FBI had definitely kept it quiet.

"I do."

"And we now know Phillip's parents were victims in that crime."

Rapp looked thoughtful. "And now Haversham is one of the ASACs here in Seattle. We should bring him in."

"Bring him in? Are you really going to order my boss's boss to come to you?"

He was already on the phone and hung up a minute later. "He'll be here in half an hour. Would you like to stay for the conversation or have me fill you in when it's done?"

"What do you think?"

"I think not even your boss's boss would intimidate you, Jane Cannon."

"You are correct, Gunther Rapp."

His eyes crinkled when he smiled. "I'm flattered you know my name."

"I should. It's written on the bathroom wall with a phone number under it. For a good time call…"

He laughed hard, and she found herself laughing with him.

Rapp wasn't laughing half an hour later when Jon Haversham planted his hands on Rapp's desk and loomed over him. "It won't take much to end this farce of a task force and your less than stellar career. You're already on thin ice, Rapp. And you too, Jane. Now I'd like to hear an 'I'm sorry, sir,' or you're both fired."

CHAPTER FORTY-ONE

JANE HAD NO IDEA HOW THEY'D GONE FROM QUESTIONS TO THREATS OF being fired so fast.

The conversation had started out nicely enough.

Rapp asked about Haversham's family, the move, how he'd liked Las Vegas, and then they'd chatted about people they both knew.

Jon Haversham had real presence. Tall and broad chested, with chestnut hair flecked with gray and a stern countenance that melted when he smiled. A handsome older man who projected confidence and sincerity.

When he'd first sat down to talk to Rapp, he'd been magnetic. But as Rapp's questions continued, Haversham's charm and affability faded. Fast.

"Fired, sir?" Rapp asked. "For what? For asking why the FBI would bury a case that should have been investigated and is now directly tied into our Code Blue Killer's motives?"

"Exactly what are you implying?" Haversham asked.

Rapp continued to speak calmly. "I'm not implying anything. I'm asking questions. Why did the Harvester case go nowhere?"

"*Agent* Rapp, I did my job in Las Vegas to the best of my ability."

Jane didn't understand his emphasis on Rapp's title.

Haversham continued, "In no way did I bury the Harvester case. We had a lot of movement on the investigation you're not privy to. Not that I need to answer to you."

"You need to answer to someone."

"Who the hell are you to take me to task?"

The questions around Haversham leaving Las Vegas hadn't hurt him any. Hell, the guy had been promoted to ASAC of a major field office. Everyone here spoke his praises.

Trust Rapp to get under her boss's boss's skin.

Watching him stand up to Haversham told her things she hadn't known about him, though.

Rapp didn't buckle under the stern glare of authority. And he didn't cave under threats.

"Just answer the question, *sir*."

She picked up on the attitude, and so did Haversham.

But screw it. She hadn't appreciated Haversham's threat to fire her for doing her job either. She kept her voice even, unemotional, and stern. "Yeah, *sir*. Why did you bury the fact that the Harvester ring that you'd been investigating reached into Seattle? That's the reason we've got the Code Blue Killer thinking he has to rectify the FBI's apparent incompetence."

Haversham's angry glare bored into her, but she refused to back down, even though she saw Rapp subtly shaking his head at her from the corner of her eye. Apparently, only he was allowed to question authority.

"I see you're learning a lot from Gunther. How to be insubordinate, how to insult your superiors, how to—"

"Stick to the truth no matter where it takes me," Jane said over him, aware she was likely kissing her career goodbye. "And for the record, I work *with*, not *for*, Agent Rapp."

Rapp blew out a breath. "Look, sir, you're missing the point. The rumors that Kaminski was involved with the Harvesters was a closely guarded secret, but I saw the case files."

"They were buried."

"Not deep enough," Jane muttered and quickly closed her mouth when Haversham glared at her.

Surprisingly, the guy was intimidating on the same scale as her uncle. Though she didn't like him all that much, she could understand why so many respected him.

"Why didn't you tell Phillip there was an open investigation, at least?" Rapp asked. "He had a right to know."

"Because I was ordered not to," Haversham admitted and sat back down, his bluster fizzling out. "The Agency screwed up. The Kaminski family couldn't be tied to what happened because evidence got lost and informants disappeared or died. The way they always do around August Kaminski."

Jane pointed out, "Then he came out here. But he's not doing much except getting his drunk kid out of trouble for killing Phillip's parents. He runs restaurants and strip clubs with his family. That's it?"

Haversham rubbed the back of his neck. "I don't know how it ties together, but I always thought the Harvesters eventually got caught because they got careless. They weren't filling their orders fast enough. Then Anton had an accident, and two donors appeared like magic."

"Why the brains though?" Rapp asked. "I've always wondered. Who would want those?"

"A collector in Reno, from what we later found out. The hearts were lost to a black-market transplant list. But the brains we tracked to a man who died not long after under suspicious circumstances. He kept the brains in jars with another two dozen in his study. He had…issues."

Jane said, "All that is beyond bizarre. Phillip started killing people two and a half years after his parents died. Why not before? Why now? Why those six people, who we know had nothing to do with the Harvesters?" She stared at Haversham. She knew she'd never get a better time to ask. "Are you working with Matthew Scott to uncover corruption in Seattle or to bury your guilt?"

He and Rapp froze.

"*What?*" Haversham asked in an icy voice.

Jane was done with all the secrets. "I know I didn't get Dan Simmons killed. And I'm pretty sure Jenn Sullivan didn't either. So why are you dirtying our reputations in the pursuit of supposed justice?" She heard Phillip's voice in her mind repeating the word, "justice." And she understood him better for it. "I could have helped you find the killer. Instead, you're possibly ruining my future with the FBI on some hairbrained scheme that makes little sense."

Haversham glared at her. "You sound remarkably like your uncle. No filter whatsoever."

"Excuse me?" Great. Someone else who knew Chris North.

Rapp nodded. "It's true. She's just like him."

"Hey."

Haversham surprised her by laughing. "Anything connected to Chris starts as a headache and turns into the migraine from hell." He muttered under his breath, swearing like the sailor he used to be. "This does not go beyond this room."

Rapp nodded. "Of course not."

"Yes, sir." Could she keep that promise? Even with her family?

"There's a little too much of what I went through in Las Vegas going on here in Seattle. The Kaminski case never closed because it's still ongoing. I brought it with me, following him."

"Huh?" Since when did an ASAC work smaller cases when he had a field office to help manage? RAs to keep track of? Caseloads to supervise?

"Don't you think it's a little strange that the Mazzucas are in the wind with nothing sticking to them? They're not behaving the way they did years ago. It's like they're learning from someone else."

"What does that have to do with Phillip losing it and killing people?" she asked.

"No, he's right," Rapp interrupted. "That puts a whole new perspective on things."

Jane normally caught on fast, and it bothered her to be in the dark.

Haversham explained, "I always thought Kaminski had someone on the inside when I was in Las Vegas. I think that someone is here now, helping the Mazzucas evade the law. It's a little too convenient that Phillip went off the rails right when the Mazzuca case was heating up. Except the Mazzucas are gone, a DEA agent is murdered, and one of our undercover agents is dead."

Jane blinked. "What?"

"Mike Stevens, an EMT and one of the Code Blue's victims, used to help the Mazzucas when they needed medical attention. He was feeding us intel. Then he died from two gunshots. A message from the family to keep our distance."

"But that's a little more subtle than usual," Jane murmured. "How did I not know about Mike Stevens?" Phillip's fifth victim, EMT1.

"Because we're not sure who we can trust on the squad. Matthew and I are working closely on this. We know you had nothing to do with Dan's death, but we wanted you out of the way so the mole would feel free to act. With you watching too closely, he or she had all but stopped sharing info with their organization."

"Why accuse Sullivan?"

Haversham sighed. "She, Williams, Jim Broderick, and Ian Tann are at the top of our suspect list. All of them came from Vegas, though Ian got here before the others. It all fits."

"It does." Jane had sensed ties between the Mazzucas and Kaminskis from the first. But making the pieces fit hadn't been easy because she'd been missing information.

"What else don't we know?" Jane snapped.

"Jane." Rapp shook his head. "I'm sorry, sir, but you should have told us."

"I know. I wanted to, but we thought it best not to. Not yet."

"We?"

Jane didn't think he meant Scott.

Rapp groaned. "*Gambol.* Lionel's in on this too?"

"Yes."

Jane wanted to slap both Haversham and Gambol for making this so much harder. "Do you happen to know who Phillip is working with?"

"No. Personally, I think he's crazy. Although August or someone in the Mazzuca crew might be feeding him names of people to eliminate.

Of the six victims, Mike Stevens is the only one who was working for us. We can't link the other vics to the Harvesters outside the fact that they were in the medical field."

"Neither can we," Rapp admitted. "And it's frustrating as hell because the answer might help us locate our killer."

Jane nodded. "If we can't find out why he chose those others or find him, he'll kill again. Soon."

CHAPTER FORTY-TWO

THE CONVERSATION WITH HAVERSHAM HAD BEEN MIND-BOGGLING AND showed how keeping secrets could hurt an investigation. Jane could have done so much more had she known about the Kaminski tie-in from the beginning.

She spent the next day studying the information they'd collected with this new lens in place, spotting connections she'd previously ignored. Three cases of illegal weapons confiscated on the waterfront nagged at her. She went down the rabbit hole of research and found two lower-level criminals working together that should have been enemies.

A Mazzuca and a Kaminski.

It would take more digging to learn when August Kaminski had moved into the Pacific Northwest. Perhaps he'd planted the seeds to grow his organization years ago. She wanted to get with Haversham to find out exactly what he knew and who he had working on it, but she knew she'd used up any good will the day before, mouthing off in Rapp's office.

While Diego and Gina worked together putting profiles of the next victims together, Rapp was in and out of the office. He appeared frustrated and angry and kept closing himself in his space.

She went back over Haversham's words yesterday, unable to stop thinking about his hints that Rapp had his own baggage to deal with. A troubled past?

Hal and Joe both respected *and* distrusted him. But had that mistrust been more about protecting Jane's heart, which didn't need protecting in the least, or because they knew something about his job history?

They hadn't said much when she'd asked. Hal never did give her that dossier on Rapp he'd promised. But she hadn't wanted to seem too interested lest they start all that nonsense about romantic leanings she didn't have, so she let it go. Still, Rapp's mysteries intrigued her.

Know your enemy, her uncle loved to say.

But anyone could be an enemy with the right incentive.

Her phone rang, interrupting her unhelpful thoughts. She welcomed the distraction though she didn't recognize the number.

"Jane Cannon."

"Hello, Jane?"

Where did she know that voice from? "Yes?"

"This is Kyle Lito."

She shot up in her chair. "Kyle. How are you?" *Where* are you?

"I'm good, thank you. Maria and I are taking a little vacation." He paused. "I talked to Phillip."

"I know."

He sighed. "I honestly don't know what to do about him. I'm so worried for him, and I don't know what's real and what's not. He told me not to trust the FBI, but he said I should talk to you."

"Why didn't you tell me you'd talked to him when I'd visited?"

"Because I hadn't. He surprised us with a visit after you left. And of course, I told him about it. I had nothing to hide." He sounded defensive.

"What did Phillip want?"

"He told us he was doing what he was meant to. He talked about justice. About what really happened to his parents." Kyle swore. "How could the FBI not tell us that? They hushed it all up! No wonder Phillip is going crazy."

"Kyle, please. I'm just learning about this with you. Can you step me through what he told you?"

"I don't know why I should. You'll just sweep it under the rug like your buddies did."

She gave him a moment to process. Kyle Lito seemed like an intelligent man. He wanted the truth as much as she did.

He sighed. "Phillip showed up the day after you did. He looked good. He'd put on weight, had color in his cheeks, a spark in his eyes I haven't seen in forever. And then he told us about people stealing his parents' organs and about the Harvester case that made the news years ago. Apparently, those criminals killed Adam and Lena. *Not* Anton Kaminski."

"Phillip found out a few months ago. I'm not sure how, but it gave him purpose. A reason to get out of the funk he'd been in." Kyle paused. "Only the truth didn't do him any favors." In a whisper, he confessed, "He told me he *killed* people. Is that true? Because a lot of what he said sounded frantic. He kept talking about someone who gives him orders now. I can't tell if he's hearing voices or is actually involved in some conspiracy. But I haven't seen anything about a serial killer targeting doctors and nurses in Seattle. So what's really going on?"

"Phillip killed six people. Two doctors, two nurses, and two EMTs. There were ten people involved in the Harvester killings, and your nephew has four more on his list. But these people are all innocent of those murders. They're symbols, stand-ins, for those who did the actual crimes."

"Dear God."

"I've met and talked to Phillip twice now. He says he's on a mission, that he's Justice with a capital J. I want to stop him before he kills more innocent people. But I don't know where to find him. Do you have any idea where he might be?"

"No, but I'd tell you if I did. His parents would never have wanted this." Kyle was crying. She could hear it. "And Maria... This will hurt her so much. We love that boy. This isn't him."

"I'm sorry, but it is."

231

"No, I mean, well, yes. It is him. But this is not the man his parents raised. Their deaths broke him. He sounded so clear and smart, like he used to be. The intelligent young man on his way to becoming a doctor. Killing people isn't what he's all about. I think someone might be using him."

"That's if he's not hearing voices."

"I hope not. Because Phillip has always excelled at whatever he does. College, the Army. He sailed through his training to become a medic. And he's a crack shot. An expert marksman like his mother and aunt." Kyle blew out a breath. "My wife's family liked to hunt. Phillip's handled firearms since he was a young boy. If he wants to kill again, he will."

"Which is why we need to stop him. Please, if there's anything you can tell me, anything at all that will help…"

"I wish I could. I'm talking to you because Phillip thought you'd help. Not like the others who buried the truth." His anger was justifiable. Jane felt it as well. "I honestly don't know. But I can tell you this. He's set on this mission to avenge his parents. He won't let you find him before he's got his targets in sight. Phillip is a lot of things, but he's not a quitter. And when he aims at a target, he doesn't miss."

CHAPTER FORTY-THREE

Jane spent Wednesday much as she had Tuesday, looking through what they knew to find something they didn't. The only good thing, if she could call it that, going on in her life was that Hal and Joe had gone *somewhere* to take care of *something* and would be back in a few days. So she had a temporary reprieve from that horrible video game she'd tried on Sunday.

Hal had said no complaining, but she really didn't enjoy the first-person shooter game where she had to kill fairies for blood gold and then run campaigns to destroy entire bloodlines. A fairyland *Call of Duty* that would probably make a ton of money but that left a bad taste in her mouth.

Killing for the sake of killing didn't appeal to her. Making the guilty pay for their crimes, through a justice system developed by a civilized society, did. Law and order made sense to her. So she empathized with Phillip Keiser for not getting the justice for his parents that they were due.

But taking that rage and pain out on innocent people who had done nothing more than share a similar occupation with the guilty? That was wrong.

Raine could blather about shades of gray all day long, but Jane contented herself with being very clear about black and white, good and bad. Phillip needed to be found, and those four potential future victims saved.

Rapp grabbed Gina and headed for her desk. "We think we have Phillip Keiser. SWAT is en route as well. But this could turn into a real nightmare."

Gina looked grim. "UW Medical Northwest. A patrol car spotted a man matching his description in the parking lot."

A hospital in the north. It made sense Phillip might target some place new. But would he let himself be seen by a patrol car? He might be hearing voices, but he was savvy enough to avoid detection. He'd be a real threat to anyone who stood in his way.

After her call with Kyle, she didn't believe Phillip would stop until he killed his last victims or law enforcement stopped him. Probably with a bullet to the head.

Rapp seemed to follow her thoughts. "I don't know that it's him either, but we'll check it out. We'll keep you updated, unless you want to come along?"

"No thanks. I'm stuck on looking through our files again. There has to be something here connecting his victims. He's been pretty deliberate until now."

"I still—" Gina paused to take a phone call. She hung up. "Rapp, let's go. There's another sighting that seems a lot more like our guy."

They raced out the door. Jane had no intention of following. As much as she'd like to be there when they found the guy, she didn't think anything but dumb luck would help detect him before the bullets started flying. If he even used guns this time.

Thus far, he'd poisoned his victims and shot them. What would he have in store for the medical admins? Fire? Knives? A bomb?

The thought made her ill. So she plugged away, working alongside Diego.

They had turned up a few interesting items when Rapp called.

Diego put him on speaker.

"It's him. SWAT has him pinned down at Swedish in Ballard, the clever bastard. We didn't think he'd go back to a previous location. Get here as soon as you can."

After he hung up, Jane grabbed her coat while Diego packed a laptop. On her way out the door, her cellphone rang. Sullivan. At a little past seven p.m., it was late for a call from her friend.

Outside, the clouds overhead blocked the sliver of moon trying to peek through.

"Heading out right now, so not a great time—"

"Jane?" Sullivan sounded off.

"What's up?" Jane nodded to her vehicle, and Diego headed for it.

"Hey, I need some help. Can you come over?"

Definitely not her normal tone. She sounded breathy. Hurt?

"Sullivan, what's wrong?"

"Nothing. I'm okay. But I need to talk to you." After a pause, she added, "It's urgent."

"And you can't tell me on the phone?"

"No."

"Okay. I need to come to you where?"

Sullivan rattled off an address in Bainbridge Island. Not at her home in the city. "Hurry, and please, keep this between us, okay? It's… I don't want this getting out before you can help me figure out what to do."

"I won't." Jane hung up and paused by the driver side door.

"Jane?" Diego tugged at the locked handle.

"I have something I need to do. I'm sorry, but you'll have to drive yourself to the scene. I'll meet you there." She didn't feel bad about not going with him. With SWAT, Rapp, Gina, and a host of LEOs ready to nab Phillip, they needed her there as much as she needed another lecture on proper FBI protocols from Agent Scott.

"Gotcha. See you soon." Diego rushed away.

Jane got into her car and sat for a moment. Sullivan wouldn't ask for help like that. Though she did value Jane's opinion, all this felt a little too cloak and dagger-ish. If Sullivan had info on the case, Scott, or Haversham she wanted to share, she'd have said so in a roundabout way. But all this mystery?

She hadn't said much.

Maybe because she couldn't.

Normally, Jane would rush over and deal with the situation, keeping her involvement quiet. But that's what Sullivan said she wanted.

Jane had no weapon on her, but since she needed to head to Bainbridge Island, perhaps a stop at the ranch would be in order.

As would a phone call she really didn't want to make, in case this situation snowballed into something worse.

CHAPTER FORTY-FOUR

Raine met her at the ranch.

"Well, well. Look who wants my help."

"You know what? Forget it." Jane knew she'd made a huge mistake calling her cousin. "I should have gone with Diego to meet Rapp and the others to grab Keiser."

"That case you're working on? You found him?"

"They think they did. I'm not sure, but Rapp sounded like this was it. I want to be there, but…"

"Come on. Spill. What do you need, exactly?"

Jane started to answer before Raine added, in a nasty tone, "Me to hold your hand? Is little Jane scared of being by herself?" She sneered.

"I'll do it myself." But what if she couldn't save both herself and Sullivan? Was Sullivan's life worth more than her pride?

"That's your problem. You want to do everything by yourself. You never let anyone help you."

I let Hal, she almost said, but it was bad enough she owed him a favor. She didn't want Raine to blackmail her as well. "You're standing here, making fun of me for asking, and then you wonder why I don't want you to help?"

Raine lost her attitude. "I'm just teasing. Besides, you still haven't apologized for being a jerk about my terminal leave."

"I'm sorry. There. Now leave me alone."

"Oh, that's sincere."

Jane didn't have time to tiptoe around Raine's precious feelings. "Well, what about you?" She grabbed her Sig, checked it, then packed two loaded magazines into her jacket. With the Sig in her shoulder holster, she added a knife in a sheath at her ankle.

Her adrenaline pumping, she stared at her laptop, studying the satellite image of the address Sullivan sent her. She had a twenty-minute drive in addition to the hour it had taken her to get over on the ferry, and she'd been speeding to make it.

"That's not a great view," Raine said, coming to stand next to her. Of course she didn't respond to Jane's "what about you?" comment. "Are you planning to storm the barn house by yourself? To what, go to Jenn Sullivan's rescue—that you're not sure she needs?"

"Forget I asked you to do anything."

Raine swung Jane around to face her. "Stop it. You obviously sense something's wrong or you wouldn't be arming up. You asked me to help, so you must feel you'll need it." Raine looked into her eyes with fiery insistence. "You annoy me. You judge me. You belittle me. And you love me." Raine grabbed both her shoulders and gave her a gentle shake. "As much as you bug me, I love you right back. And I'm a better shot than you are. Take me with you. With any luck, you won't need me."

Then she shocked Jane anew by yanking her in for a hug.

It had been a long time since Jane had felt such a mire of emotion. Love, worry, and pain balled up, knotting inside her. Then she let out a breath, and it flowed through her, there to strengthen her, to be used if needed.

She pulled back, uncomfortable yet relieved that they'd gotten past their arguments. Their connection remained, ratty and worn, but with such a strong foundation, it would never break.

"What's going on, Jane?" Raine asked again.

Jane gave her a quick rundown of the Code Blue Killer case and the supposed mole at the Agency.

"Your boss suspects Sullivan might be one of them."

Jane nodded.

"What do you think?"

"I thought she couldn't possibly be guilty. Now I don't know."

"Then be smart. Let's go see what's so important and hush hush that your FBI buddy can't say over the phone. We'll hope she's not as smart as you think she is."

They headed to Jane's car, but Raine didn't get in.

"I'll meet you there. I'll park away from the address. But I'll be there. Count on it."

"I will. I do. Count on you, I mean." Jane didn't know why she suddenly choked up. They'd rarely worked together, but when they had, Raine had had her back. And Jane would have hers.

"You should, little cousin."

The moment passed. "I hate when you call me that."

Raine grinned. "I know."

The drive passed in relative quiet, the moon's light shrouded by clouds and overhanging branches. Despite the lack of snow, the Ponderosa Pines and Douglas Firs felt heavy, hiding private driveways and plots of land in between forests and ferns.

Sullivan had been out of touch for over an hour. The area the woman directed Jane to was located in one such hideaway, surrounded by a thick forest. Jane turned twice and had to backtrack once, having missed a turn onto a narrow drive lined with gravel.

The driveway went back a good hundred feet or more. For a while, only her brights penetrated the gloom. Then she saw the bright lights of the home, a large, two-story barn house surrounded by open grass and patio stone. To one side sat a detached two-story garage with an ADU above.

She had no idea where Raine might park. Trusting her cousin, Jane took her time leaving the car, scanning. Listening.

Silence. Not even a television from inside the house.

The place had to be worth a good bit. Looked to Jane like something out of a designer magazine. Sullivan didn't have that kind of money, so whose house was it?

Jane itched to grab her gun, tucked away under her jacket, but she forced herself to remain loose as she walked up the porch steps onto the spacious landing and knocked.

Sullivan answered the door, her features wan.

She didn't look to be planning Jane's demise, but she didn't look glad to see her either.

No, Sullivan looked…scared.

"Ah, Jane. I'm so happy you're finally here." Rob Williams smiled at her over Sullivan's shoulder. "Come on in and join the party."

As she stepped inside, he closed the door behind her. In the living room stood two men Jane had never before seen. Along with Junior Mazzuca.

CHAPTER FORTY-FIVE

A DIFFERENT PERSPECTIVE

GUNTHER RAPP SURVEYED THE SCENE IN FRONT OF HIM: SWAT positioned around the University of Washington Medical Center's main entrance, flashing police cars parked to cordon off the area, medical staff and patients gathered under warming tents while others were escorted to adjacent buildings for protection.

"This isn't going to end well," Gina Holtz murmured, standing with him by the perimeter while they watched the LEOs do their job.

"I know. I'm surprised he let us get this close."

Gina turned to him, a surprised look on her face. He'd come to know the three people in the small task force well in the short time they'd worked with him. Gina dotted her I's and crossed her T's, a professional to the core who believed in the Agency's values and mission without a doubt.

She'd go far in the organization...if she could get out of her own way. Gina followed orders and gave her all, but if she spotted anyone coloring outside the lines on her watch, she turned stubborn and hard to work with. Case in point—Jane Cannon, who made her own lines and colored wherever the hell she wanted to.

He glanced around, not seeing the cause of his most recent

headaches, and spotted Diego chatting with a few officers outside a tech van. He didn't know if he should worry or not that he didn't see Jane.

"You don't think we found him on our own?" Gina asked. "Phillip wanted us to find him?"

Rapp nodded. "Phillip Keiser's been one step ahead of us since he started."

"But Jane spotted him in Ballard."

That had been unexpected. But then, Jane Cannon didn't fit the norm. She had an uncanny sense, a way to follow the evidence in directions not easy to predict. "I think we got lucky there."

"Hmm." Gina didn't say much more.

They waited and watched while the negotiator spoke with Phillip through a radio he'd dropped off. Rapp didn't like how much they hadn't known when being assigned this mission.

He was only working while on temporary leave from his real job. The moniker of "agent" served as a helpful if not legitimate tool to further Gambol's agenda. Yet, despite being a temp assignment, he still wanted to find the killer and put him away before Keiser took any more lives.

Damn Gambol for withholding the truth about Haversham's involvement. Maybe Haversham didn't know about Gambol's deal with Rapp, but the big-wig knew enough to call him out for being on "thin ice."

Rapp flexed his arm under his jacket, conscious of the wound he'd gotten in service of his country that had yet to fully heal. Another reason he'd been stuck out here in Seattle—to recuperate.

He understood Jane a lot more than she realized. Also falsely accused of being disloyal to job and country, both he and Jane continued to fight the good fight.

He glanced around again, wondering where she was. She should have been standing with them while they waited to learn Phillip's fate. Rapp could only hope they got to him before he killed again.

"Uh, are you Agent Rapp?" a young officer asked as he approached.

"I am."

The officer nodded. "Can you come with me please, sir? The suspect is asking to talk to the FBI."

Rapp had a feeling Phillip would rather talk to Jane. They seemed to have built a rapport.

"Lead the way."

Rapp followed, curious about the connection Jane had formed with their killer. He could easily see the appeal from Phillip's perspective. Jane was around Code Blue's age, attractive, smart.

He still didn't understand what it was about her that drew *him*. Rapp had seen better looking women. Wined and dined dignitaries, doctors, lawyers, and other intelligent ladies, attracted as much to their brains as their bodies.

But she had something else he couldn't put his finger on. He even liked Jane's prickly personality. Not that he ever mixed business with pleasure, but if he did, he'd certainly have asked her out by now. She intrigued him on a multitude of levels, and her sharp ability to follow clues and turn them into real leads made her an asset.

Why would her boss burn her just to find a mole in his squad? He would have been better off using Jane to find the leak. But then, Rapp didn't care much for Matthew Scott. Everything he'd read about the guy suggested a rich kid using his parents to be a big shot.

"He's in there." A detective handed Rapp a vest, which he donned, then had two armed officers escort him to where Phillip could see him. Rapp paused just outside the lobby, beyond the closed door but protected by a cement column from gunfire.

"I don't see a weapon," Rapp murmured, eyeing the lobby through glass.

In it, a small crowd of people cowered by the back wall while four people sat on their knees in the center, their hands behind their backs. Two women and two men. All four looked petrified. The pallor of the oldest man suggested a health problem.

He spoke into a handset someone provided. "Phillip, I'm Gunther Rapp."

"I know who you are." Phillip smiled. He wore neither ballcap nor hoodie, nothing to obscure his features, and matched the photos they had of him. He looked All-American handsome, someone who should be on a baseball card grinning at his fans, not on a wanted poster.

And he knew Rapp.

Another connection to someone feeding him information, but who? Not Gina and not Diego. Rapp had secretly been keeping tabs on the team.

As for Jane, Team Ten were legendary. Once he'd met Hal and Joe and seen how they treated her as one of their own, he definitely knew he could trust her.

Which left Gambol and the people he'd been talking to—including Haversham and everyone associated with August Kaminski.

"Phillip, I'm here to talk. Just tell me what you want. And let those people go. They're innocent, the same way your parents were. They're not the ones at fault."

"I know who's guilty," Phillip's dreamy smile said he wasn't firing on all cylinders. He'd have been taken out by a sniper by now if he hadn't already promised a larger threat if anything happened to him.

"What can I do?"

Phillip held up the gun in his hand before pointing at the younger woman kneeling by him. "You know who's guilty."

"Yes, the Harvesters."

"No. Who's *really* guilty?" He shifted his finger on the trigger, ready to fire.

"Law enforcement who covered up the real criminals."

Phillip shifted his aim, so the muzzle pointed to the floor. "Correct. But I'm willing to make a trade."

Rapp had a bad feeling he knew where this was going.

"I'd rather have talked to Jane, but since she's not here, you'll do."

How did he know she wasn't there? "Tell me what you want."

"You for them."

"All of them?"

"Yes. But you have to drop the vest, the weapons, and walk toward me. Just you. The FBI for innocent civilians."

"You can't, sir," one of the men closest to him said.

"Deal." Rapp would hear about this later. But he had the best chance of getting those people free from this nightmare. He could only hope he wouldn't regret not returning his mother's phone call yesterday.

He didn't want her last memory of him to be forgetting to wish his oldest brother a happy birthday.

CHAPTER FORTY-SIX

JANE WALKED INTO THE LIVING ROOM AND PAUSED, HANDS UP, WHILE Junior removed her gun, magazines, and knife. Sullivan took a seat on the couch while Junior gave Jane a pat-down. It was a little more intimate than professional but not too gropey.

A part of her wondered hysterically in Raine's voice, *Too gropey? You're a moron.*

"On the couch, Agent Cannon." Junior smirked at her while his goons held their guns close, ready to shoot.

She joined Sullivan on the couch and waited for the fun to begin.

To her surprise, Junior stepped aside, giving Williams the floor.

"Thanks, guys. You're sure he's tied up in the back?"

One of the goons nodded. "Still out cold, too."

"Good." Williams shot Sullivan a cold smile. "Loverboy wouldn't have lasted even if he wasn't soon going to burn up in an unfortunate fire."

"Fire? What...?" Sullivan gaped. "Rob, you can't!" She started to get up, but Rob slapped her hard. Her head snapped back, and she sank onto the couch.

"Shut up. You ruined *everything.*" He glared with hatred.

Behind him, the Mazzucas laughed.

Junior slapped him on the back. "You're all right, man. We're going to doublecheck that all the rooms are doused in gasoline. I think Bucky's still doing the greenhouse."

The taller goon nodded. "Yeah. I ran out. I'll go get more and flood it."

"Then, whoosh," the other goon added with a grin. "Flame on."

They left, and Junior paused before saying, "You did a half-decent job, Jane. You too, Jenn. But sloppy work leads to sloppy outcomes." He smirked at her. "It's okay. You couldn't have foreseen this. And it doesn't matter anyway. Even if they stop that mindless idiot, Keiser. You know why? Because you'll never stop what's coming. There's too much at stake." He winked, turned on his heel, and left.

It was just Sullivan, Williams, and her. And Jane's many questions.

"What the hell, Williams? I thought we were friends," Jane bit out.

"So did I, Jane. But Jenn wouldn't play nice." He turned to Sullivan. "I tried to keep you out of it, you know."

"How?" Sullivan snapped. "By selling out to the Mazzucas? How could you? You're a great agent, Rob. Why ruin your life like this? For money?"

"Of course, for money." He sneered. "And that's ironic, coming from you. You spread your legs for your CEO boyfriend, and that's okay. But a few harmless dates with your best friend are impossible since I don't have the cash."

Jane prayed Raine was out there either listening in or preparing to take out Junior and his guys. Jane could handle Williams so long as she didn't have to worry about the others.

"This is because you're jealous of Sullivan's boyfriend?" A stupid question, but Jane wanted to see his reaction.

He glared and took a step in her direction. Then stopped and smiled. "Not bad. Make me angry and I'll get close enough so you can take me down the way you took down our guy at the gas station. That idiot was only supposed to scare you. He got greedy because Junior offered him more if he'd kill you, but only to see if the loser would go through with it. I mean, none of us thought he'd succeed."

"Thanks." Jane crossed her arms over her chest and settled onto the couch. Williams wanted to talk. She'd let him. "So explain all this. Money? Really? You're smarter than that. You've got an ulterior motive."

"You think he's smart?" Sullivan snorted.

Shut up. You're going to make him unbalanced and unpredictable.

But Sullivan wouldn't look at Jane to read her warning. Instead, she glared up at Williams. "You know why I wouldn't go out with you? Because we're not supposed to fraternize, that's why. It had nothing to do with your personality, which I used to love." She sniffed.

Jane didn't know if Sullivan meant to or not, but she thought it was a nice touch. At least she'd been smart enough to compliment Williams and not aggravate him.

He seemed to soften. "Jenn. You should have tried harder. We could have made us work."

"But we'd never have worked if I knew you worked for the Mazzucas."

"He doesn't. Not really," I said.

Williams's slow smile said more than words would have. "So smart, aren't you, Jane? You worked it out."

"What?" Sullivan looked from him to Jane and back. "Tell me."

"It all leads back to the Harvesters," Jane said, watching Williams.

"No, it all leads back to a fight over territory in Camden."

"New Jersey?" Sullivan asked.

Williams nodded. They all heard a door slam, a vehicle start, and then the sounds of vehicles crunching away down the drive. "Good. We're finally alone. Yes, Camden, New Jersey. One of the roughest places in Mid-Atlantic. The Mazzucas were only an idea when they ran up against the start of the Kaminski organization. And yes, they are a full-fledged syndicate. But they're smart."

"I knew it." Jane felt vindicated, a brief bonding with her friends when they both nodded.

Until she saw William's pistol.

"You caught on faster than we liked. Just like Jon Haversham did."

"Did you join the FBI and then turn? Or were you always one of them?" Sullivan asked, her voice small.

He sighed and crouched down to look at her at eye level, yet far enough away so they couldn't rush him without getting shot. "I'm sorry, Jenn. I genuinely like you. Always have. But I was groomed to do this, to plant myself where I can do the most good for the family."

"Which side?" Jane asked.

"Leo Mazzuca's brother knocked up my mother before he died. I've always been a part of them."

Sullivan shook her head. "The FBI would have known. The background checks..."

"Were legit. I never had any connection to the family on paper. Heck, my aunt still thinks my mom was raped. But the Mazzucas were there for me. Helped with money, with things we needed. All they asked for was a little help to keep them in the clear. And here we are. The Mazzucas got into organ theft a few years back."

"Not the Kaminskis?" Jane asked.

"Not...exactly. My family got a little reckless. But I was in Vegas to help. I put a stop to any investigation that pulled the family into it. We blamed some crackpots instead, made it seem like it was all about money and not about the power that came from our buyers."

"August Kaminski," Jane said. "Tell me about him."

"Aw, Jane. That's above your paygrade."

"I know he works with your family. That he's quiet and stealthy and invades like a hidden parasite, sucking up all the riches until there's nothing left. Then he kills the host and moves on to the next one." She paused, watching Williams but not seeing a reaction. "He told Phillip Keiser who to kill, didn't he? So that we'd be distracted while he hid your family from us and destroyed any evidence to nail them on RICO charges."

"I don't know what you think you know." He winked. "But wow, that'd be pretty clever if it happened."

"One thing that's bugging me though. How did Phillip pick his targets? That's been driving me nuts."

"Oh right. You're stuck on the Code Blue Killer case." He snorted. "We've been keeping track of that since the task force started. You could almost say it was our idea." He laughed.

"The victims?" she prodded.

"Well, one of them, Stevens, used to help us when we had medical needs. He was one of the EMTs who bit it. Turned out he was a snitch. So he got what was coming. The others pissed off Leo in one way or another. I'm not sure on the details, but we used the Keiser wacko to take out the trash. No loss there."

"And the rest of them? They're also on your list?"

"What rest?" He frowned. "He did the job. He's on his own now. I think aliens are telling him who to kill. The guy's looney."

"You were never my friend, were you?" Sullivan sounded broken up.

Jane studied her, worried about her state of mind.

"I'm sorry. Maybe if we'd slept together, if you'd taken a chance on me, you might have seen what we could have had. But you threw me over for wonderboy in the back." Williams didn't seem too upset about it.

"Your *friends* nearly killed her on the pier. Why should she want you?" Jane asked.

He shook his head. "No. That was all a mistake, and your fault." He aimed his gun at Jane. "They were there for you. You kept looking into things, checking into Las Vegas and the Harvester case. That was old news. You became a problem." He turned to Sullivan. "I am sorry about that." He glanced down at her injured leg. "I wish—"

Sullivan launched herself at him before Jane could react.

The gun went off. Sullivan sagged to the ground. Blood seeped under her.

"And that's why women don't make good FBI agents, Jane," Williams said as he stood. "They're too emotional."

CHAPTER FORTY-SEVEN

"Let me help her." Where was Raine?

Williams backed up and motioned to Jane with his gun. "Go ahead. But any sudden moves and you'll be bleeding out with her." He sounded tough, but as Jane looked into his eyes, she saw regret.

For all his posturing, Williams did care for Sullivan. Just not enough to keep her safe.

Jane hurried to her friend and pushed her onto her back, staring at the blood around her belly.

Sullivan stared up with glassy eyes and a weak grin. "Not my week, huh? First the leg, now the gut. Jackass shot me."

Williams scowled. "You shouldn't have rushed me like that." He ripped a curtain from the wall and threw it at Jane. "Put that over the wound. She'll be okay."

"I don't know, Rob. Hurts a lot." Sullivan started to slur, "R-rright over an old scar, at least."

"She needs help." Jane hadn't forgotten that his friends had been soaking the house in gasoline. Williams didn't expect any of them to live through tonight. "You could have done all this and gotten away with it. But you got greedy."

"How did I get greedy? Trust me, I'll get away with this. You've been so clueless. For years, I've been giving them information. No one ever knew."

"Haversham did."

"He did not."

"Why do you think he transferred here? He's building a case against you."

Williams blinked. "You're lying."

"Why would I lie?" She increased pressure over Sullivan's belly until Sullivan subtly angled the pressure toward her hip. Jane masked the shift, hoping that meant Sullivan wasn't gutshot. "You shot her, Williams. You're clearly going to kill me too. I have no leverage. But at least I'll go out knowing you're going down."

"Shut up." He pulled out his phone, trying to keep an eye on her while dialing at the same time.

She didn't try to take him down. She'd need to get closer. Jane knew she could take him, but she couldn't risk him shooting Sullivan again.

"Hey." Sullivan tugged at her hand.

"What? Does it hurt?"

"Duh. I got shot. It hurts." She coughed, and a trickle of blood seeped from her mouth.

Jane froze. "Did the bullet hit your lungs?" Typically, a gutshot would have internal bleeding Sullivan might cough up. But no bleeding from the mouth unless Sullivan vomited.

Sullivan whispered, "No. I hit my face when I landed and bit my lip."

"Good." Jane sighed with relief.

"That's not—better." Sullivan's breathing hitched. "But do you think..."

Williams was whisper-yelling into his phone. Walking away from them yet keeping them in sight.

"Think what?" Jane asked, praying Raine would show up soon. What if her cousin had gotten hurt dealing with the Mazzucas?

"...you could call me Jenn?"

Jane blinked. "Huh?"

"You never call either of us by our first names," Williams said as he returned, appearing shaken.

"Oh. Sorry. Old habit I picked up from my Marine Corps days. The only people I ever call by their first names are my family."

"You're weird." Sullivan closed her eyes.

Jane swore. "Sullivan! Jenn. Open your eyes."

She gripped Jane's hand though her body sagged. Jane could only hope Sullivan wasn't as injured as she let on.

"Oh my God. She's... She's *dead.*"

Williams blinked. "She's not dead."

"What do you care? You're going to kill us soon enough." Jane tried to will a tear, but unlike Raine, she'd never been able to fake emotions on command, and especially not tears.

Crying was for wimps. Plus, Sullivan's grip remained tight. *Thank goodness.*

Now to use that to her advantage.

"I don't think you meant to kill her," Jane said quietly as she stroked her friend's hair with her free hand. "I think you probably would have let us go."

"I—I mean... I would have." Williams sucked in a breath and let it out in ragged gasps, swearing and praying and swearing some more before he let out a whoop of laughter. "Sucker. You're all going to die. You, her—ding, dong, the witch is dead. Even that loser boyfriend of hers in the back. This is his house, you know. I meant to kill you all. I'm only sorry she's gone too quickly. I'd have liked to have hooked up once before she died."

Jane scooted back from Sullivan, her jeans covered in blood, and pulled the curtain she'd been using to stem the blood flow with her. "She used to tell me all the time you were her best friend."

"Yeah, well, I guess she wasn't too bright, was she?" Yet for all Williams kept trying to act like he didn't care, Jane saw the loss register. He kept staring at Sullivan, looking at her with eyes that cared.

Jane sat, trying to appear lost, her mind on how long it would take her to throw the bloodied curtain at Williams' face before attacking him. *Come on. Come closer. Look at her.*

But Williams wouldn't. She needed something to distract him, damn it.

A pane of glass broke behind him. He turned. Fired.

Jane was on him. She slung the wet curtain around his face then knocked the gun from his hand and kicked it away.

"You're good. Take him out," Raine said. "We're safe."

Jane focused on Williams. The traitor.

She drove him to the ground.

Behind her, Raine called for help on her phone and rushed toward Sullivan. A man joined her, but Jane didn't look up from her opponent, letting the rage flow as she got to her feet.

With a feral grin, she let Williams rise. He lunged for her, tearing at the blood-drenched fabric swaddling his head.

Jane broke both his wrists and popped his knee with a kick.

He shrieked and folded like a battered chair as her leg sweep took him down and kept him down.

"That's what you get for being a traitor and a fool." She tied him up using a set of flex cuffs Raine tossed to her.

"The others?" Jane asked, breathing hard. She itched to break the guy's neck. "Who's your friend?"

The man next to Jane kept talking to Sullivan—to *Jenn*—in a low, calming voice, holding his sweater against her belly.

"This is Dash, Jenn's boyfriend," Raine said by way of introduction.

Dash didn't look away. "Thanks."

"Anytime. I just love beating up scum," Jane growled and shoved Williams away from her.

"Nice job." Raine nodded with approval as she studied the creep.

They listened to him whine and cry some more before Jane went in search of her phone and weapons, squirreled away on a table in the other room.

"So what happened?" Jane asked as they heard sirens closing in.

"I called them as soon as I saw we had more company. I took out the goons outside at the end of the driveway, away from the house." Goons—just like Jane had mentally described the Mazzuca stooges. Great minds thought alike. "But the head goon didn't make it." Raine frowned. "One of those morons shot him by mistake. I left him tied up and bleeding out. I doubt he'll live."

"Too bad," said Dash as he glanced up, rage in his eyes. "Because I'd like to kill him all over again. He trashed my place, beat me up, and threatened Jenn with revolting things."

Jane noted the black eyes, swollen mouth, and the way he cradled his side. He probably had bruised or busted ribs.

"Ambulance is on its way," Raine reminded her.

Jane approved of Dash. He hadn't crumbled in the face of adversity and continued to care for Sull—Jenn. *This will take some getting used to.*

A glance at her phone showed dozens of new messages.

She returned Gina's call. "What's up?"

"Where have you been?" Gina bit out.

"It's a long story. What's going on? Do you have Phillip in custody yet?"

"We have a situation here."

Jane grimaced. "He didn't kill anyone did he?"

"No. But we've been in a standoff until about ten minutes ago. Now we have an entirely different situation."

"How so?" Jane rushed for the door.

"Don't worry. I got this," Raine yelled after her. "You're welcome!"

"Thanks." Jane said to Gina, "Sorry. I'm on my way. Tell me."

"Phillip wanted to talk to you, but he settled for Rapp."

"What does that mean, exactly?" She started her car and raced for the ferry.

"Phillip traded the guilty civilians he held for one 'real' bad guy. An agent."

Her heart raced, but she had to clarify, "Rapp?"

"An unarmed, unprotected Rapp. Yes. And even worse, SWAT found evidence of some small tanks filled with a mysterious fluid outside the facility, wired to timers that are counting down."

"You're kidding."

"Phillip's going to go out with a big bang. Literally."

CHAPTER FORTY-EIGHT

With a lot of luck and friendly guards at the ferry, Jane made it to the city in less than an hour. She kept Gina on the phone. News that Jane was on her way put Phillip in a good mood.

The police escort to UW Medical Northwest shaved off a ton of time, though she worried that Phillip might decide waiting didn't fit his master plan.

Why had he let his targets leave though? Why bring in Rapp?

What game was he playing now, and did he even realize he might be controlled by someone else? Who the heck was pulling his strings? Because it was more than the Mazzucas, no matter what Williams said.

She arrived without a protective vest or weapons, which she left in the trunk of her car against protocol. But she had more important things to worry about.

Fortunately, she hadn't taken any major wounds from Williams, that twerp, and Raine had given her steady texts on Dash's status as well as Jenn's condition. *Thanks for looking after Sullivan,* Jane sent her.

You're so weird. Call her by her first name. That last text from her cousin calmed her. Made her smile.

"You find death coming for you funny?" Gina asked, clearly nervous and trying not to show it as she met Jane near the hospital.

"I find it hilarious." She noted Diego hovering nearby. "What are you holding there?"

"We want a closeup view. Put this on." He handed the small camera and mic to her, and she attached it to the collar of her sweater since it looked like an ornamental pin.

"I like this." So would Hal.

"Thanks." Diego flushed at the praise. Then he jumped in for a quick hug. "Please don't die."

"I won't."

Jane was touched until Gina added, "And don't get Rapp killed."

"Aw, I knew you cared."

Gina huffed. "Go on. Be safe."

Jane hurried to the front of the building and held up her arms, showing herself weaponless. After lowering her arms, she said into a radio one of the SWAT guys had handed her, "I'm here and unarmed."

"Enter," Rapp answered.

Good. He was alive. Walking slowly, she entered, noting the locations of the small, weird mystery tanks inside, hooked up to wires that disappeared into the walls. The door swung shut behind her, leaving her in the lobby with Rapp and Phillip.

Phillip sat at a desk, a semiautomatic resting in front of him.

Rapp sat on the floor, his legs splayed and resting back on his hands.

Jane had the feeling she'd interrupted an interesting discussion. Rapp didn't appear upset, and Phillip was smiling.

"What did I miss?" She walked near Rapp but stopped when Phillip lifted a hand. "Where do you want me?"

"That's what I like about you, Jane. You're a pleasure to work with." Phillip pointed to a nearby chair off center of the middle of the floor. "Please, sit there. And know if you did sneak a weapon in, I'll shoot him in the head before you get off a round."

"Understood."

He smiled. "Excellent." After she settled, he asked, "Where were you?"

During her travel from the island, she'd debated on whether or not to tell him the truth. She'd decided he'd appreciate her honesty. "Well, it's been an exciting night." She felt Rapp's attention narrow on her.

While she explained everything that had happened, she waited for Phillip to chime in with some detail. He didn't.

She finished with, "Sullivan's at the hospital now, and we don't know if she'll make it. Her new boyfriend seems a decent sort. He cared about helping more than he did about saving his own skin."

"That's a good quality in a partner," Phillip agreed. "My parents were like that."

"I heard amazing things about your dad," Jane agreed. "And everyone loved your mom. The florist next door to her bakery couldn't say enough about her or her baked goods."

Phillip grinned. "Ah, Mrs. Knof. She'd pretend to be cranky, but she always gave my mom a fresh bouquet to start the week, free of charge. She was such a nice woman." Unexpected tears filled his eyes. "It's been so long since I've been around nice people."

Rapp caught her eye, but she didn't need him to tell her Phillip had held on this long for some reason. He now had an excuse to end things since she'd finally arrived.

"Phillip, how can I help you?" Jane asked.

"Just by being here, you're helping. I called a reporter the other day, and I told him everything. How the FBI covered up a serial killer —that's me. I also gave him my name, so don't blame anyone on the task force for giving me up. This spectacle … I imagine it'll be hard to hide this. Although I bet you could if you wanted."

Jane shrugged. "I don't much care. My job isn't about PR. It's about protecting lives. And I know he doesn't care." She nodded to Rapp. "Or he'd have fired me on day one. I don't play nice with others."

"Seriously. She's not kidding." Rapp chuckled.

Phillip glanced from Rapp to Jane. "I like you both. He's got military training. You can tell."

"I know."

Rapp sighed. "Hard to hide proficiency from a fellow expert."

"Thank you." Phillip had to be the nicest—well, only—serial killer Jane had ever met.

"Phillip, can I ask you a question?"

He glanced at his phone before placing it back down. "Go ahead."

"Did someone tell you to do all this? Or did you hear it from God or someone inside your head?"

He paused for a moment then broke into laughter. "Oh, wow. Thanks. I needed that." He let out a loud breath. "So that's what you thought? That I was looney tunes? Bats in the belfry?"

"Hey, you're killing people and on a mission. It's not farfetched to think you had a 'higher' purpose." She glanced up, as if looking to a higher power.

"Fair enough. Yes, Jane. And Gunther. He told me I can call him that."

Yes?

"An actual human being, alive, not a god, whispered certain truths to me. He set me on my path. Sure, you'll all call me insane and say I'm dealing with grief and other traumas I'm obviously suffering. But Mike Stevens' name came from my special friend. I had to work to fill in the others around him, so that you wouldn't see the true victim until it was too late."

"But we know about Kaminski and the Mazzucas now," Rapp confessed. "I told you that."

"You did, and I appreciate that knowledge. I also appreciate that you haven't been sharing everything we talked about with the group outside."

Well, they hadn't been until Jane had arrived. Diego and Gina were getting all this in real time.

"I told you once, Jane, that I am Justice. And I am. I'm not crazy or grieving. Well, maybe I am. But that grief cleared my vision, enabled me to see that not everything is in black and white. We're all shades of gray."

She scoffed.

Phillip frowned. "What?"

"I just had this conversation with my cousin. She says I'm too black and white, that I need to see that the world exists in shades of gray. But I think that's just an excuse to allow yourself to break rules that should remain unbroken."

"Interesting. And wrong." Phillip stood.

She saw Rapp tense, but he remained still.

"I learned a lot in the Army. My family dedicated itself to service. I tried to be the best soldier, the best medic, son, and student. I admit, something in me broke when my parents died, because we all know they might have been saved if some scum hadn't butchered them for parts."

"But Phillip, that crime ring was under August Kaminski's leadership. He's the one you're really mad at," Rapp said.

Jane still didn't understand why Phillip was determined to punish everyone but his grand-uncle, who deserved his wrath. He'd even forgiven his cousin, who had actually crashed into his parents.

"That's what you all think. You don't really know."

"And you do?" Jane asked gently. As much as Phillip acted like he had all his ducks in a row and a clear focus, his actions were those of someone with a few screws loose. He hadn't gone to the press when he'd learned about the organ harvesting. He hadn't contacted any authorities. Hell, he hadn't even contacted the FBI to get help.

Instead, he killed innocent people under someone else's directive.

"Who gave you your marching orders?" Rapp asked.

Phillip studied him and Jane, shaking his head. "You still can't see it. But then, you don't have to. I'll die, and you." He looked at Rapp, "You'll go back to missions overseas." To Jane he said, "And you'll go back to fighting crime at the Seattle field office. You both think you're helping. And to an extent you are. But when it all comes crashing down, you'll finally start to see what I've been saying."

He motioned to the room to Jane's right. "If you hurry and get in there, you might escape the blast. But you have to be quick. Thanks for coming to my TED talk." He laughed, a sound bordering on hysteria.

Then she noticed the device in his hands. Some sort of trigger.

Rapp rushed her into the small, empty closet just as Phillip waved goodbye.

A blast of heat threw her and Rapp against each other and the wall.

CHAPTER FORTY-NINE

JANE WOKE TO MUTED VOICES AND HOSPITAL SMELLS. TO HER RIGHT, A bouquet of flowers and a small balloon on a stick told her to *Get Well Soon*. Another next to it said, *Congrats! It's a girl!*

Funny. Jane didn't recall giving birth.

She blinked at the IV and felt bruised all over when she took a deep breath. Her right forearm had been plastered in a pink cast.

She hated pink.

"I told them it's your favorite color," Raine said as she came into Jane's vision, knowing full well she liked blue. Then Raine leaned in and raised each of Jane's eyelids to look into her eyes. "She's back."

Jane tried to shake her cousin off and felt woozy. "Cut it out."

"They have you on some nice pain meds. Enjoy." Her cousin leaned in to kiss her on the cheek. "That's what you get for trying to be a hero."

The past came rushing back. "The others?"

"Well, let's see. Jenn Sullivan is recovering nicely. They sewed up a small tear in her hip that bled a lot but that didn't do much damage otherwise. Her cutie boyfriend is glued to her hip, so that trauma bonding might be something to watch out for. Your hot merc, Rapp?"

Jane nodded.

"He's banged up like you but only suffered a major concussion. I think he fell on you, and that's why you're more banged up than he is."

"He'll hate that." Jane laughed, probably harder than the idea warranted. Stupid drugs.

Raine grinned. "The Mazzucas are all in custody, well, except for Junior, who's dead. I told you his guys shot him by accident. Williams is under arrest and in surgery to repair one of his wrists. Nice job." Raine gently squeezed her good hand. "Hmm. What else?"

"Does the family know about all this?"

Raine made a face. "I think Hal has been watching from some hidden camera somewhere. He warned me to stick to you like a fat, happy tick."

"Gross."

"Yeah, Hal's not all that poetic. He and Joe are wrapping up their 'thing' early," she said, using air quotes. "They'll be here soon. Oh, and you have some visitors that want to come in. Are you up for that, or do you want me to keep them waiting?"

Jane felt like crap, but she also wanted answers. "Bring 'em in." She had so many questions still buzzing in her brain. She just needed to focus to get all the alphabet soup in her mind to make sense. "ABCs," she muttered.

Raine frowned. "Are you sure you can handle visitors?"

"And water."

Raine fished an ice chip out of a nearby cup for her instead and slid it between her lips. "There. Enjoy. I'll be back."

She left, and Gina and Diego entered.

"Oh, cool. War wounds!" Diego grinned and held up a Sharpie. "Can I be the first to sign?"

"Be my guest."

Gina studied her. "You look better than I'd expected for having two hundred pounds of Marine thrown on top of you."

Diego paused to look at Gina, who flushed.

"Okay, that didn't sound at all how I meant it. Rapp is waiting to come in. He feels bad about landing on you when the explosion hit."

"Bring him in." Jane wanted everyone to explain what happened after the big boom.

Gina flagged him in.

Rapp entered, looking wan. Almost brittle, which made little sense considering his large stature. He hadn't lost any muscle mass or limbs from the blast that she could tell.

When he saw her, he smiled with relief. "Oh good. You're not dead."

Diego snickered, and even Gina cracked a smile.

"What happened?" Jane needed to know.

"Well, after I traded myself for the hostages, Phillip let me inside. We chatted for close to an hour before you arrived. He would sound sane and super smart one minute, mentally unwell the next. I still don't know if he got his mission from a real person or someone he thought was real. None of his motivations made sense."

Jane struggled to understand what he said when Gina explained.

"Yeah. It makes no sense that he doesn't blame August Kaminski for organizing the Harvester ring that killed his parents, or the crash caused by his drunk-ass son. But no, Phillip goes after a bunch of medical people that August has grudges against. Supposedly. The only one we can really confirm was Mike Stevens."

"What about Rob Williams?" Jane asked.

Rapp chuckled and eased into a seat next to her bed. "You did a number on him. Nice work, by the way."

"Thanks."

"He's doped up on pain meds, but I overheard that your boss managed a confession from him. He's definitely the mole, and he started years ago. He ditched the evidence on Kaminski in Las Vegas. And he's been throwing off your squad in the Seattle office since he arrived on site. With him gone, you guys should be back on track."

She blinked to keep her eyes open. "Only one?"

"One what?" Diego asked and handed the pen to Gina. She studied it then wrote on Jane's cast. Diego said, "Ah. Got it. Only one mole, yes. That's the theory everyone's sticking with. But you know everything in that HQ is going to be under close scrutiny. I'm glad I'm heading out soon."

Jane blinked. "You're leaving?"

"You'll miss me, won't you?" Diego gave her a smug smile. "Chicks dig brains. I know you and Gina are gonna want my number, so I sent them to your phones."

"Gee, thanks." Gina rolled her eyes and handed Rapp the marker. "Come on, Diego. You're not gone yet. We have a bunch of after-action reports to get to."

He groaned. "*Nooo.* I'm out of energy drinks."

Gina shared an amused smile with Rapp and said, "We'll get you some. My treat."

That perked him up, and he left with Gina.

Rapp stood slowly, cradling his side.

"Broken or bruised?" Jane asked and felt sad all of a sudden. "You're leaving?"

"Soon but not yet. And I'm only bruised." He grabbed a tissue. But instead of letting her wipe her stupid face full of stupid tears, he did it for her. So gently.

He confused her.

"I'm sorry for body slamming you when that bomb went off. Or I should say, bombs. Phillip made some fun incendiaries. He toasted the lobby, but the closet was reinforced enough to protect us. In other odd news, we're still sifting through the rubble for his body." His voice came to her from a distance.

"He got away?" Her eyes refused to stay open.

She felt pressure on her cast. Then a whisper and a brush of something on her cheek.

Closing her eyes, she dropped into sleep.

CHAPTER FIFTY

A WEEK ON MANDATORY RESTRICTED DUTY AT HOME WAS CRUEL AND unusual punishment.

Especially because her entire family had returned.

All of Team Ten, including Uncle Chris, had descended on the ranch like a horde of concerned locusts.

"You need anything, Jane?" Hondo asked. His hair stuck up, a result of twelve hours of sleep after coming off his own light duty. Apparently, in an effort to teach Malcolm the difference between left from right, he'd gotten into an altercation with Malcolm's mighty fists.

Hondo stood about Jane's height and had ten years on her but two fewer fingers. Their bomb expert swore a ton and had a mouth that didn't quit. Often to his detriment.

Malcolm, who normally never took offense, had had a bad day. The guy fought like a demon, so why Hondo had even thought about screwing with him made little sense. But the fight had eased tensions among the many varied personalities in the group, as it usually did.

"I'm good, Hondo. Thanks." Jane smiled at him, sitting in her room at the ranch and wishing she was back in Seattle. Alone. Where it was quiet.

He walked away but left her door open. She stared at the door, willing it to close. It didn't, and she didn't have the energy to get up.

She hadn't been hurt that badly, or she hadn't thought. But she'd spent a lot of time sleeping or resting. It felt like forever since she'd jogged. She hated feeling so helpless.

Hal and Joe surged into her room with grand smiles and carrying a tray of bacon and orange juice. At four in the afternoon.

Still, they were her favorite foods, so Jane happily thanked them.

While she ate, they caught her up on all she'd missed since...yesterday.

"We said nothing to your uncle about that thing I did," Hal said.

"You told Joe?" She shot him an accusatory glare.

"I overheard him muttering to himself and made him talk."

Hal sighed. "He's huge and he threatened me. I had to tell him."

Joe smiled. "Don't worry, Jane. I'm a vault. A very big, very scary vault. I say nothing. Never, to anyone."

"Say what?" Uncle Chris asked in a gruff voice. He'd been mothering her for a week. His constant presence bugged her, and she knew it bugged him. He hated feeling helpless as much as she did.

Joe and Hal jumped.

"Nothing at all. Just catching Jane up on all the gossip." Hal clapped a hand on Joe's shoulder. "We're heading out with Smith and Minjun tonight. Want us to bring you back anything?"

Chris paused. "Nah, but if you head out to Poulsbo tomorrow, make sure to drop off some goodies from Sluys to Grace."

Jane watched their eyes glaze over but could empathize. Sluys baked her favorite treats. Despite not having a sweet tooth, she always tried to grab a Viking cup, a type of cinnamon roll that was to die for.

Her uncle grinned at her and added, "And get a few Viking cups for the kids." Meaning her and Raine.

Hal and Joe nodded and left them alone, but as Hal moved through the doorway, he turned, twisted his fingers over his lips, and threw away an invisible key.

Jane, still irked at being called a kid, would have smacked her uncle if she'd had the energy for it. "Why am I so tired?"

"Physical trauma takes a toll." He sat on her bed. He looked the same as always. A tall, older man with a square jaw, and brown eyes, so dark they looked black, that seemed to see right through a person. He had a rangy strength with big hands and big feet, and he still palmed her head in his hand as a sign of affection. As if her noggin was a basketball.

"You look good," he said, studying her. "I know it's killing you not to be at work, but you have a concussion, Jane. This ain't the movies where you can get blown up and punched and shot and be back at work by two. Make sure you heal right so you're good to go when you're operational."

"Aye, aye, Colonel."

He grinned. "Smartass."

"Speaking of, have you and Raine made peace yet?"

He groaned. "And here we were, you and I, getting along just fine. No, the girl won't talk to me. Every time I find her, she has an excuse to duck out." He frowned. "I think a few of the boys are helping her avoid me."

"Probably Shawn and Minjun."

"I know. Minjun's slick with that smile. Even I can't stay mad at him."

She chuckled. "Is it weird for you to be home with everyone?"

"Kind of." He rubbed his short, salt and pepper hair, the sophisticated cut at odds with the hard warrior who liked nothing better than to slam a few beers while betting on who could belch the loudest and longest. "We need the downtime though. It got a little rough on our last mission." He got that angry look on his face she liked directed at anyone but her. "Shawn and I had a talk."

Better him than me. "What did he do?" Shawn was the youngest member of Team Ten, the newest hire just a few years older than Jane. She thought of him as an older brother rather than an uncle, like the rest of the guys.

"A little bit too much fun stabbing people. In his defense, those same people had done some terrible things to the children in that

271

village. I'm just making sure he has his head on right. We don't kill for fun."

"I know." She thought about it. "Hold on a minute." She texted Raine to come to her room.

Her cousin texted, *Is the coast clear?*

"Go hide behind the door," she said to her uncle and texted Raine, *Yep. Come in.*

Once her cousin entered, her uncle shut the door behind her, trapping them all together.

Raine glared at her. "Traitor."

"We need to talk. All of us." Jane gave Raine a sad smile, and her cousin's lower lip quivered.

"Aw, hell." Uncle Chris sighed and held open his arms. "Come here."

Raine darted in for a hug.

Jane gave them some time before saying, "Uncle Chris, Raine is on terminal leave. She needs something different in her life. She's smart enough to know what works for her. She just needs time to find something new to challenge her that will let her look in the mirror and have pride with what she's doing again."

To Raine, she said, "Uncle Chris has been where you are. He's done things he didn't like but that were necessary in the line of duty. If you won't go to therapy, then talk to him or Sven about it." Sven, their resident linguist who looked like a modern-day Viking, was also the team counselor and confidant.

"Honey, you can always talk to me. You know I don't judge." Uncle Chris stroked Raine's hair, then tugged her with him out of the room. "Oh, and one other thing," he said to Jane, holding onto Raine's arm—likely so she wouldn't bolt. "Matthew Scott called. Call him back. You and I will talk about Gunther Rapp later, after I'm done with this one."

"Talk about Rapp?"

He left, so she called out after him, "Talk about what, exactly?"

There was nothing to talk about. In fact, she had to get back to work before the task force split up permanently. She wanted to at least say goodbye before everyone went somewhere else.

As much as the team had annoyed her, Gina especially, she'd miss working with them.

And Rapp… Well, she'd miss working *with* him, not *for* him.

She smiled and decided to take a nap. She'd talk to Matthew Scott tomorrow.

In person. Right after she finished the sweets Joe and Hal were sure to bring her.

CHAPTER FIFTY-ONE

JANE ENJOYED HER VIKING CUP MORE THAN SHE'D THOUGHT SHE WOULD. It was like a cinnamon roll but had an open middle filled with cream cheese frosting. Between the yeasty dough, the delightful cream cheese, and the gooey cinnamon, she loved everything about it.

Raine devoured two and a donut shaped like a man, glazed with maple frosting. The rest of the guys continued to give them a hard time about their poor diets.

Raine answered by flipping them off while Jane challenged them all to keep up with her on a cross country run just as soon as her head stopped throbbing so much.

That shut them all up, except for Shawn, who told her to bring it on.

She accepted her uncle's company when she went to the Seattle field office Thursday afternoon. He needed to talk to some people there, and she let him do the driving, content to relax on her way to work.

Work. Her real job.

She hadn't been by to see the Code Blue crew and she needed to. But she didn't want to say goodbye yet, and she didn't know why. She didn't get overly emotional about departures, as change and moving on was a way of life.

But she'd miss Rapp, Gina, and Diego. *And that's okay.*

Jane found it difficult to allow herself feelings sometimes. But she already felt vulnerable due to her concussion. So she cut herself some slack.

Before they entered the lobby, she pulled her uncle aside. "You tell no one we're family." Too many higherups had heard about the legendary Chris North. She didn't want his infamy affecting her relationships at her job.

Bad enough Matthew Stone knew about it. Jon Haversham too. But she didn't think they'd say anything. It wasn't like Jane worked in covert operations or undercover.

"I swear. Nag, nag, nag." He grinned, his eyes crinkling. "Go be a boss and text me when you're done." He slid away like a shadow. Quiet and unassuming.

She took the stairs, needing to get back into fighting shape a little at a time. She wore jeans and a plain navy tee since nothing else would fit over her bulky cast. She'd been secretly amused, and even touched, to see everyone's comments. Some more than others.

Gina's *Air Force #1* still made her chuckle.

When she entered the office, her squad looked delighted to see her. Everyone crowded her and laughed at her pink cast, especially when she told them her cousin had a sick sense of humor. Catching up felt good, like coming home. And she appreciated how much she'd missed this.

Matthew Scott stepped out of his office and gifted Jane with a genuine smile that made him look almost human, less model-FBI man.

"Jane. Welcome back."

"Thank you, sir."

"Everyone already knows, but you're officially back to work, completely reinstated, just as soon as you're medically sound. OPR cleared you of everything."

The room erupted in cheers.

"Please, come into my office."

She promised the gang she wouldn't leave right away after her meeting with the boss and sat across from him at his desk.

"First, I'm sincerely sorry for how this all happened. Your suspension, Dan Simmons, and Rob and Jenn." He rubbed his eyes, and she was taken back to the image of him in his house, rubbing his face in exhaustion, disheartened at the thought of any of his people being suspect.

"I understand."

"Do you? When Jon and I talked about it, our actions made sense. We really did have an email with those odd messages from Dan Simmons implicating you. We've since learned Rob Williams planted it. You were getting too close to his business with the Mazzucas."

She'd wondered about that. "What else has Williams shared? Did he kill Dan?"

"Yes. Shot him at the warehouse the night Dan went missing. He never liked Dan to begin with, and when he learned about Dan's undercover role in undermining the Mazzucas, he alerted the organization. They disappeared when Rob took over the surveillance unit, yet he made it so we couldn't be sure what happened. Arranged it to seem like we'd had a technical issue with files missing and a lack of reporting. It's still a huge mess."

"You look tired." She hadn't meant to say that out loud, but she felt a little bad for him.

He gave a surprised laugh. "You know, I think I've missed you, Jane. You're always honest. Sometimes to a fault."

She flushed.

He smiled kindly. "You look much better. Does your arm still hurt?"

"Not so much. I should be fully healed in another month and a half. It was a slight radial fracture. My head is the problem, but I should be fine soon. I'd like to come back next week and start catching up on my caseload."

"A good idea. As long as medical okays it."

She nodded. "What happens to Williams now?" He'd never, ever, be "Rob" to her.

"He's in custody. I don't think he'll tell us much we don't already know. His loyalty to the Mazzucas remains firm. I think we'll have a tough time turning him."

She agreed.

"On a good note, Jenn Sullivan is doing better. It'll be a while before she's back, but she sounds as eager as you do to return to work."

"She's a great agent. She was pretty strong against Williams."

Scott nodded. "I've read the report you gave. Would you mind going through it again with me?"

She explained all that had happened, including her cousin's part in being there as back up. Fortunately, Junior really had been killed by his companion. Jane had no need to hide any bodies or lie about Raine's involvement.

"This all wraps up then." Scott folded his hands atop his desk. Graceful yet masculine. She wasn't sure if she'd liked him better when he was a total tool or now. "I appreciate your candor. I'm glad to have you back."

"Thanks. I'm glad to be back." She paused.

"Yes?"

She stared into his blue eyes, reminded of the hassle he'd been before she'd left. "If you want the office to function like a team, stop making us hate you."

He blinked. "Come again?"

"I don't mean we hate you. But we hate all the micromanaging. You either trust us or you don't. The mole is gone now. Williams is toast. But the rest of us take pride in our jobs and want to protect our citizens and our country. Trust us to do that without a bazillion meetings every day. It gets in the way of our work."

Perhaps Jane shouldn't have said all that. But it had needed to be said.

He nodded, solemn but also possibly amused. "Again, I appreciate your honesty."

"Yeah, well." She stood and held out her good hand. "No hard feelings."

He stood to shake her hand, the contact affirming. His smile faded. "I won't take all your hard work for granted, Agent Cannon."

The scent of his cologne wrapped around her fuzzy head. She gently tugged her hand back. "I guess I'll head out. But I'll be back next week. Tuesday morning okay?" She had some medical appointments Monday.

"Perfect."

She was at the door when he added, "One more thing."

"Sir?" Jane turned around to see him holding a marker.

"Don't I get to sign the cast?"

CHAPTER FIFTY-TWO

Friday afternoon, Jane entered the task force's office, aware this might be her last time swinging by.

Boxes lay all over the place, files being stacked neatly by Gina and Diego while Rapp carried equipment from one room to another.

"Hey, Jane." Diego saw her and hustled over.

She allowed him a hug and nodded to Gina, who joined them.

Rapp came over as well and declared a late lunch for everyone, on him, now that the team was all together.

They celebrated closing the case by ordering in some amazing pizza and local root beers Jane made a note to remember.

"So what's next for everyone?" she asked. "I'll be heading back to the field office next week."

Diego answered, "I've been assigned to a special task force on cybercrime in Denver for a little bit. It was either that or Atlanta, and I'm not into all that heat."

Gina grinned. "And there's the fact that Colorado's fine with the legalization of a certain substance…"

"There is that." Diego enthusiastically bit into another slice of pizza.

"What about you, Gina?" Rapp asked. "Made up your mind?"

"I'm sticking around in Seattle." She shot Jane a look, as if Jane might object.

"Good for you. Seattle's great."

Gina nodded. "I'm settling in. The Agency has an opening I'm eager to join. I think I can bring a lot to the team."

Jane realized they had a spot open in her squad since Rob Williams was gone. "Who are you going to be working with, do you know?"

"Monica Pearson, I believe. I met with her a few days ago. She seems solid. Plus, I'm happy to get back to cybercrimes."

Rapp said, "Tired of violent crimes already?"

"Aren't you?" Gina shot back. "I hear you're heading back into the field. Are you working national security or partnering with another agency?"

"Something like that."

"The mysterious Agent Rapp," Gina said. "I'll drink to that."

They clinked bottles. Chatter turned to Gina's sister, who lived in Kirkland and was planning to get married come summer. To Diego's planned ski trip with some "bros" he met gaming online that he planned to hook up with in Denver. Rapp remained quiet, content to listen.

"What about you, Jane?" Gina asked. "What do you do for fun when you're not catching killers?"

Jane did her best not to squirm in her seat. "I like reading. And my cousin's back in town. To stay, I think. So that will be interesting."

"Is she anything like you?" Diego asked and wiggled his brows, prompting a laugh out of her.

"No. She's a hothead who speaks before she thinks." True but not exactly kind. "But she'd give me the shirt off her back if I needed it. And she's smart. Sometimes too smart for her own good."

Rapp chuckled. "Sounds like my brothers."

"How many do you have?" Gina asked.

Jane still suspected Gina had a crush on him, but she didn't show anything but polite interest while waiting for his answer.

"Three brothers. Two are twins." He made a face. "The oldest is a doctor. Talk about too smart for his own good." He grinned, sincere appreciation in his smile. "Then there's me, the perfect son."

Diego snorted and Jane choked on her soda, which made Gina laugh.

"And the youngest, the twins, both cops. We're supposed to have some big family reunion this summer if I'm in town. Not sure I will be."

"They live here?" Diego asked.

"In Oregon, actually. I'm the renegade for moving around so much. The rest of them live in Central Oregon."

"My uncle has property out there," Jane mentioned.

Discussion then moved to popular spots in Oregon.

The conversation felt nice, Jane realized. Being around other people—these people—felt like snuggling under a warm blanket on a cold, wet day.

She'd miss them when they broke up. But all good things had to come to an end, she supposed.

Jane stood. "Well, guys. I guess this is goodbye to you two." She glanced at Rapp and Diego. To Gina, she held out a hand. "See you around."

Gina shook it, squeezing hard once before letting go. "Not if I see you first."

"Ha. Nice one." Diego fished an energy drink out of the refrigerator and came back to ask Gina a few questions about Denver, since she'd been through not too long ago.

Jane walked to the exit, feeling a literal sense of closing the door behind her before moving on to bigger and better things.

Rapp stopped her with a hand on her shoulder, his expression blank as he listened to whoever was on the other end of his cellphone.

She felt his tension. "Rapp?"

"On our way." He tucked his phone into his pocket. "Jane, there's something we need to see." He added to the others, "I'll be back in a few. Don't drink all the root beers. I'm talking to you, Diego."

"Hey, man. Gina's doing it too!"

Then Rapp tugged Jane out the door, a sense of urgency in his step.

"What's wrong?" Jane didn't fight him, just followed his frantic steps to his vehicle.

"They found Phillip's body."

"Finally dug him out of all that debris from the hospital, eh?" Jane had figured they would have combed through the mess sooner, but apparently Phillip's bombs had done real structural damage to the building because of where he'd placed them. Plus, he'd used some extra special compound to make a bigger boom.

Hondo had been impressed while looking over the devices as a courtesy to Gambol.

In any case, it felt good to put the final piece of the case to rest. With a new case file started on the Kaminskis, they were on the way to cleaning up the chaos left in Phillip's wake.

"No, they didn't find him at the hospital." Rapp got into his SUV.

Jane buckled up as Rapp turned them around and jammed his foot on the accelerator. "What do you mean? Phillip didn't die in the bombing?"

"No. He left a note for you, Jane." After a pause, Rapp glanced at her and added, "And he's not the only body they found."

CHAPTER FIFTY-THREE

To Jane's surprise, they arrived at the warehouse where Dan Simmons had made his last official appearance before being murdered.

Flashing lights strobed across the building's wall and crime scene tape draped around the warehouse and adjacent building on the dock.

"Seriously? They found the bodies here?"

"What's the significance?" Rapp raised the yellow tape and flashed a badge at the officer standing close by while he and Jane ducked under it.

"This is where we were surveilling the Mazzucas." She looked over her shoulder at the apartments on the other side of the street. "We set up back there, fifth floor. We couldn't see too much, but we kept track of comings and goings. Until, of course, the few days prior to Dan going missing. The Mazzucas just up and left with no witnesses."

They walked into the center of the dock to find it empty.

"Over here," one of the detectives said when she spotted them. Jane recognized her as the same woman who'd interrogated Harding with Gina a few weeks ago and found it curious the detective would be so far away from her precinct. "How's Gina doing?"

"Better now that I'm out of her hair," Jane confided.

The detective grinned but said nothing else.

They entered the large warehouse space and stopped.

In the middle of the cement floor, a dozen dead bodies lay sprawled in a large circle, each covered in blood. Leo Mazzuca especially. He'd been shot in each eye, his sockets dark, heralding a hard death.

And in the middle of the circle, Phillip lay flat on his back, smiling at the ceiling. He stared, unseeing, a blanket of blood pooling under his head and neck from a bullet wound at his temple.

Flat on his belly lay an envelope.

Jane and Rapp stood back while the forensic team did its job, but to Jane, it was clear Phillip had arrived to clean up a mess. His mess or someone else's?

"Why?" she mused aloud. "He was presumed dead. He could have used the time before we found out he hadn't died at the hospital to get away clean. Make a new life for himself."

"Maybe that voice that told him what to do insisted he stay." Rapp crossed his arms over his chest as they watched. "I'm glad we found him, but not like this. He was messed up, no question. But he started the ball rolling on fixing corruption in the Agency."

The media had been all over the incident at the hospital, as well as the Code Blue Killer. Fortunately, or unfortunately, depending on one's perspective, the FBI's internal problems hadn't come to light with the press, though questions were being asked.

On the one hand, Jane wanted the rot exposed so it couldn't grow back. On the other hand, she didn't like the idea of the public losing faith and trust in an organization that genuinely helped people. Either way, Jane had never been so happy *not* to be in public relations.

However, the news reports also thought Code Blue had killed himself in the bombs he'd set. Because that's the message Phillip had left them.

One of the forensic team walked over to Jane and Rapp. He had gloves on and held the envelope that had been sitting on Phillip.

"Jane Cannon? This is for you. You can look at it over there." He nodded to a table, beside which more tech and lab equipment had been staged.

She headed over with Rapp, careful to stay clear of everyone still processing the scene. It would take months to get everything back from Quantico.

After donning the gloves one of the techs handed her, she opened the flap of the envelope and pulled out a handwritten letter.

In black ink, Phillip had written the following, which Jane read out loud, "I only ever wanted to help. And so I end my life by helping one final time. These were not good people, Jane. Not like your Agent Rapp, Agent Holtz, and Diego Rivera. And you, Jane. You stand for honesty and integrity. I'm glad we're on the same side."

"Not quite," Rapp murmured, reading over her shoulder.

Jane continued. "I know what I said before. But I've changed my mind. You *can* stop what's coming. There's *always* too much at stake... but you can win when you have the courage and commitment of brave soldiers and Marines to win the war." Jane paused and glanced at Rapp. "War? What war?"

"Maybe the war on crime. Or the war on violence. I'm curious about how he knew to come here. Did he bring everyone with him? How did he convince them to meet him here? Or did he maybe kill them elsewhere and stage this scene?"

A nearby detective overheard and commented, "No. He shot them here. We got a call an hour ago about shots fired. But we were dealing with some crazy who lit himself on fire down near the market. By the time we got here, everything was silent and locked up tight. When we got in, we found it like this."

Jane frowned. "How did Phillip know about our investigation?"

"My bet is Rob Williams let it slip at some point, and Phillip, acting like the arm of justice, decided to make peace with the way he went out. We'll know more when all this is processed, I'm sure."

As she and Rapp drove away, she asked him, "Will we know more? The task force is done."

"Gambol will likely assign the cleanup files to someone in Seattle. Maybe even you."

"If I'm unlucky."

They both smiled.

"Do you think this is done then?" Jane couldn't have said why, but she felt as if they had left something unfinished. And it bothered her.

"I hope so. It's done for me at least. I'm reinstated and back with my unit."

"I don't suppose you'll tell me what you got suspended for."

Rapp looked serious when he answered, "I could, but then I'd have to kill you."

She just stared back at him. "Like I haven't heard that *a million* times before." A favorite tease Hal, her family—all of them, including Raine—continued to use on a daily basis.

He chuckled. "But it's true. Suffice it to say the guilty has been found out. I'm clean and mean and ready to—"

"Just stop. Please. Keep your black ops-ness to yourself."

"Ha. You know, there's nothing stopping you from joining Team Ten. I guarantee your uncle would be giddy to have you."

"Not for me. I'm more a rules kind of gal. Besides, I like my job."

He nodded. "And you're good at it, even if you do bristle overmuch with authority."

"I do not."

"Case in point."

Jane huffed. "Whatever, Rapp."

He grinned but didn't answer.

They drove back to the office in contented, and complete, silence.

CHAPTER FIFTY-FOUR

Friday morning after a lovely, quiet Thursday night spent *alone* in her apartment, trying not to dwell on Phillip Keiser's final words, Jane took the ferry back to Bainbridge Island.

She had promised to spend the weekend with family at the ranch, and she was way overdue for a visit with Jenn Sullivan.

Fortunately, Jenn had only stayed a few days in the hospital before being released into her aunt's care. Like Jane, Jenn had spent her time sleeping and recovering. Now, it sounded as if she'd turned into a huge pain in the butt.

At the door, Jane was met by an older version of Jenn. It still felt odd to think of Sullivan as a *Jenn*, but Jane was starting to get used to it. The more she used it, the more natural it would become.

"How wonderful. You must be Jane. Jenn's been talking about you." The older woman yanked Jane in for a hug. "You saved her life. Thank you so much." She pulled back, tears in her eyes.

Jane felt awkward. "Yeah, well. It seemed like the thing to do."

The woman laughed and wiped her eyes. "Oh, and I'm Susan. Come on in." Susan closed and locked the door. "Jenn's in the far room in the back. I'll be there in a minute. I've just got some cookies in the oven."

"I came at the perfect time then." Jane smiled, immediately thinking back to Lena Keiser, who would never bake another batch again, and Maria Lito.

For all that Phillip had done bad things in search of righting a great wrong, he'd lost so much more than his way. From all accounts, the Keisers had been admirable people who helped many. The loss from their passing, along with Phillip and his victims, would be felt for a very long time.

She found Jenn's room easily enough, with sunlight streaming through the blinds, flowers everywhere, and a large sleigh bed with a scowling woman in the center of it. Jenn's hair stood on end, and her robe looked soft but threadbare in spots.

"Dressed up just for me, eh?" Jane asked with a smile.

"Screw you. Took you long enough to come visit." The smile that blossomed on Jenn's face made the bright room even brighter. "So what's the scoop?"

"I'll tell you, but first, what's with the garden in here?"

Jenn blushed. "Turns out Dash is a terrific guy after all. He keeps saying I saved him. I didn't."

"I think you did. You kept a cool head and Rob's attention on you and not him. I also read in the report that you talked him and his mob guys out of killing Dash outright. Not sure how you did it, but kudos."

"Thanks." Jenn's smile faded. "I still can't believe Rob was selling out. It hurts, you know?" She patted her chest. "You think you know someone. But I guess you don't."

Jane sighed and sat on the edge of her bed. "I know. I don't know how I never saw it. I'm usually a pretty good judge of people." The knowledge Williams had been guilty and right in front of her would bother her for a very long time.

She'd suspected something wasn't right with the Mazzuca investigation for a while. Perhaps if Williams hadn't set her up to get suspended, she'd have figured him out. She hoped.

"Are you feeling okay?" Jenn asked.

"I should be asking you that."

"Oh, I'm good. They sewed up all the holes, so I'm told. The angle of the wound was such that it went through fatty tissue and lodged in my hip. It did bleed a lot, and it hurts, but I'm thankful every day he didn't shoot me in the stomach." She nodded to a bullet on her side table. "That's the little bugger they dug out."

Jane stared, aware Jenn's life could have turned in a much different direction. "Do you think Williams pulled his shot? Or that you just got lucky."

Jenn teared up. "I'd like to think both."

"Oy. Don't cry. Your aunt will kick me out for disturbing you. And I'm really here for the cookies."

Jenn laughed and wiped her eyes. "So what's the scoop? And hey, I didn't get to sign the cast!" she added as Jane pulled out of her jacket, feeling overly warm. "Pink. Really? Although with all that writing, it's more like pink and black and blue. And green? Who used a green marker?"

"My idiot cousin." Jane smiled as she said it, pride in her family and herself filling her with joy. "We got the bad guys in the end on this one. And don't tell anyone, but I don't think Matthew Scott is as bad as we thought." Jane filled Jenn in on her conversation with their boss and on all she'd learned about the case. Including the death of the rest of the Mazzucas.

"Wow. Code Blue cleaned up one case for us, didn't he?" She groaned as she tried to sit up.

"Cookies," Aunt Susan announced and scowled at Jenn. "Hey. Quit moving around so much."

"That's what I told her," Jane said, sucking up so she got first dibs on the sweets. "Thank you."

"Anytime, honey. And you can call me Aunt Susan."

"Will do." Jane smiled, at ease being the good kid, the good agent. But not always the good friend. She eyeballed Jenn. "You know, Aunt Susan, Jenn is lucky to have you. She always talks about you."

She did, though Jane had rarely paid attention. Now, she'd do better. Or at least she'd try.

Jenn beamed. "Oh my gosh. You're really using my name. I'm overjoyed."

"Shut up."

Aunt Susan bit back a grin. "I'll leave you two alone. I have some more baking to do."

Jenn groaned as she inhaled the cookies and nibbled on one. "I can't help myself around these."

"Ah, should you be eating that?"

"Shot in the hip, I said. I'm good." Jenn held onto the cookie as if Jane meant to steal it. "You know she bakes for Swan's Bakery."

"These are the cookies from that place in Lynwood Center?" Jane took another off the plate. "Geez. I need to stop by more often."

They laughed and chatted, less about work and more about Jenn's boyfriend and Jane's kooky family. So many cousins and uncles and friends that meant so much to her.

At one point, she glanced down at her cast and read what Matthew Scott had written. *Welcome back.* And then Rapp's scrawl: *Don't worry. I'll be back to work WITH you soon enough.*

"Hey, me too," Jenn had grabbed a pen and motioned for Jane to come closer.

"You need a marker."

Jenn signed in purple. *Thanks, Life Saver. JENN.*

"Come on."

"Have I told you how much I love how you turn pink when you're embarrassed? I can't wait to get back to the office to tell everyone how you saved my life and broke Rob in three places."

"Well, that part was satisfying." Jane doubted she'd ever look at the people she worked with the same way again. Maintaining trust was such a delicate balance.

"Did you ever doubt me?" Jenn asked.

"Maybe for a minute."

Jenn perked up. "Because I'm sly and totally able to con people?"

"Because you and Williams both came from Vegas and knew Haversham."

"Who was innocent." Jenn shook her head. "Jane Cannon, Superstar FBI Agent? Ha."

"Fine. You got me there."

The rest of the morning passed with more laughs than Jane had expected.

And it was nice.

* * *

TUESDAY MORNING, when she returned to work, she wore a smile as she sipped a latte and got back to her cases needing attention. The files had been covered by the team as best they could, but they were all slammed with work that never stopped accumulating. When one criminal went to jail, another took his place.

But that was part of the thrill in her work, a constant challenge that would never grow boring. And Jane knew she made a difference.

Hours later, a text from Gambol interrupted her. *Great work. Thank you. Bonus from Uncle Sam. Check's in the mail.*

Jane snorted and muttered to herself, "Check's in the mail. Yeah, right." To Gambol, she sent, *Happy to help.*

Her phone chimed again. *You impressed Gunther. Not an easy thing to do. Do you mind if I call you again sometime? I might have more work for you if you're available.*

Available? Jane had nothing but time to help clean up the riffraff trying to turn her city—her country—into chaos.

Anytime, she texted him.

Then she got back to work.

* * *

The story continues in Collateral. Keep reading for a sneak peek of book 2 in the Jane Cannon Series.

Join the LT Ryan reader family & receive a free copy of the Rachel Hatch story, *Fractured.* Click the link below to get started: https://ltryan.com/rachel-hatch-newsletter-signup-1

COLLATERAL: CHAPTER ONE

An urgent manhunt through Seattle's Capitol Hill in the summer heat hadn't been on FBI Special Agent Jane Cannon's bingo card, but never let it be said she couldn't adapt. "It's all about timing."

"No kidding," fellow Agent Jenn Sullivan replied from the driver's seat of the vehicle. "Four banks in three months? How are these guys getting away with it? They're not that organized or skilled. Just lucky."

"Sometimes luck is all you need," Jane said just as the SUV they'd been looking for popped up in front of them.

"You're a little freaky, you know that?"

Jane grinned and radioed in the suspects' location.

The trio of bank robbers had hit a small bank and fled with the police on their tail. The suspects avoided the cops thanks to traffic then disappeared in the city. Only to pop up in front of Jane and Jenn, who'd been out on another case when they'd gotten the call about a robbery in progress.

Unfortunately, their current location, in a residential neighborhood near Volunteer Park, didn't bode well.

"I don't like finding them out here," Jenn said as they flashed lights and gunned it after the SUV.

"Keep tight on them."

"No, I think I'll hang back so they can get away," Jenn drawled, full of the sarcasm that made her one of Jane's favorite coworkers...and friends.

Jane still didn't know how to feel about getting so chummy with her peers. She liked a certain formality at work, especially after one of her last coworkers had nearly killed her. Then again, the ex-agent had nearly killed Jenn as well, so they had that trauma to bond them.

Studying the way the SUV kept speeding up and slowing down around traffic, Jane said, "He's going to stop and let them out."

"No way, they're—Well, damn. You're right."

"Stop the car," Jane ordered, already unbuckling her seatbelt.

"Jane, wait!"

The car had barely halted before Jane was out, chasing after one of the suspects while the other darted in the opposite direction. The one she followed, according to reports, had shot and wounded a police officer during his escape.

Yep. Caucasian, short brown hair, dark-blue tee-shirt, crossed pistol tattoos on right arm, jeans, scuffed Nikes. *Got him.*

"FBI. Stop!"

He peered over his shoulder as he ran, saw her, swore, and ran faster.

Toward Volunteer Park.

The lovely weather beckoned people outdoors, and the park would be full of families and children hoping to indulge in the playground, botanical garden, and art museum.

Jane ran faster and heard the squeal of tires. Probably Jen chasing the SUV. Jenn would also call for back up to nail the other suspect who'd escaped on foot.

Now Jane could only hope the idiots would be more caught up in escaping than in taking a hostage.

Jane was literally in *hot* pursuit. Today's temperatures made it one of the warmest days on record for June.

Though known for their cool, wet days and grand vistas of Mt. Rainier, Seattle could get unreasonably humid in the summer, especially in the middle of June, turning everything hazy while the city sweltered.

Despite sweating under her collared tee-shirt and cargo pants, Jane indulged in the thrill of the hunt, picking up speed.

The suspect looked over his shoulder, saw her, and tried to run faster.

But Jane ran daily not only to keep in shape, but because she liked it. And she was *fast*. Like a deer, according to her family. None of them could keep up with her.

This guy, while close to her age, didn't seem like a marathoner. The jerk was flagging.

She ran through the trails, cutting across grass and weaving in and out of people before heading back onto a path full of runners. People stopped and stared, pointing. She saw a few take out their phones to record.

Her focus narrowed on the dirtbag who thought it okay to target small banks, hurt the people working there for fun, and attack LEOs —law enforcement officers—who arrived to arrest them.

To date, this particular trio of thieves had shot two police officers and wounded civilians while stealing from four banks.

Jane's anger fueled her. She'd nearly caught up to her suspect when he veered toward a group of children. The young woman with them froze in fear while the children stared, wide-eyed, unsure how to react. One screamed.

"Get out of the way," she yelled, put on a burst of speed, and launched herself at the suspect, catching him at the knees.

He fell, and they rolled together in a tangle of limbs.

The woman with the children recovered to run to safety with her charges, along with a couple of other onlookers.

The suspect rose to his feet, panting. "Back off, pig."

"FBI, you're under arrest." She gulped air as she stood and tapped the badge visible on her belt.

He struck out, landing a lucky blow on her shoulder. Though it hurt, his proximity allowed her to grab his arm, jack up his elbow, and twist him into a wrist lock.

He had weight on her and height, but she had tactical advantage.

She'd been battling men twice her size for over a decade, and she knew how to fight dirty.

Before he could punch her again, she doubled down on the wrist lock and had him shrieking in pain. He bent low under the pressure.

One hard knee to his face laid him out flat, blood dripping from a broken nose.

In seconds, she had him on his belly, groaning, his hands behind him as she cuffed him. A pat-down proved him unarmed.

She read him his Miranda rights while people clapped in the background.

As she came back to herself, her adrenaline racing, she hoped she hadn't looked as if she *enjoyed* using brute force to take him down. Or that the crack of his nose and subsequent gushing of blood satisfied that urge in her to seek vengeance for the good people he'd hurt.

Because FBI Agent Jane Cannon was no vigilante, and she shouldn't—*didn't*—take pleasure in causing others pain.

Normally, she wouldn't. Jane believed in justice, in law and order.

But she also believed that the guilty deserved to be punished. And this creep had intended to take *children* hostage.

The sweat dripped down her face, and her clothes stuck to her, the oppressive summer sun baking her.

A glance at the nearby kids, staring with excitement, assured her of their safety, and she started to relax, satisfied that she'd been a hundred percent in the right.

Fulfilling her duty to protect and serve.

The suspect under her unleashed a string of profanity, which had those children's eyes growing wide.

But protecting and serving didn't mean she had to color inside the lines all the time.

Jane leaned down and whispered, "One more word out of you, and I'll *accidentally* snap your wrists. Both of them. Try defending yourself in prison without the use of your hands." She wouldn't have. But he didn't know that.

That shut him up fast, and he lay motionless until the police arrived to take him into custody.

She gladly gave him up. "How's the officer who got shot? Do you know?" she asked the nearest cop as she wiped her face with her short sleeve.

"Doing okay last I heard." The officer grunted. "Nice takedown."

"Thanks." She nodded at him. "He's unarmed. Ditched his weapon earlier in the chase."

"I heard. We got him now." The cop escorted the suspect with another officer away from the crowd. "Let's go, buddy. This is not your lucky day."

And speaking of lucky… Jane hurriedly dialed Jenn. "I got our perp. Did they find the other suspect who ran?"

"And hello to you, too. Not that I know of, but we did get the driver."

"Good. Can you pick me up at the museum? I'm at Volunteer Park." The spot was a short walk away and bound to be air conditioned.

"Sure. Be there in twenty."

Jane disconnected, but before she could make her way to the museum, a little girl approached.

She wore shorts and a tank top, her dark curls balancing oversized pink sunglasses atop her head. The little girl held an unopened bottle of water and couldn't have been more than seven or eight. "Excuse me."

"Yes?"

"Did you catch the bad guy?"

"I did."

"Wow. That's cool. Are you a police officer?"

"FBI."

"This is for you." The girl handed Jane the water, and Jane thanked her, too hot and tired to reject it. She drank down every drop.

Before she could thank the kid again and leave, the girls' friends surrounded Jane, along with several people in the park now brave enough to approach.

Jane spent an eternity waiting for Jenn, deflecting questions about her ongoing investigation into the bank robbers while answering questions about the FBI and performing what her boss liked to call "community outreach."

Jane considered it a worthwhile endeavor. For someone *else.* Someone who liked dealing with masses of people.

Sometime later, Jenn smirked as she drove them back to the field office. "So, what was that all about? You being all social and friendly with Seattle's citizens. You feeling okay?"

"Just doing my job, ma'am." Jane would rather face another armed suspect than deal with the public.

Unfortunately, Jenn knew that and mocked her all the way back to the office.

But at least they'd caught two of the suspects. Now to find that last one before he hurt someone else.

COLLATERAL: CHAPTER TWO

JANE SPENT THE NEXT MORNING CRUISING 3RD STREET, A FEW BLOCKS inland from the ferry. The area was one of several seeing a bad surge of fentanyl cases. It also happened to be a purported hangout for the last of the Trinity Bank Robbers—a stupid name, but some reporter had dubbed them as such due to having three members.

Their suspect turned out to be a lot smarter than Jane gave him credit for, considering his partners had turned on each other the moment they'd been questioned. Eric Garcia and George Mancini were done. But Doug Lewis, according to his now ex-girlfriend, had left her behind to visit a relative in California.

A few dash cams supported her story, and they had him on I-5 heading south.

That he'd left the city so soon after the robbery and had thus far evaded the police told Jane they were dealing with a smarter than average criminal. His friends identified Doug as a twenty-seven-year-old wannabe law school student.

The co-conspirators had told the police everything they knew, which turned out to be quite a lot. Doug had engineered all the planning. Eric provided the car and knowledge of the city streets, and

George cozied up to the pretty, single bank tellers for inside information on their targets.

Both men in custody faced major jail time and couldn't afford decent attorneys. Doug promised to be another story. His background interested her. She also suspected he *wouldn't* be heading to California. Not after his careful evasive measures.

She drove into South Lake Union where she'd arranged to speak with his aunt. The woman met her in the vestibule of her unassuming apartment building, surrounded by other unassuming apartment buildings, then walked up the stairs to her equally unassuming flat.

"I don't have a lot of time before my shift starts, but I've got a pot of coffee still going. Would you like some?" Linda Lewis waved Jane into a tidy, fresh smelling space. A bouquet of flowers sat in the middle of a two-person kitchen table.

Everything in the home had been scaled for a small space, so it didn't feel overwhelming. And the bright colors gave the place an air of repressed energy. The décor seemed a mix of IKEA and thrift store, but the overall effect was charming.

A lot like Linda Lewis. The older woman had laugh lines around her eyes and mouth, bright blue eyes, and dark hair threaded with gray. Attractive, softening around the middle, and at first impression, kind.

"No coffee, thank you, Ms. Lewis. I have a cup in the car waiting on me."

"Please, call me Linda."

Jane followed Linda into the living room, sat on the couch the woman pointed to, and whipped out a small notepad and pen. "I'm here about your nephew."

Linda sighed. "Timmy or Danny?"

"Doug."

Linda blinked. "Dougie? He's normally the one I *don't* have to worry about."

The woman was in for a rude awakening. "Unfortunately, Doug has been linked to some serious crimes."

"My Dougie? Doug Lewis?" Linda left her seat and returned with a photo of their suspect.

Jane nodded.

Linda sat, flabbergasted. "But that boy's been on the straight and narrow since elementary school. He graduated high school then college at the top of his class and got a job as a paralegal for a law firm while he's saving for law school. He's such a smart young man. You must have the wrong person. What's he supposed to have done?"

Jane already had information on their suspect from his partners. Doug Lewis had a mother, father deceased, and two aunts. He had lived with his Aunt Linda until he graduated from Edmonds Community College.

"Bank robbery."

"No. No way." Linda shook her head, emphatically. "He's on the right side of the law, Agent Cannon."

"What can you tell me about Eric Garcia and George Mancini?"

What little outrage left in Linda deflated. "Oh, well. That explains it."

"Explains what?"

"Those boys have been nothing but trouble for years. Always getting into one scrap or another, and my nephew would bail them out. I've been raising him since he turned thirteen and his mother disappeared. Sad to say my younger sister has been addicted to one thing or another forever. I was glad when she left because I was finally able to give Dougie some stability."

Jane nodded and made a few notes. "Your first thought was that your other nephews, Timmy or Danny, might have done something. Why's that?"

"My older sister's boys have been in trouble for one thing or another the past few years. But I thought they'd straightened out."

"By trouble, you mean...?"

"Minor stuff like bar fights and being stupid in public."

"Drunk and disorderly?" Jane offered.

Linda shrugged. "Just boys being boys, mostly. Nothing violent, though they did break a window at a convenience store that took them forever to pay off. But bank robbery? No. I don't believe they'd get that bad or that Dougie could possibly be involved." Linda's lips firmed. "But Eric and George? I'd believe it of them."

"Why's that?"

"Those two are cousins who come from a family that does a lot of questionable things. Like stealing to feed their drug habit. I tried to get Dougie to stop hanging around with them, but he promised he was keeping them out of trouble. Even when Eric got busted for selling pot in high school, Dougie did his best to support him." Linda wiped a stray tear from her cheek. "He's such a good boy."

A good boy who'd been robbing banks and getting away with it. Jane had a feeling Dougie only showed his aunt what she wanted to see.

"Where does Dougie live now?"

"He used to live in an apartment a few blocks from here. But he moved a month ago, and I don't have his new address yet. I think he and Eric and George were living together in some temporary place. Rent being what it is, it only makes sense for him to have roommates. Law school isn't cheap, and he's been doing his best to save."

Linda waxed on about all of Doug's glowing traits. A nice young man. Good-looking, smart, a hard worker. He always brought her flowers and checked in to make sure she had everything she needed. From what Linda gathered, Doug was close to going to law school full-time.

"Thank you for your time, Linda. I'm sorry to be the bearer of bad news. But if you hear from Doug, please tell him to call me. If he is in this mess thanks to his friends, he can only help himself by talking to me to get him out of trouble." She stood and handed Linda a card.

Linda nodded and stood with her. "I will. You'll see. My boy had nothing to do with this. He's probably helping them by trying to get them out of trouble. If I hear from him, I'll tell him to call you."

"Thank you. We want guilty people to go to jail, not innocents. And it seems like it's time for Eric and George to stop dragging Doug down."

"Yes, yes. Exactly. I'll call him and tell him to call you right away."

"Good. I don't want the police to think he's dangerous if he isn't."

Linda paused on the stairs outside her apartment. "Dangerous?"

Jane nodded, her expression grim as she met Linda's eyes. "Eric shot and wounded several police officers in the course of their robberies. He and George are in big trouble."

Linda paled. "Oh my God. I hadn't realized. I'll call him right away and let you know what he says."

Jane didn't hold out hope that Doug would comply, but she thanked Linda again and left.

After following up on a few places Eric and George thought Doug might go, she was just leaving a food truck area when a woman approached, staring at Jane in shock.

"*Olivia?*"

Jane frowned. "Excuse me?"

The older woman, likely in her fifties, scrutinized Jane from top to bottom. "Is it really you?"

Ah, a case of mistaken identity. "I'm sorry. I'm not Olivia."

All hope faded from the woman's eyes. To Jane's shock, she dropped to her knees and sobbed. Then passed out.

COLLATERAL: CHAPTER THREE

A COUPLE OF PASSERSBY HELPED JANE GET THE WOMAN TO A NEARBY bench, then scattered. Jane stuck close. After a few minutes, the fainter revived enough to wave off the need for an ambulance.

"I'm sorry. It's been a long day, and I'm tired." Dressed in a shabby tee-shirt and threadbare jeans, she did look exhausted. Limp hair hung around her face like a faded yellow curtain, and her eyes filled with a despair that made Jane pay attention.

"My name's Jane. You're looking for Olivia?"

"Yes. Do you know her?"

It hurt to have to say no. "I'm sorry, but I don't."

The woman sighed. "I didn't think so. But I'm always out here, trying. Olivia's my daughter. She went missing two years ago, and I've been searching for her ever since."

"I take it she looks like me?" Jane sat next to her and thanked a nearby food cart employee for the bottle of water he handed to the older woman. "What's your name, ma'am?"

"Oh, sorry. I'm Andrea. Andrea Wilson. Olivia Wilson, my daughter, went missing when she was twenty-two. A day after her birthday." Tears spilled from Andrea's eyes. "I miss her every day."

Jane felt awful for the poor woman, but when she glanced up and saw the food cart employee, the younger guy rolled his eyes before walking away.

"Did you report her missing to the police?"

Andrea nodded. "Right away. But she had a habit of sometimes leaving, and she'd gotten into drugs. Nothing serious, but the police didn't see it that way. Except Olivia never came home. And that's not like her. At all." She paused and added softly, "From the back, you look just like her. But you're probably a few years older. She'd be twenty-four now."

Jane was a good thirty-one, though she had often been told she appeared younger. Olivia's mother wore desperation like a tattered cloak, so it was no surprise the woman would zero in on anyone who resembled her daughter.

Jane didn't want to give her false hope, but she also wanted to help. "I tell you what, Andrea. I'll ask around and see what I can dig up. And I'll tell my friends too. Would you mind giving me your number so I can let you know if I find anything?"

"Oh, thank you." Andrea fished out a crumpled tissue from her pocket and blew her nose. Then she gave Jane her number. "I'm so sorry for passing out on you. But for a minute, I could have sworn you were her."

"I understand." Jane helped steady her when Andrea stood. "Are you sure you're okay? Is there someone you can call to help you get home?"

"Oh, no. Again, I'm just tired and grieving. But I need to get back before my youngest gets home from school."

Jane didn't point out that most children didn't attend school in the summer, or that Andrea looked more like a grandmother than any toddler or teen's mother.

"She goes to an art program in the summer," Andrea said with a watery smile. "So talented. Just like her big sister. I'm sorry for bothering you."

"No problem at all." Jane watched her leave then walked to the street vendor who'd rolled his eyes. "What's the story?" She nodded to

Andrea, who looked so frail that a stiff wind would blow her over before she disappeared from sight, lost in the crowd.

"Look, I like Andrea and all, but come on."

"What's your name?"

The young guy gave her the side-eye. "Who wants to know?"

Jane sighed and flipped her badge at him. "Agent Jane Cannon."

"I'm Pete Boser." His eyes widened. "Oh, wow. Are you working the case?"

"No. I came by looking for someone else." She described Doug Lewis and showed a picture of him on her phone, but Pete hadn't seen him around. "So what's your problem with Andrea?"

"Well, I mean, I feel sorry for her. Ever since her daughter disappeared, she's been here nearly every day asking people if they've seen her." He nodded to a nearby pole where a picture had been tacked. One of a young woman looking a lot like Jane.

"But...?"

"But she's constantly bugging everyone, asking about her. And a lot of the time, her other daughter has to come drag her home. The kid's like, maybe thirteen, I think? I don't know. But the girl looks sad and skinny, like she isn't eating enough or getting the help she needs. I just think the mom is too busy looking for one kid and not taking care of the other."

Pete seemed sincere, and Jane added him and his contact information to her notepad. "If you hear about or see my guy, let me know. And if anything happens with Andrea, call me about that too."

He nodded.

Jane left, perturbed. Knowing she wouldn't be able to leave Andrea's case behind, she grabbed the photo of the missing girl off the post. Maybe Olivia had run away. Maybe she'd taken up with some guy or girl. Hung with a bad group. OD'd on drugs. Or she could have been trafficked. The picture showed a vibrant woman with attractive features and a beautiful smile.

Sadly, bad things happened to pretty girls all the time

Knowing that Jenn was working on a human trafficking ring, Jane was determined to pick her brain and see if Jen couldn't look into

Olivia's disappearance. And Jane would see what the local LEOs had to say about it as well.

It couldn't hurt. Besides, she had just about caught up on paperwork. At least, for the minor cases, they'd been able to close in the past two months. Considering that of her fourteen pending cases, more than half had been ongoing for years, she didn't hold out hope to close anything else anytime soon.

Though finding "little" Dougie Lewis would really make her day.

Unfortunately, when she returned to the office, she learned that he'd vanished. All the called-in IDs on their bank robber turned out to be unsubstantiated. The other robbers, now in custody with a court-appointed public defender, had no idea where their buddy might have gone. Doug's ex had given them everything she knew, which wasn't much, except the fact that the bank where she worked had terminated her employment.

They had no leads but Linda.

And Jane wasn't holding her breath.

* * *

Jane Cannon's story continues in Collateral. Grab your copy here:
https://a.co/d/0hypK0Kt

Join the LT Ryan reader family & receive a free copy of the Rachel Hatch story, *Fractured*. Click the link below to get started:
https://ltryan.com/rachel-hatch-newsletter-signup-1

THE JANE CANNON SERIES

Blind Trust
Collateral

ALSO BY L.T. RYAN

Find All of L.T. Ryan's Books on Amazon Today!

The Jack Noble Series

The Recruit (free)

The First Deception (Prequel 1)

Noble Beginnings

A Deadly Distance

Ripple Effect (Bear Logan)

Thin Line

Noble Intentions

When Dead in Greece

Noble Retribution

Noble Betrayal

Never Go Home

Beyond Betrayal (Clarissa Abbot)

Noble Judgment

Never Cry Mercy

Deadline

End Game

Noble Ultimatum

Noble Legend

Noble Revenge

Never Look Back

Bear Logan Series

Ripple Effect

Blowback

Take Down

Deep State

Bear & Mandy Logan Series

Close to Home

Under the Surface

The Last Stop

Over the Edge

Between the Lies

Caught in the Web

The Marked Daughter

Beneath the Frozen Sky

Rachel Hatch Series

Drift

Downburst

Fever Burn

Smoke Signal

Firewalk

Whitewater

Aftershock

Whirlwind

Tsunami

Fastrope

Sidewinder

Redaction

Mirage

Faultline

Switchback

Mitch Tanner Series

The Depth of Darkness

Into The Darkness

Deliver Us From Darkness

Cassie Quinn Series

Path of Bones

Whisper of Bones

Symphony of Bones

Etched in Shadow

Concealed in Shadow

Betrayed in Shadow

Born from Ashes

Return to Ashes

Risen from Ashes

Into the Light

Blake Brier Series

Unmasked

Unleashed

Uncharted

Affliction Z: Fractured Part 2 (Coming Soon)

<u>Alex Hayes Series</u>

Trial By Fire (Prequel)

Fractured Verdict

11th Hour Witness

Buried Testimony

The Bishop's Recusal

The Silent Gavel

Improper Influence

<u>Stella LaRosa Series</u>

Black Rose

Red Ink

Black Gold

White Lies

Silver Bullet

<u>Avril Dahl Series</u>

Cold Reckoning

Cold Legacy

Cold Mercy

<u>Savannah Shadows Series</u>

Echoes of Guilt

The Silence Before

Dead Air

<u>Danny Cortez Series</u>

Dead Man's List

Shadow Directive

Widow Protocol

Jane Cannon Series:

Blind Trust

Collateral

* * *

Receive a free copy of The Recruit. Visit:

https://ltryan.com/jack-noble-newsletter-signup-1

ABOUT THE AUTHORS

L.T. RYAN is a *Wall Street Journal* and *USA Today* bestselling author, renowned for crafting pulse-pounding thrillers that keep readers on the edge of their seats. Known for creating gripping, character-driven stories, Ryan is the author of the *Jack Noble* series, the *Rachel Hatch* series, and more. With a knack for blending action, intrigue, and emotional depth, Ryan's books have captivated millions of fans worldwide.

Whether it's the shadowy world of covert operatives or the relentless pursuit of justice, Ryan's stories feature unforgettable characters and high-stakes plots that resonate with fans of Lee Child, Robert Ludlum, and Michael Connelly.

When not writing, Ryan enjoys crafting new ideas with coauthors, running a thriving publishing company, and connecting with readers. Discover the next story that will keep you turning pages late into the night.

Connect with L.T. Ryan
Sign up for his newsletter to hear the latest goings on and receive some free content
➔ https://ltryan.com/jack-noble-newsletter-signup-1

Join the private readers' group
➔ https://www.facebook.com/groups/1727449564174357

Instagram ➜ @ltryanauthor
Visit the website ➜ https://ltryan.com
Send an email ➜ contact@ltryan.com

* * *

K.T. CROWE served in the United States Marine Corps as a communications officer. A self-professed bibliophile with a degree in English, K.T. loves nothing better than putting action into words and letting her characters tell their own stories. When not writing, she's either reading, hiking in Central Oregon, or hanging out at the local coffee shop dreaming of new ways for her heroes and heroines to save the day.

www.ingramcontent.com/pod-product-compliance
Lightning Source LLC
Chambersburg PA
CBHW072129250626
47159CB00007B/2615